UNFORSAKEN

"Do you intend to hate me the rest of your life?"

Startled, Olivia whirled around to see Matthew standing just inside the doorway, his arms folded across his chest. She hadn't seen him in several months. Her throat tightened. Summoning every ounce of pride she had, Olivia raised her chin and said, "I have better things to do than hate you."

"But you do," he countered. "Don't pretend you don't."

"Why would I do that?" she countered, wishing she felt nothing for him at all. "To spare your feelings?"

"Olivia, you know I'm sorry for what happened, but I can't change things."

Without invitation, he walked inside her office and closed the distance between them. She backed away, refusing to look at him. Her lips were trembling, and she could feel her eyes filling with tears. She started to turn away from him but a gentle hand on her shoulder stopped her.

His arms closed around her and she buried her face against his shoulder. She knew in this moment that she loved him still.

She glanced up. Olivia knew he meant to kiss her and could not summon the strength to refuse.

Praise for *UNFORGIVEN*:

UNFORSAKEN

Lisa Higdon

Zebra Books
Kensington Publishing Corp.

http://www.zebrabooks.com

ZEBRA BOOKS are published by

Kensington Publishing Corp.
850 Third Avenue
New York, NY 10022

First Printing: August, 2000
10 9 8 7 6 5 4 3 2 1

Printed in the United States of America

To Anita Beasley, my junking buddy,
who wanted a southern book.
The best things in life are found on the side of the road.

November 12, 1864

My darling Matthew,

When you read this letter, all my prayers will have been answered. Countless times each day, I lift your name in prayer, beseeching the Lord to keep you alive and safe, and to allow my words to reach your eyes.

I am thankful that you were with my brother when he died, that Ryan was not alone or without comfort. I regret that he died with a troubled heart, worrying needlessly for my happiness, and I doubly regret that I could have spared him this distress but chose not to.

Ryan was right to fear that Father would forbid us to marry and that he would go to any length to destroy our happiness. Even so, he should not have asked you to break our engagement, but this I know he did out of love. What Ryan did not know was that our father passed away one month before you wrote to me of his death. I dared not inform Ryan of Father's death for fear he would return home out of concern for me. I would not risk him being hanged as a deserter for my sake.

So, Matthew, please be comforted to know that nothing stands in the way of our happiness, and our engagement need not be broken. I will wait for you as long as necessary and look forward to the day we are reunited.

Faithfully yours,
Olivia

Prologue

June 1865
Wilkes County, Georgia

Please, Lord, please let him be on this train.

Olivia Chandler breathed the same prayer as every other person thronging the depot. An eerie hush hovered over the crowd as the train screeched to a halt in a cloud of soot and smoke. finely sprinkling everything and everyone with coal dust. Too late, Olivia covered her mouth with a handkerchief, but her eyes were already stinging from the grit.

If Matthew wasn't on this train, she would be forced to face the very real possibility that something awful had happened to him and notice of his fate had failed to reach her. Indeed, it had taken two months for news of her brother's death to reach her and another month before Matthew's letter arrived. Mail had become as much a luxury as white sugar and coffee.

She clung to the hope that her reply had reached him by some miracle, assuring him that nothing stood in the way of their happiness. If only her brother could have died with that peace of mind, but had he known of their father's sudden death, Ryan would have returned home, even if it meant desertion.

Men in tattered gray uniforms began emerging from the heaving train, and the silence dissolved into cries of delight as loved ones caught sight of one another.

Aunt Eula kept a reassuring hand on Olivia's elbow, but the older woman's own anxiety began to mount as one by one soldiers other than Matthew Bowen debarked and were swept into the loving arms of their families.

"There he is!" Olivia cried at last out before Matthew set foot on the first step of the platform. Forgetting decorum, she shouldered her way through the crowd and rushed onto the platform just as he turned round. Breathless, she held out her hands. "Matthew! Thank God, you're home."

His eyes widened, and he didn't reach for her hands. "Olivia . . . what are you doing here?"

"I've met every train for three days. I just knew you'd be on one of them. Oh, Matthew—"

"Didn't you receive my letter?"

"Didn't you receive mine?"

He shook his head, and panic began to well inside her. Perhaps something horrible had happened after all. Like most men returning home from the war, he was noticeably thinner and his face appeared haggard and pale.

"I was afraid you wouldn't," she told him, fighting to keep her voice calm. "We haven't had mail for months. I wrote to tell you not to worry. There's no reason—"

"Matthew, don't forget the other bag."

The female voice silenced Olivia's explanation, and she turned to see a young woman stepping off the train with her hand braced against the unmistakable swell of her abdomen. She made her way to stand beside Matthew and direct a questioning smile toward Olivia.

"Are you a relative of Matthew's?"

The woman went on to say something else, but Olivia couldn't hear anything other than the hammering of her own heart. She glanced back at Matthew, hoping for a denial of the obvious, but the guilt and contrition in his eyes was all the confirmation she needed.

She tried to back away from the couple, painfully aware of the drama unfolding before half the population of the county, but Matthew's hand on her arm prevented her from stumbling down the steps.

"Livvy, after I wrote that letter. I didn't think you—"

"Take your hands off me," she said in a voice eerily quiet. Anger flooded the gaping wound in her heart, but she wouldn't add to her own humiliation by losing her composure. "There is nothing to explain."

"Olivia, darling, what's wrong?" Aunt Eula appeared atop the platform and observed the trio. Her face grew flushed with realization and understanding. "Oh, dear. Dear Lord, let's get you home."

Without a word, Aunt Eula s delicate fingers formed a steel band around Olivia's arm and led her down the platform steps, whispering, "Don't look back, dear. Don't look back."

Olivia felt like Lot's wife being led away from Sodom, and the comparison almost made her want to laugh. The crowd parted before them, and they swept past the curious glances and hushed whispers. Only when they reached their buggy and Olivia saw the pitying expression on their driver's face did she crumble.

Catching her by the upper arm, LeVon kept her from falling and calmly assisted her into the buggy. "Miss Olivia . . . are you going to be all right?"

"Just get us home," Eula instructed as she settled herself beside Olivia. "As quickly as you can."

Olivia sank to the bench before her bedroom window and listened.

"Miss Eula, please believe me. I never meant to hurt Olivia."

Aunt Eula's answer was swept away by a sudden breeze that rustled through the limbs of the gnarled oak tree and stirred the sheer curtains.

"If I could just speak with her, just once."

This time her aunt's words were clear. "Matthew, there is nothing you can say that wouldn't make things worse than they already are. Let her alone."

"I never received a letter from her," he insisted. "I didn't know . . . I had no idea she was waiting for me. Please, believe me, if I had known, I swear I would never have—"

"I believe you, dear." Eula's voice was always so calm and soothing, and Olivia could picture her laying her hand upon Matthew's arm and smiling up at him. "She doesn't want to see you. Try to understand, she's not ready to hear what you have to say."

"You will tell her I came to see her, won't you?"

"Of course I will."

They exchanged good-byes, and Olivia knew her aunt would be upstairs in a matter of minutes, trying to make her believe it was all a huge misunderstanding. Well, very few misunderstandings show up with suitcases and a baby on the way. In front of the whole county.

Tears threatened again, and she bit the inside of her lip until she tasted blood. She would not shed one tear over that man.

She turned at the sound of Eula tapping on the

door as she stepped inside the room. "Matthew came by again; he asked me to tell you—"

"Why do you bother to knock when you have no intention of waiting for an answer?" Eula only smiled, and Olivia apologized for her ugly mood. "I heard what he had to say, but that doesn't mean I believe him. Even if I did, what difference would it make now?"

Chapter One

December 1865

"Merry Christmas, Miss Chandler."

"How'do, Miss Olivia."

With a slight smile, Olivia nodded in reply to each eager acknowledgment and made her way to the back of Parson's General Mercantile. She knew better than to allow herself to be dragged into a conversation. They all either worked for her, owed her money, or both, and anyone who didn't most likely wanted to.

The holidays were an especially trying time. There was something about Christmas that prompted the beholden to believe money was a burden to those who had it. She supported her church's efforts to provide for the needy year-round, but want was constant.

"Well, well, Miss Olivia." Eli Parson beamed at the sight of his wealthiest patron. "Doing a little last-minute shopping?"

"Just a few things." She handed him her list. "And I wanted to pick up the package from Montgomery Ward."

"Right away, Miss Olivia."

Parson turned to gather the items neatly penciled on Olivia's list, leaving her to linger at the counter. Ordinarily, groceries were delivered to the house, but Olivia needed to claim the present she'd ordered for Aunt Eula and had Mr. Parson hold for her at the store. Eula was notorious for snooping and wasn't above peeking at her own gifts ahead of time.

A late afternoon dusting of snowflakes had fanned her languid holiday spirit, and Olivia decided to walk to the mercantile, admiring the cheerful decorations in almost every storefront window, claim the package herself and buy the last-minute items Maddy needed for Christmas dinner.

Olivia glanced around the store and realized this was her first visit since the holiday season and noted the effort Mr. Parson had made to create a festive atmosphere for his customers. The sharp scent of cedar boughs and pinecones filled the store, and jars of peppermint candy were prominently displayed. The toys arranged near the counter drew her attention.

A doll carriage bearing two lace-trimmed passengers was surrounded by brightly painted wooden blocks. Nearby, a stuffed rabbit patiently awaited his guests at a miniature table and chairs set for high tea.

When she was certain no one could see her, Olivia plucked one of the dolls from the carriage and fingered the lacy bonnet framing the angelic face. Olivia tilted the doll slightly, so the blue eyes stared up at her beneath a fringe of dark black lashes. She could just imagine how delighted a little girl would be to find such a doll waiting for her on Christmas morning, and it was a shame no one had purchased her.

"Miss Chandler?"

The storekeeper's voice startled her so that she almost dropped the doll.

"Everyone has admired that doll," Mr. Parson said by way of dismissing her chagrin. Being the consummate salesman, he added, "I thought surely someone would have taken her home by now."

Awkwardly, Olivia replaced the doll. "I'm sure someone will."

He shook his head. "Maybe next year. Most youngsters will be lucky to get hard candy and oranges. It'll be a long time before we can put this war behind us."

"We're better off than most," she reminded him. Their town was one of the lucky few spared Sherman's destruction, and not one acre of land had gone under the tax collector's gavel. Instead, Olivia was blamed for everyone's misfortune, and she let them think what they liked. "And things are getting better every day."

"Yes, they are," he hastened to agree. "They are indeed."

She accepted the box containing her purchases, inhaling the tangy scent of lemons and cinnamon sticks, and made sure the present for her aunt was tucked well beneath the other items.

Olivia bid Mr. Parson a pleasant holiday and turned to make her way out of the store. Once again, she was beset with well-wishers and polite acknowledgments. She turned to wish everyone a Merry Christmas just as she reached for the door, but the door swung open to admit another customer, along with a sharp blast of cold air.

Olivia hastened to thank the person holding the door open for her and found herself staring up at Matthew Bowen. The polite words died on her lips along with her smile.

She hadn't seen him in several months, but the change in him was stark. His features were no less handsome but held a weariness far beyond his years, and she couldn't help but notice the threadbare jacket he was wearing. Her throat tightened, holding back anything she might have said, and it saddened her to know he was struggling to survive.

His eyes, never leaving hers, warmed with affection, and it galled her to think he was actually happy to see her. If anything, he should be ashamed to look her in the eye.

Neither of them spoke, but Olivia was painfully

aware of the gaping eyes of every person in the mercantile. Their broken engagement had been grist for the gossip mills for months, and tongues would wag over this innocent encounter and whatever her reaction to it would be. Gathering her cape around her shoulders, Olivia opted not to react at all.

Without so much as a nod, she made her way out of the store, hesitating only a moment when his voice reached her ears.

"Merry Christmas, Livvy."

Her steps never faltered, but the endearment knifed through her heart. No one, not even her parents, had ever called her anything but Olivia. Only Matthew had bestowed upon her enough affection to merit a pet name.

To her horror, her eyes began to burn with tears, and she wished desperately that she'd taken the buggy to the store. All she could do was hurry down the street, swallowing back her tears, and pray no one would try to stop and speak to her. Once inside the safety of her office at the mill, she let herself relax enough to gulp deep, calming breaths.

I will not cry. I won't.

She didn't. Instead, she crossed the room and began sorting through the neatly stacked papers on her desk. The ledgers were all in balance, and the men had been given their pay vouchers that included a generous Christmas bonus in addition to having a half-day Christmas Eve and all day Christmas off work with pay. Olivia Chandler's workers were loyal, and that to her was worth losing a day's profit.

Indeed, she prized allegiance, whatever the cost. She'd been scarred once by betrayal and vowed it wouldn't happen again. What she couldn't understand was why seeing him hurt so badly. She had put him from her mind, refusing to grieve for someone who cared so little for her, and avoided social occasions he was likely to attend.

Several of her so-called friends accused her of being bitter. Well, maybe she was, but she had reason to be.

She had even gone so far as to move her church membership to the New Hope Methodist Church. Nothing came between Olivia Chandler and a grudge, not even God. Still, it galled her to think of all the ladies at the First Baptist Church whispering about her and shaking their heads in disbelief at her refusal to be gracious about her situation.

To hear them, one would think Olivia should have welcomed Matthew's wife with open arms and wished them well. The last straw had been receiving a written invitation to attend a baby shower the ladies had planned for the new bride. Hell would freeze over before she would wish that woman anything but misery.

Matthew Bowen had been the kind of boy every man wanted for a son, and the last young man a mother wanted courting her daughter. He was wealthy and handsome but had the reputation of being reckless and defiant, caring nothing for society parties or debutante balls. He scoffed at the idea of some husband-hunting female adding his name to her dance card.

No wonder everyone had been stunned when he began to pursue Olivia, whom they considered plain and awkward.

Suddenly, she grew angry at the thought. She had been love-struck, easily manipulated, and he had taken advantage of her innocence. Or had he simply assumed she would be so grateful for a husband, she would take him on any terms? If anything, she was lucky to be rid of him.

"Do you intend to hate me the rest of your life?"

Startled, she whirled around to see Matthew standing just inside the doorway, his arms folded across his chest. Summoning every ounce of pride she had, Olivia raised her chin and said, "I have better things to do than hate you."

"But you do," he countered. "Don't pretend you don't."

"Why would I do that?" she countered, wishing she felt nothing for him at all. "To spare your feelings? Oh, my, I would never forgive myself if I caused you a moment's grief."

"Olivia, you know I'm sorry for what happened, but I can't change things."

"I'd say you've already changed things enough." Indeed, every dream she'd held on to throughout the war crumbled when he'd stepped off that train, dragging his bride along with him.

Without invitation, he walked inside her office and closed the distance between them. She backed away, refusing to look at him. Her lips were trembling, and she could feel her eyes filling with tears. She started to turn away from him but a gentle hand on her shoulder stopped her.

His arms closed around her and she buried her face against his shoulder, hating him for seeing her cry. She couldn't help remembering another time she had cried in his arms. The day of her mother's funeral, she had slipped away from the house and hidden in the woods. It was nearly dark when he found her huddled against the trunk of an ancient oak tree. Her father had been furious with her for running off and sent Matthew and her brother, Ryan, to find her.

"It's all right to cry," he had whispered, resting his cheek against her forehead.

They had been little more than children, but Olivia knew in that moment that she loved Matthew Bowen. Just as she knew in this moment that she loved him still.

She glanced up, and he smoothed a tear away from her face with the pad of his thumb. Olivia knew he meant to kiss her and could not summon the strength to refuse. He lowered his mouth to hers and kissed her as if she were something fragile The touch of his lips awakened forgotten memories of stolen embraces, and she shuddered in his arms. He drew her more closely to him, and the kiss lost its sense of reverence.

Her lips parted easily beneath his and he deepened the kiss. Her arms found their way around his neck and his mouth left hers to seek the sensitive flesh at the base of her throat.

The feel of his hands on her breasts drew a gasp of alarm that he easily silenced with another hungry kiss. He was expertly searching out the tiny buttons of her blouse, and she was helpless to resist. She had resigned herself to never seeing him again and now found herself drowning in the taste of his kisses. The warmth of his hands burned her flesh as he lowered his head to kiss the swell of her bosom.

With the slightest touch, he traced the cleft between her breasts with his tongue, and she combed her fingers through his hair, holding on, feeling dizzy and too weak to stand

"Olivia," he whispered, lowering both of them to the floor. "I know you want me, I know you love me."

She could only nod, her lips throbbing from his kisses and her mouth greedy for the taste of him. Consumed with passion, lust and desire, all of which she had denied herself, she made little protest when he smoothed his hands under her skirt and over her legs, lingering on her thighs and cupping her buttocks.

He kissed her again, and it was she who deepened the kiss, tightened her arms around his neck. A sense of urgency flared between them, and he wrested her body free of her undergarments and fumbled with his own clothes.

She felt him hesitate, and he searched her face before easing her thighs apart. He kissed her again and tentatively thrust his body into hers, moving forward when her nails dug into his shoulders. A sharp stab of pain startled Olivia, and she gasped, "No, don't. We can't—"

"Shh, sweetheart," he murmured against her lips. "It'll pass and then I'll make you feel so good."

Another movement of his hips gained complete penetration and she cried out in panic, desperately pushing him away from her. "Stop it!"

He froze momentarily, his expression grim and disbelieving, but he rose to his feet as if anxious to be away from her. She sat up and felt the utter degradation of what she had allowed to occur. This was the man who had betrayed her, spurned her, humiliated her before the entire county, and now with just a few kisses, he had her willing to be his whore.

His back was toward her as he adjusted his clothing, and she hurried to do the same. What a picture she must make, sprawled on the floor with her blouse gaping open and her skirt twisted up around her waist. She scrambled to her feet before he turned back around. When he did, she faced him as defiantly as she could.

"Don't you dare say I forced you," he challenged, and she was surprised by the anger in his expression.

"Surely to God, you don't think I would breathe a word of this to another living soul." The cool tone of her own voice surprised her for, inside, her heart was racing and her stomach felt tied in knots. "I would rather die than have anyone know I allowed you to ruin me."

His eyes narrowed. "Or that you wanted me to."

Her control snapped, and her own rage rushed to the surface. She resisted the urge to slap him, but her reply was no less stinging. "At least I'm not the first woman to make that mistake."

He advanced on her, grasping her shoulders. "Olivia, listen to me."

"No!" Wrenching herself from his arms, she staggered back and clutched the gaping front of her blouse together. "I want you to leave."

"Not until we've said the things that need to be said."

She shook her head, backing away from him. "I have nothing to say to you. Go home ... home to your wife."

The contempt in her voice made each word sound like a curse, and his eyes narrowed. She wanted him to be angry, to hurt the way she did. "And home to your *baby*."

Right away, Olivia regretted the spiteful words but desperately needed something—anything—to shield her wounded pride. She didn't look away, daring him to retaliate, but he only looked at her with regret and walked out of the office without a word. Wasting no time, she rushed to close and lock the door.

Her fingers remained clenched around the solid brass knob, and she let her forehead rest against the door's smooth mahogany finish.

"I will not cry." Her voice was no more than a ragged whisper, but the words penetrated her heart. The tightness in her throat lessened and she realized she had no more tears left.

* * *

Matthew had sworn to forget about Olivia, not to let what might have been haunt him, but the most unlikely things would bring her to mind. He had no right to want her, to long for her, to need her so desperately. It was little comfort to know that she was no longer the sweet, bashful girl he remembered when he was to blame for the bitterness in her heart.

"Promise me . . ."

"Anything. What do you want?"

"Promise me that you . . . won't marry my sister."

"What?"

"Look, I'm dying, I know that."

"Ryan, just hold on. Wait until the doctors—"

"I'm dying, damn it! Listen to me. If you marry her, Father will disown her, and she won't have me to protect her."

"I can take care of her."

"He'll ruin you just to punish her. Just promise me you won't marry her."

Matt swore out loud and slammed the ax blade into the log, splintering the wood in two, and savored the sharp pain that ricocheted up his arm and stung his shoulder. He'd been a fool to listen to Ryan, a fool to let the ranting of a dying man cloud his judgment. Ryan had been his best friend since they were boys, and he felt bound to honor his last wish. It seemed only right. Matt resolved himself to the fact that Olivia would never be allowed to marry him or dare defy her father.

Even if he had received her reply to his letter, it would have been too late. He'd already made the biggest mistake of his life.

He just couldn't get over the way she'd looked at him that day in the store. For an instant, her heart had been in her eyes. and he knew that she still cared for him. Just as quickly, the warmth in her eyes had vanished, and she regarded him as something she wanted to avoid stepping in. He deserved her contempt, but facing it was a different story.

His only reason for confronting her was to make her understand that he had not betrayed her, and in doing so he'd wronged her even more. He had been a fool to ever touch her, let alone kiss her.

It had all been too much. The feel of her body against his, the taste of her tears mingling with his kisses. Something had snapped inside him and he couldn't resist her. Wild ideas ran through his mind. They would run away that very night. Leave everything behind and go where no one would find them—but Olivia wasn't ready. Not for him, not for desperate actions and certainly not for physical passion.

She'd been a virgin, deserving courtship and seduction, not a hasty tumble. In his haste, he'd ruined everything. She felt violated and hated him all the more.

He glanced past the weathered barn, toward the fields that lay barren as far as the eye could see, and tried to see some sort of future. Come spring the land would be tilled and sown, and the rest would be up to the Lord. Rain or drought, Matthew hated knowing that his very existence hinged on the whims of nature.

His father had considered himself a farmer, not a gentleman planter, and Matthew had learned early the realities of work in the field. Only now was he thankful for that experience. While so many displaced southern aristocrats were struggling to learn the concept of living by the sweat of their own brow, Matthew was already preparing for the labor that awaited him.

His father had taught him hard word and the war had taught him hardship, but nothing had prepared him for poverty. The war had taken everything. His father had died while he was away, and the livestock was quickly looted by soldiers and fleeing refugees. Only the land remained, and that in itself was a miracle.

Still gazing across the barren fields, he tried to picture them green and bountiful, but all he saw, all he felt was emptiness.

Chapter Two

Spring 1867

"I don't mean to sound critical, Olivia, but it isn't wise to court contempt."

"Courting contempt? I assure you, my intentions are not that honorable."

Everyone at the dining room table laughed, but she didn't miss the nervous clattering of silver on china. Olivia rather liked shocking people either by words or actions, but words always garnered a more immediate response. Indeed, Rodger nearly choked on his coffee, and the preacher's wife turned a bright shade of pink.

Rodger Kirk was Olivia's cousin on her mother's

side of the family, and he and his wife, Ada, always joined them for Sunday dinner. What had started out as a one-time invitation somehow became a weekly tradition, but Olivia didn't mind their presence as much as she did their presumptuous attitude toward their status as *family*. If she and Aunt Eula were hurting for money and had nothing to put on the table, it was doubtful Rodger and Ada would even darken their door.

Rodger forked a second helping of baked ham from the serving platter onto his plate, clearing his throat before he spoke. "The mill is doing well enough on its own without dealing with carpetbaggers and Yankees."

Olivia paused thoughtfully, as if contemplating her cousin's advice. "I'd be a fool to turn away business. Besides, the opinions of the people in this town are the least of my worries."

Olivia watched the uncertainty flicker in Ada's eyes, always amazed at the depth of the woman s hypocrisy. If it weren't for her husband being related to the Chandlers, Ada Kirk would be poor as Job's turkey, but she was scandalized whenever Olivia provoked the disapproval of the town matrons. Ada was hard pressed to maintain her social standing and not jeopardize her bread-and-butter.

"Olivia has to do what she thinks is best for the business." Aunt Eula never hesitated to speak in defense of her niece. "After all, that mill is the only thing that kept this town from ruin."

That and Northern trade, war or no war. Olivia's

father had seen little reason to cut his ties to Yankee industry just because there was a war on. When the knowledge became public, Olivia, not her father, bore the brunt of resentment for not stopping the practice. Instead, she doubled the business and saved the town from financial ruin, but her treachery was never forgiven.

"You're absolutely right, Miss Eula." Rodger hastily latched onto something upon which he could agree. "Half the men in town work for us, and their wages are the livelihood for every other business there is."

For us. Olivia was tempted to remind Rodger that no one worked for him. He worked for her just like every other man at the mill, but she remained silent. Aunt Eula had once observed that Rodger had very little to be proud of and needed every shred of importance he could scrape together.

Rather than having an unpleasant disagreement, Olivia chose the simplest tactic to hedge Rodger's doubtful loyalty. "We wouldn't be getting the extra business if Rodger hadn't worked so hard on restoring that old warehouse in the first place."

Rodger beamed and gave his wife a knowing look. Ada managed a weak smile. "Oh, I was happy to do it, you know that. I told you we'd need that extra space, and I was right."

Why must he always point that out? Even a broken clock is right twice a day.

Rodger glanced at the other guests and went on to say, "With all the extra business, that old building will pay for itself twice over."

"And this year will be the most profitable since the war," Olivia predicted, amused at how quickly he took the bait and stopped worrying about contempt. "The weather has been perfect, and getting the cotton to market is all that matters."

"I couldn't agree more," Rodger said over his coffee cup. "Everyone is optimistic, and Matthew Bowen told me himself this year will be his best ever."

The dining room fell silent, and Ada gaped at her husband in openmouthed disbelief. Olivia felt the nervous glances skittering in her direction, and her fingers trembled as she reached for her own cup, causing it to rattle on its saucer. Poor Rodger babbled on about the possibility of adding new machinery to the gin, blissfully unaware of his blunder, and Olivia listened intently. She would be damned if she would so much as flinch at the mention of *his* name.

"It's such a lovely afternoon, why don't we have dessert on the patio?" Aunt Eula said by way of dismissing the uncomfortable silence and rose from the table. The guests followed her lead. "We have pecan pie, and I know that's your favorite, Reverend Peeler."

Olivia rose from her chair but let the others file out of the dining room before exhaling the ragged breath she didn't realize she was holding. Bracing her palms on the table, she hung her head and berated herself for giving a damn what anyone thought, but it was obvious they'd all expected her to crumble at the mere mention of Matthew Bowen's name. Even

Aunt Eula had eyed her warily for a moment. She only wished there had been no reaction to hide.

Two years. It had been two years and she still couldn't forget him. How could she, when he had doomed her to being an old maid? She'd had her share of gentlemen callers, but none to whom she cared to explain what had taken place that fateful Christmas Eve. The thought almost made her laugh. With her money they probably wouldn't care if she was a saloon girl.

"If you don't get out there on that patio, they'll figure you're in here drying your eyes."

Olivia's head snapped up, and she glared at the housekeeper. "I don't give a damn what they think."

Maddy only smiled, a knowing look in her eyes. "No, but you care plenty what Ada Kirk goes blabbing to her friends."

"That her husband is a babbling fool?"

"Everybody knows that." Maddy turned her attention to the task of clearing the table. "But they all wonder just exactly what your feelings toward Mr. Bowen are after all this time."

Chapter Three

Speculation over Olivia's feelings grew even more that fall.

While most of her neighbors were struggling to get back on their feet, Olivia prospered, along with the lumber mill and the cotton gin. She made no apology for profiting from the destruction of the war, and was absolutely brazen about dealing with the Union Army and would-be carpetbaggers. Behind her back, most folks called her a traitor, but her treason fed their children.

Cotton was in demand, and Olivia surprised the factors in Savannah and Charleston who thought to deal with her any differently than they had her father.

He kept detailed records, and she followed his example and accepted nothing less than top dollar.

She parlayed the profits by paying off the Yankee tax collectors and acquiring control of almost every acre of land in the county. Landholders would repay her with a percentage of their crops over a ten-year period, and she allowed them to keep their homes. For this she was labeled an extortionist, a vulture preying on the misfortune of others, but no one opted to take their chances with the tax collector.

"There are plenty of folks who'd give their eyeteeth to change places with them."

"Olivia, darling, you really must be more sensitive toward their circumstances," Aunt Eula urged as they hurried up the front steps of the church. "Times are hard and—"

"Everyone has a sad tale to tell." She paused before stepping inside. "Would our being homeless make things easier for them?"

Eula's lips thinned in disapproval but she said nothing more.

Once inside, Olivia was surprised by the solemn assembly. For weeks, every member of the church had anxiously awaited the arrival of today's speaker, a missionary just returned from the South Sea Islands. Several polite nods were exchanged but there was none of the usual chatter before the service and certainly none of the excitement she expected over such an interesting speaker.

The minister solemnly asked everyone to stand and opened the service with prayer.

"Heavenly Father, we ask your blessings upon this church and this community. We pray comfort and reassurance for those who have lost loved ones. We pray especially for Matthew Bowen in the loss of his wife—"

Olivia's Bible slipped from her hand and landed with a heavy thud on the floor. Her head began to swim, and she dared not reach down to retrieve it for fear she would topple to the floor herself. She forced her attention back to the minister's words, positive that she had not heard right. Instead, he droned on about the plight of a father left to raise a young child without a mother.

When the prayer concluded, every bowed head raised and turned expectantly toward Olivia, but she exchanged only a brief look of surprise with her aunt before returning her attention to the minister, as if he had prayed for nothing more significant than clear skies for a picnic.

It was a fitting day for a funeral. Drizzling rain had begun at dawn and lulled only long enough to ensure the service would not be canceled. As the carriage neared the cemetery, Olivia noted the dark clouds on the horizon and hoped for a downpour.

"Please don't make me do this."

Her aunt ignored her plea and glanced out the window. "Thank goodness the rain didn't keep folks away."

"Aunt Eula, no one expects me to attend. In fact, some might consider it improper."

"If you don't put in an appearance, you'll never be able to show your face in this town again." The severe tone was so out of character for Eula that Olivia was quite taken aback. "It's one thing to avoid someone socially, but not paying respect to the dead is an affront even you can't buy your way out of."

Olivia opened her mouth to rebut, but Eula was already stepping out of the carriage and thanking LeVon for his assistance. She had no choice but to follow despite her every instinct to remain safe inside the shadows of the carriage.

Stares of disdain and reproof assailed her immediately, and a rush of whispers reached her ears. Her insides quaked and she remained rooted in place, holding tightly to the handle of the carriage door.

"Please, Aunt Eula, I'm begging you."

"You can't turn and run now. You'll look like a fool."

"Stay close," Olivia whispered to the driver. At his understanding nod, she forced herself to follow her aunt's confident steps toward the gates of the cemetery. Several men were gathered just outside the entrance, and they all tipped their hats and spoke in a solemn manner befitting the occasion. Their wives, however, felt no obligation for polite pretense and stared daggers at Olivia, only to look away when she met their glances with haughty disdain.

"Don't get your back up," Eula warned in a sharp whisper. "Remember why we're here."

"I'm here because you forced me."

As with her earlier protests, the comment went unanswered, and Olivia was actually pleased to see her cousin Rodger coming toward them.

He offered his arm to Eula and nodded to Olivia. "You should have let me know you would be here. You would have been welcome to ride with us."

"We hadn't planned on it." Olivia accepted the arm he offered her and allowed herself to be led to the graveside, where the mourners were already beginning to assemble. Thankfully they were forced to take a place in the back.

A narrow strip of tarp had been erected as an awning over the open grave and the simple coffin was draped in a modest spray of flowers. Olivia had to look away, holding tight to Rodger's arm, and she prayed desperately that the sick feeling in her stomach would pass.

"All right, cousin?" he asked, patting her hand in a reassuring gesture. She nodded and moved to stand behind her aunt, who sought out a place beside Rodger's wife.

"Do you know what happened?"

"Fever of some kind," Rodger whispered discreetly. "I can't believe you're here."

She glanced up at him, trying to read the meaning in his quiet remark. "I'm sure everyone else feels the same."

Even Ada glanced back at Olivia, obviously aghast, no doubt mortified to be in her company. Poor Ada, how would she be able to denounce Olivia's presence

when standing right at her side? Olivia only smiled
slightly and nodded, knowing she had Ada completely
discomfitted.

The minister cleared his throat a little louder than
necessary, but it served to draw everyone's attention
back to the purpose of the gathering. For the first
time, Olivia caught sight of Matthew standing before his wife's grave, and her heart constricted with
anguish for him. Dressed in a dark suit that had
seen better days, he looked so much older than he
should, and she was heartbroken to see the desola-
tion on his face.

It hurt even more to know she had no right to offer
sympathy or contrition, and he might even resent her
presence here today. Still she couldn't tear her eyes
away from him. Throughout the entire service, her
gaze remained fixed on the stark figure he made, his
eyes downcast and his face betraying none of the
sorrow he must be feeling.

Olivia was thankful he never looked her way. She
wished she could think he might never even know
she'd been there, but she had no doubt there were
many in the community who would feel honor-bound
to tell him how shameful her presence had been and
how much they disapproved. Her back stiffened at the
thought, and she glanced over the solemn assembly.

Hang them all! What right had any of them to judge
her actions? If it weren't for her, not one of them
would have a roof over his head or food on his table.
They all knew it, too, and hated her all the more.
How silly she'd been to think her actions noble, but

she preferred wealth and comfort to admiration any day.

The thought gave her solace, and a satisfied smiled played upon her lips. She looked up to find Matthew's gaze riveted on her face, his expression grim. Olivia felt every ounce of blood rush from her head even as her face flamed. Dear Lord, not only had he noticed her, but he'd caught her grinning like a possum. She wished the ground would open up and swallow her.

Instead the rain began again and she hung her head slightly, ducking the raindrops and his sight. The rich scent of damp earth filled the air and Olivia shuddered, acutely aware of being surrounded by graves, old and new alike. She hated cemeteries, always had, and today she felt that hatred more intensely than ever.

The first time she'd ever seen a graveyard had been the day her mother was buried in the family plot. It was August, stifling hot without a breath of air stirring, but her father had seen that they were all dressed in proper mourning clothes. Black from head to toe. Her father insisted on maintaining the decorum befitting their family's prestige, despite the merciless heat.

She dared peer up at her father just before the service began. There had been nothing sorrowful in his countenance, only solemn composure as he shook hands with the minister and bid him to proceed. Tears stung her eyes and she squeezed them tight, pretending to pray. Father had warned her not to make a spectacle of herself by blubbering in front of the whole town, but she feared she would suffocate from holding back her tears.

The minister concluded the service with a prayer, and folks moved to extend their sorrow to Matthew. Olivia resisted her aunt's insistent tug on her sleeve, refusing to further humiliate herself, and turned toward the exit where her carriage was waiting.

She'd taken no more than two steps when the cries of a child reached her ears, frightened, confused cries, and she froze in place. For some reason, she turned around. She had to find the source of those cries, and she was sorry she did.

Olivia turned just in time to see the minister's wife struggling to comfort a little girl, not even three years old, but the child wanted her father, and Matthew didn't hesitate to reach out for her. The little girl flung herself into his arms and hid her face against his shoulder, and he absently stroked her wavy hair while listening to an earnest expression of sympathy from one of the mourners.

The scene completely undid her, and Olivia whirled around and hurried to the carriage, not even waiting for the driver to help her climb inside. She collapsed onto the seat and let her head fall back against the upholstered cushion, smothering her own cries beneath her gloved hand.

"Olivia?" Eula's voice was harried when she joined her a few minutes later. "Are you all right?"

She nodded, forcing herself to speak despite her

constricted throat. "Please, hurry and close the door. Let's go home. Now."

Eula settled herself opposite Olivia and the carriage lurched forward. Why had she let herself be dragged to that funeral? She was the last person who should have been there, let alone be overcome with emotion. She could only hope no one had noticed her dash out of the cemetery.

"You should have spoken to him, dear."

She glanced up. "He saw me. He knows I was there."

"But he doesn't know why."

"I was there because you insisted that it was the right thing to do."

Eula reached inside her reticule and withdrew a lace handkerchief, offering it to Olivia. When she finished drying her eyes, her aunt said, "Then you should feel proud of yourself."

Olivia knotted the hanky around her fingers, remembering the way that child had held on to Matthew for dear life, and felt ashamed instead. She had never seen the child, never bothered to ask about her, or even acknowledge her existence. It had been so much easier to think of her as an unfortunate indiscretion rather than a little girl who deserved her compassion rather than her disdain.

Chapter Four

Spring 1868

There were certain advantages to being an old maid. Perhaps *advantage* was too strong a word, but Eula Chandler felt entitled to a few privileges, one of them being the right to meddle in the lives of those she cared about. Olivia tried not to let it bother her, knowing her aunt had the best intentions, but there were days she feared her patience had been tried to the limit.

"Now, aren't you glad you came with me today?"

"Glad is hardly how I would describe it." Olivia snapped the reins and turned the buggy onto the main road. If anything, she was frazzled. "I had no idea we'd be there all day."

Indeed, she had little patience for the sick and the shut in, but Eula thrived on them and felt responsible for every wretch in the county. Today she had sworn delivering food was all they would be doing and that it would take no time at all. Olivia hadn't even intended to go inside, but her aunt couldn't carry everything by herself. Indeed, Olivia had to make two trips from the buggy into the house, wondering how any sick person could eat so much.

"Olivia," Eula admonished. "We must always ask ourselves what Jesus would do."

Despite her irritation, she smiled at her aunt. "He only fed five thousand."

"Hush up and drive."

It was no short trip to reach the more rural area, and the morning was completely gone. It didn't help that the trip required driving right past Matthew Bowen's farm, coming and going.

She had managed not to even look in his direction coming out, but the silence had her mind wandering and her eyes followed suit. She managed to stop herself before completely turning her head toward the farmhouse, but not before Eula noticed the direction of her thoughts.

"Look, Olivia. There's Matthew."

Olivia glanced toward the house but saw no one. She turned back to tell her aunt that she was mistaken when she caught sight of the wagon approaching them.

Eula waved. Olivia snapped the reins, urging the horse on, and vowed not to give him so much as a passing nod.

Eula thought otherwise. "We must stop, dear. He has seen us."

"Of course he has seen us. He'd have to be blind not to see you waving like a carnival barker."

"Olivia, don't you dare drive past that wagon." When she didn't respond, Eula threw down the gauntlet. "He'll think you're afraid to speak to him."

The horse gave a startled snort when she jerked on the reins and frowned at Eula. "Nothing could be further from the truth."

"That's good to know." Eula smiled brightly and called out, "Good afternoon, Matthew. What a nice surprise."

"Hello, Miss Eula." He reined the team of horses to a stop. "Miss Chandler."

She winced at the formality but merely nodded in reply.

"I envy you ladies, taking advantage of this fine weather for a drive in the country." He let the reins dangle between his fingers, his eyes never leaving Olivia, and she felt acutely self-conscious. "Unusually warm for April."

Too warm, she thought, hoping her face wasn't as flushed as she felt. She opened her mouth to make her excuses and be on their way, but Eula cut her off.

"Just lovely. When Olivia suggested taking a drive, I just couldn't resist."

Olivia gaped at her. What in the world was she up to? The last thing she wanted was for Matthew to think she was driving past his house in hopes of seeing him.

Matthew glanced at her, his eyes slightly narrowed. His uncertainty was obvious, but she knew any contradiction of her aunt's statement would only make her appear to be denying an ulterior motive.

Though it was barely noon, it was obvious Matthew had already put in a full day's work. The sleeves of his shirt, faded almost white by the sun, were rolled up to the elbow, and several buttons were left undone at the collar. She could see that his chest was bare and quickly looked away. Unfortunately, her eyes were drawn to his forearms, tan and muscular, and the memory of those hands on her breasts made her shrink inside her elegant traveling suit.

His eyes narrowed again, ever so slightly, but this time it had nothing to do with whether she had purposely driven past his farm. He knew exactly what she was thinking, and there was no mistaking the warmth rising to her cheeks.

Olivia gathered the reins for a quick departure and gave Eula a warning look. "I'm sure Mr. Bowen has better things to do than chatter on about the weather."

Eula wasn't fazed. "Where is that pretty little girl of yours, Matthew?"

His expression softened at the mention of his child, and he replied, "One of the sharecroppers sent his daughter to watch her for me today."

"Today? Don't you have a regular nursemaid?"

A warning sounded in Olivia's brain and she twisted the reins tightly around her fingers. The last thing she needed was Matthew Bowen thinking she was concerned about his personal life. It was none of her concern whether he had one child or ten, let alone a nurse to care for them.

He smiled and shook his head. "Nursemaids are a thing of the past, Miss Eula. I make do with whatever help I can get."

"How dreadful. I can only imagine how difficult that must be for you, and she's such sweet thing."

Olivia cleared her throat and managed a polite smile. "We really should be on our way."

His smile faded and he looked her up and down one more time. "Yes, Miss Chandler. I know you're anxious to get on with your . . . drive."

Before Eula could say anything else, Olivia snapped the reins and urged the horse into a trot. She ignored her aunt's disapproving glare.

"Olivia, you were not raised to be so impolite. I was not finished speaking with him."

"Then it's a good thing I managed to escape when I did."

Eula's annoyance vaporized and smug certainty took its place. "Just what are you running away from, Olivia?"

She didn't answer, concentrating instead on driving the buggy. The horse could fly and still not get her home fast enough.

* * *

"Damn!" The skillet clattered noisily against the stovetop, and Matthew swore again.

He wondered how many fingers he'd have left by the end of the week. Those he didn't burn off he would most likely slice away with the butcher knife.

He looked back to find Sarah gaping at him from her highchair, her eyes wide with alarm.

"Everything's all right, sweetheart," he tried to reassure her. "I'll have your breakfast ready in a minute."

Determined that he could at least manage scrambled eggs, he turned back to the stove and reached for the skillet once again, this time armed with a pot holder. He spooned in a bit of bacon grease, watched it melt and slide across the pan. He broke the first egg into the pan and then another. They began to sizzle and he whisked the yolks and whites together until the eggs were done.

Scrambled were easier than fried, he'd learned that quick enough, and he'd given up on bread of any kind. At first, meals hadn't been much of a problem. Ladies from the church had provided a steady stream of food for the two of them. Gradually, the dishes became accompanied with stern admonitions that he owed it to his child to marry again and less than subtle references to unmarried female relatives: daughters, nieces, and sometimes themselves!

A man couldn't work his land if he was burdened with tending to a child, they would say over and over, and the last straw had been a stern warning that Sarah would be better off in an orphan's home if he refused to take a wife. His scathing reply had put an end to the covered dish brigade, but he'd rather eat his own cooking than listen to anyone suggest he should give up his little girl.

Remembering the pot holder, he took the pan from the stove and raked the eggs onto a plate. They were a little runny, but he managed to conceal that fact by scraping the worst of it onto his own plate. When he placed her breakfast before his daughter, she looked up at him doubtfully.

Ignoring her spoon, Sarah tested the eggs with her fingers, and her expression became even more skeptical.

"Eat up, darlin'," he urged, seating himself across from her. "We've got a lot to do today."

And he had no idea how he would get any of it done and tend to Sarah, who was still more baby than child. He'd already lost a week and a half in the fields thanks to unreliable help. Twice, he'd thought he'd found someone to watch the little girl while he worked, but both girls had quit after only a few days. One got married and ran off in the middle of the night, and the other was offered a housekeeping job for a lot more money than he could pay.

Now he was right back where he started, and his options were limited. He had married once out of necessity and vowed it would never happen again, but he would lose everything if he didn't get his crops planted.

His grim thoughts were interrupted by the unmistakable sound of a horse and buggy approaching the house. Foregoing his own breakfast, Matthew reached for his coffee cup just before going outside. He suspected such an early morning visitor would not be bringing good news.

To his surprise, he found Eula Chandler bringing her buggy to a halt in front of the house. He hurried to help her down. "Hello, Miss Eula."

"Matthew, dear, how are you?"

"Fine, just fine. And you?"

"Just splendid." She smiled up at him, and he swore he saw mischief in her eyes. "As you can see, I'm driving my own buggy, something a lady wouldn't have dreamed of in my day."

"It's a little early for a drive, isn't it?"

She smiled even more at his teasing. "No, I came to speak with you."

He waited, but she didn't elaborate. After an awkward silence, he asked, "Would you like to come inside?"

"Thank you, I would."

He was even more puzzled. He'd expected her to decline the invitation and state her business. Instead, she seemed intent on nothing more than a leisurely visit. They crossed the porch, and he moved to open the screen door leading to the kitchen. Before he reached for the latch, Eula caught sight of Sarah perched at the table.

"Isn't she a pretty thing?"

"Yes, ma'am. And a handful, too."

"Most children are at that age." She nodded, smiling to herself. "In fact, that's the reason for my visit."

He let his arm drop to his side and the screen door snapped shut. "Sarah?"

"How are you going to manage taking care of a small child and tending all this land?"

He hesitated. "It's a challenge."

"You'll be spending all your time in the fields," she pointed out. "It can't be easy finding someone to watch her, and when you do come home, I'm sure you're exhausted."

She wasn't telling him anything he didn't already know, but hearing it from someone else made the situation sound much more bleak. He only shrugged and said, "It isn't easy."

Eula fingered a tiny button on the cuff of her sleeve, carefully considering her next words. "Wouldn't it be easier for her just to stay with someone for the next few months? A relative, perhaps?"

Matthew felt too guilty to admit to anyone that he'd already considered the option. "My aunt in Texas would be glad to take her, but it would take weeks to get there and back, and then I might not see her until next year."

"What about right here? With me and Olivia?"

He nearly strangled on his coffee. "You're not serious."

"Of course I am. Lord knows we have plenty of room, and you could see her as often as you like."

"Olivia can't stand the sight of me, why would—"

"Surely you don't believe that." Eula didn't wait

for his answer. "Olivia was hurt, but that was a long time ago. If that's how you feel about her, no wonder she didn't want to make the offer herself."

"It's not—" His voice faltered and he barely stopped himself before insisting that he knew that Olivia's contempt for him went beyond the broken engagement and had not lessened in the past few years. Not one bit. If anything, she hated him even more, but he didn't regret what happened between them. For a few moments, he had seen desire in her eyes and had felt the heated passion of her response. That was worth any amount of animosity.

"I just don't think it would be a good idea," he said at last, schooling his thoughts to the matter at hand. Eula Chandler was the last person with whom he should be discussing Olivia. "I'll find someone to watch Sarah."

The older woman drew her shoulders back and eyed him with a look that made him squirm. "You must think of the child, Matthew Bowen. Not your own pride."

She wouldn't let him deny it. "Whatever happened between you and Olivia is in the past. Refusing our help now only hurts your little girl and does nothing to atone for whatever wrong was done."

Without another word, she brushed past him and went inside the kitchen. He could hear her talking with Sarah and the child's cheery response. What was he supposed to do?

His pride wouldn't do him much good if he lost his land and had no home for his daughter, but he hated the thought of sending her away, even temporarily. Sarah was still confused by her mother's death and often asked when her mommy was coming home. How could he explain sending her to stay with strangers? Would she believe that she would be able to return when her mother hadn't?

At last, he stepped inside his own kitchen. Eula Chandler had seated herself at the kitchen table next to Sarah and had the child completely enraptured with a story about a gingerbread man who ran away when someone failed to close the kitchen window.

"Would you like to help me make some gingerbread men . . . just like that one?" Sarah nodded earnestly in reply. "Wonderful, but we mustn't forget to close the window."

Eula's expression was very solemn and she managed to look quite startled to notice Matthew standing just inside the door. Her face brightened as if she'd just had a wonderful idea. "Do you think your papa would let you come to my house and help me?"

Sarah glanced toward her father, her eyes brimming with anticipation. How could he say no?

Chapter Five

"Go ahead. Say it."

Olivia watched her best friend struggle with her feelings. At last, all Nancy Potter could think to say was, "I just don't see how you can *deal* with those people as if the war had never happened."

By *those people* she was referring to most of Olivia's clientele at the lumber mill. Nancy had arrived at the mill just in time to see Olivia shaking hands with the local Union Army commander and thanking him for sending her more business.

"I know the war happened, but we lost and these are the consequences."

"Olivia!" she gasped. "You make it sound . . . like nothing."

"If they don't buy lumber from me, they'll buy it somewhere else. And what do you think would happen if I lost the business? Every man at the mill would be out of a job and sooner or later his home. All that will do is give the Yankees more to buy up and use against us."

Her friend made no reply and they walked on in silence. Olivia had tried to ease Nancy's discomfiture by inviting her home for tea, but her real motive was needing someone to talk to about a delicate subject.

Olivia's home sat at the far end of one of the loveliest streets in town, and the clear spring weather only served to enhance the picture-book setting. Dogwoods and tulips were in full bloom, and the branches of the trees lining the street almost touched, creating a shady canopy.

Tentatively she broached the subject, hoping to sound nonchalant. "Aunt Eula and I saw Matthew Bowen yesterday."

Her friend only nodded. "Did he have the little one with him? She certainly is pretty."

"No. He said he had managed to find someone to keep her for him while he worked."

Nancy's steps halted and she looked surprised. "You actually *spoke* to him?"

"Of course." Olivia only shrugged. She had never breathed a word about her fateful Christmas Eve encounter with Matthew to anyone, not even to her best friend, but Nancy knew that her hurt and resentment ran deep. "It would have been impolite to do otherwise."

Nancy gave a very unladylike snort of disbelief. "Since when have you bowed to decorum? Under any circumstances?"

Olivia resumed walking, ignoring her friends good-natured teasing, but said nothing. Nancy was at her elbow. "You have to tell me what was said."

"I do?"

"You do. Every word."

"My goodness, to hear you, one would think the exchange of a few pleasantries meant—"

"A chink in your armor?"

"What armor? You're talking nonsense."

"Tell me what he said."

"Nothing more than a few comments about the weather and the fact that nursemaids are a thing of the past." She came to a halt, resting her hand on the iron gate to her front walk. "I can't imagine how he manages taking care of a child and working all that land alone."

"Olivia Chandler, you vowed you wouldn't spit on that man if he were on fire and now you tell me you're concerned about his child?"

"I didn't say I was concerned," she quickly denied her friend's interpretation. "I just can't imagine how anyone can work and tend to a small child at the same time."

"They can't," Nancy didn't hesitate to conclude. "That's why men remarry so soon. Look at Joe Nathan. His wife died and left him with a houseful of children . . . ten, wasn't it? Well, his wife wasn't dead a month before he married her sister!"

"That's disgusting." Olivia frowned. "Besides, caring for one child isn't the same as ten."

"It's worse. At least in a large family, the older ones can look after the little ones."

Olivia didn't like the turn of the conversation, not one bit. "Well, I suppose you think he should marry the first woman he can find. Maybe he should hang around the funeral parlor so he can have first pick of the new widows."

A smile crept over Nancy's features, and she barely smothered her laughter behind her gloved hand. "I never thought I would live to see the day. Olivia Chandler, you are jealous."

Olivia's eyes narrowed and she hurried up the walk, not looking to see if her friend was following, but she heard Nancy's footsteps close behind her own.

"Don't deny it. You are absolutely pea green."

"Just what am I so jealous about?"

"Your pride won't let you offer to help Matthew, but it's killing you to think of all the women who will."

"I would never envy a woman who would be willing to be nursemaid to a houseful of brats just so she can have a husband."

"Olivia," Nancy's tone became reproachful.

"Well, why haven't you married one of those needy widowers?"

"Because I was in love once," she replied. "And once you've known love, you'll never settle for anything else."

"I'm sorry, Nancy." Olivia hadn't meant to drag up painful memories. "I was speaking theoretically."

"I know."

Nancy's husband had been killed in battle just before the end of the war, and Olivia knew she still grieved despite the brave front she put on for everyone.

They had married just two weeks before his regiment left to join the fighting, and had seen each other only twice in all that time. Olivia had often wondered what might have happened if she had married Matthew before he left. No doubt her father would have locked her in her room if any such thing had even been suggested.

"Aunt Eula says we should offer to do something," she spoke quietly, more to herself than her friend. "Something to help Matthew with the child."

"What would you do?"

Reality washed over her and she snapped her head up as if the matter was irrelevant. "Oh, I don't know. Perhaps offer to hire a nurse for the child."

They stepped inside the spacious foyer and began removing their gloves; all the while Nancy studied her with obvious disapproval. "You can't always throw money at your problems, Olivia."

Olivia turned around, her feelings smarting from her friend's criticism. "This isn't my problem. I'm willing to help, but—"

Before she could finish, a loud crash sounded from the kitchen, followed by shrieks of delight and cries of dismay. Aunt Eula's voice could be heard clearly. "Come back here! You're all wet!"

Suddenly, the door leading from the dining room burst open, and Olivia barely dodged a collision with a barreling youngster and her aunt, who was is pursuit.

"What in the world?" Nancy was laughing, and Olivia scowled at her.

Olivia hurried into the parlor to find her aunt draping a towel around a tiny naked body despite the little girl's protests.

"Will you *please* tell me what is going on here?"

Eula and the child both gaped at her.

"Olivia, darling, this is Sarah. You know, Matthew's little girl."

"But, I didn't—" Olivia's words were lost as Sarah grasped the sudden opportunity and fled from Eula's hold, streaking out of the parlor and down the long hall leading to the back porch. "I never said—"

Eula wasn't listening; instead she took off after the girl, calling out for Maddy.

"Looks like you've got your hands full for the afternoon." Nancy stood in the doorway of the dining room. "I'll just run along now, and we can have tea another time."

"You can't—"

Olivia stopped herself before insisting that her friend stay, and . . . do what? The truth was, she wanted to leave herself and not face whatever her aunt had gotten her into.

Nancy was already out the front door before Olivia could reach her. Rushing out onto the front porch,

Olivia tried to stop her. "Don't just run off. Let me find out—"

A shrill squeal interrupted her and Olivia look up, dismayed to see the little girl far outdistancing Eula. Without a stitch of clothes, the child ran lickety-split around the side of the house into the front flower beds, trampling tulips and buttercups. Ladies out for their afternoon stroll stood gaping at the spectacle, and Nancy waved good-bye with a smile.

"Sarah, come back here!"

Oblivious to Eula's exasperation, the child giggled all the more and dashed toward the back once again. Hesitantly, Olivia followed the path they had taken around the house and found Aunt Eula leading her wayward charge up the steps. The child's hair was a mass of dark curls, still dripping wet, and her eyes were bright with mischief. Olivia could tell little else about her for the towel draped over her shoulders, except, of course, that her bare feet were muddy from a dash through the flower bed.

"Aunt Eula, we need a chance to think this over."

"What do we need to think over?" Eula brushed past Olivia and led the child into the kitchen. Maddy hurried to hoist the little girl back into the tub of water, scolding her for running off and for tracking dirt on the freshly mopped floor.

"There is a great deal to consider."

Eula motioned for her to be quiet and led her out into the hall while Maddy bathed the little girl for the second time.

"You would actually consider turning away a motherless child?'' Eula's hushed tone didn't disguise her disappointment. ''You were raised better than that, Olivia Chandler. And you of all people should sympathize with her situation.''

Indeed, Olivia remembered very well the overwhelming sense of loss at her own mother's death, but she resented the comparison. ''I was much older than she is, and—''

''You loved your mother less when you were younger?''

''Don't twist my words around.'' Olivia cringed inwardly, hating the way she sounded. ''I only meant—''

Maddy led Sarah into the hall, once again clean and draped with a towel, and issued the child a stern warning. ''Don't let me catch you traipsing through this house with muddy feet again, you hear?''

Sarah nodded, and Maddy returned her to Eula. With hardly a glance in Olivia's direction, her aunt dismissed the entire conversation, saying only, ''We'll talk about this later.''

Eula held out her hand to Sarah and led her toward the stairs. ''Come along, child. We have to get you dressed before your papa gets here.''

Olivia breathed a sigh of relief. Matthew was coming for the child, so the arrangement was only fleeting. Thank goodness. When he arrived she would offer her solution to his problem—a full-time nursemaid to care for the girl and ease her own conscience.

She followed Maddy into the kitchen. ''Will it be too much trouble if Mr. Bowen stays for supper?''

"Of course not." Maddy stooped to open the oven door and check whatever was baking inside. The wonderful aroma of apples and cinnamon filled the kitchen, and Olivia remembered how Matthew always bragged on Maddy's apple pie. "He'll be coming for supper most every night."

"Every night?" Obviously Maddy remembered as well.

"As long as the child is staying with us." Straightening up, she closed the oven door and began checking each of the simmering pots on the stove. "I say it's for the best. The child won't think he's took off and left her."

"Well, it seems you and Aunt Eula have everything worked out," she snapped. "I wish you had taken the trouble to ask my opinion."

Maddy eyed her with a solemn expression. "We figured you was Christian enough not to have any different opinion."

Olivia opened her mouth to rebut but said nothing. Instead, she turned and left the kitchen without a word, refusing to accept the dilemma everyone seemed determined to force upon her.

"Good evenin', Mr. Bowen. Come right on in."

"Hello, Maddy." Matthew stepped inside the foyer of the house he knew so well as a boy. Glancing around the spacious entryway, he was astonished to see that the interior of the house was just as he remembered. Nothing had been changed or even rearranged. It seemed a lifetime since his last visit, and it saddened him to think how much *had* changed since that time. "It's good to see you."

"Daddy!"

He turned at the sound of his baby girl's voice and smiled at the sight of her running toward him. He knelt down and scooped her into his embrace, savoring the feel of her arms around his neck. "Hello, sweetheart. How's my girl?"

"I had a baf'," she informed him, leaning back to study his face. "Got soap in my eyes."

"Well, you look awfully pretty." Lowering the child to her feet, he took her hand and twirled her about as if waltzing. The dress she was wearing was one he'd never seen, and it was obviously brand new and very costly. "Where did you get the new dress?"

"Eu-la give it to me." She stepped back and hiked the skirt up to her waist. "Lace panties, too."

He laughed at her and smoothed the dress back in place. "Those aren't for showing off."

Maddy shook her head. "Lord have mercy, this child ain't timid, that's for sure."

Glancing up, Matthew caught sight of Olivia watching them from the parlor, as if she'd stumbled upon a snake and was trying to decide if it was poisonous or not.

"Good evening, Mr. Bowen." She smiled slightly, almost wincing from the effort. "I'm pleased you could join us."

He rose to his feet, not liking the way she spoke to him as if he was a stranger one bit, but he could scarcely protest. Sarah held tight to his hand and led him into the parlor. "Thank you for inviting me."

"Matthew! I didn't hear you come in." Eula swept inside the parlor and smiled at Sarah. "What does your papa think about you being so gussied up?"

"She looks like a princess." Sarah beamed at his compliment and Matthew glanced at Olivia, trying to guess her thoughts.

"Well, dinner is on the table," Eula told them all. "Let's not let things get cold."

Matthew tried to concentrate on Sarah's jubilant tale of nearly escaping her bath and picking flowers for the table, but he was so tired he could barely get through the meal. At last they all rose from the table and he bid Sarah kiss him good night before he left.

"No-ooo!" she cried, flinging her arms around his neck. "I wan' go with you!"

He swallowed hard. "No, honey, you're going to stay here, but I'll be back to see you tomorrow."

"No, Daddy, please." she begged, her tiny face puckering with misery. "Don' go."

"I have to, sweetie." He was at a loss and looked to Olivia for help.

"Miss Olivia and I want you to spend the night here," Eula cajoled the unhappy child. "Won't that be fun?"

She shook her head miserably. "No, no. I want Daddy."

"What about Miss Nellie?" Eula shook her head. "She'll be so sad to know you left her."

A tug of war ensued and the child was torn. Matthew asked her, "Who is Miss Nellie?"

"My ba-by," was the hoarse reply. "She's upstairs."

"Let Daddy tuck you in and then he'll be back tomorrow," Eula suggested.

At last she nodded, and Eula told her she was a brave little girl. "Olivia, dear, I had Maddy make up the trundle bed in your room.

Olivia's face paled. "My room?"

"Of course, dear. She can't sleep in a room all alone in a strange house, and my room doesn't have a trundle."

An awkward silence followed that implied Olivia was to lead the way, and her reluctance was obvious. At last she said, "This way."

He followed her up the stairs, bearing Sarah's limp form. He heard her yawn in his ear and knew she would be asleep before long. Olivia paused before the door of her bedroom, and he was surprised by the blush on her face.

Once inside, he felt suffocated by the delicate, feminine things. The room smelled of flowers and perfume, and he guessed the tiny bottles covering the top of the dressing table accounted for that.

Olivia bent to retrieve a tiny nightgown that lay folded on her bed and awkwardly held it out to him. He eased the little girl to her feet, but she slumped against him, rubbing her eyes. Olivia reached for the buttons of her dress just as he did and his fingers brushed against hers. He drew back as if burned.

Indeed, the feel of her skin in such an intimate setting was more than he could bear.

She methodically went about the task of removing Sarah's dress and petticoat, all new and costly, and drew the nightgown over her head. He turned back the covers on the narrow bed beside Olivia's and placed the sleepy child on the starched white sheets. Olivia presented him with a doll and whispered, "Miss Nellie."

He nodded and laid the doll beside his daughter and smiled as she embraced it. "Good night, sweetheart." He brushed a kiss against her forehead. "Sweet dreams."

Tears budded in her eyes once again, but she whispered, "G'night, Daddy."

He hated leaving her. She was too young to understand why she couldn't stay in her own home, why someone else had to care for her while he struggled to hold on to the land. It had been hard enough making her understand that her mother wasn't coming back, that death was forever.

He brushed a single tear from her face. "You be a good girl for Miss Olivia."

She nodded, and he forced himself to his feet and turned to find that Olivia was waiting outside in the hall. "Just leave the door open," she said as he stepped out of the room. "I'll stay up here with her. So she won't be afraid."

He studied her in the soft light spilling out of the bedroom, deciding she looked older but hadn't aged. There was a staid elegance about her, and he fought the urge to trace the gentle curve of her face with his fingers, just to see if it felt as soft as it looked. "I'll never be able to thank you enough for doing this."

Her only response was a slight nod of her head. "Good night, then."

Knowing he had been dismissed, he nodded. "Good night."

Olivia closed the door behind her and sank against the smooth polished surface. She couldn't do this. She just couldn't. There was no way she could endure seeing Matthew Bowen at her dining-room table every night when the slightest touch of his hand nearly overwhelmed her.

Already she felt bereft of his presence, the room oddly empty, and she caught the masculine scent of shaving soap and leather that lingered behind to taunt her. She folded her arms, as if to shield herself from the very thought of him, and crossed the room to turn the covers down on her bed.

She hesitated before turning to retrieve her nightgown from the armoire and peered over the side of the bed. The little girl had drifted off to sleep, clutching the doll to her chest, and Olivia studied her for a long time.

She was a pretty child, and the resemblance to her father was evident. Still, Olivia couldn't ignore the features she'd obviously inherited from her mother. She'd only once actually spoken to Matthew's wife, and she cringed now at the memory. She'd been hurrying down the street, on her way to the mill, when she'd encountered a group of women gathered in front of the dry goods store. Matthew's wife had stood in the center, holding her new baby, while everyone ooh'd and aah'd over the child.

They'd all seen Olivia, and there was no way to turn and run. Instead, she nodded politely and tried to walk past them without stopping. But someone couldn't resist calling out to her, "Olivia, don't you want to see the baby?"

She could have kept walking but the sweetly spoken dare had galled her to the core. She turned and glanced at the child and the mother.

"She's just an angel," the new mother said. "And looks just like Matthew."

"Well, I'm sure you're both relieved by that."

With that she turned and continued on her way, ignoring the collective gasps of shock and indignation. Let them say anything they liked about her except that she was a coward.

Tonight she had felt so awkward, standing there while Matthew coaxed the child into staying behind, and shaken to realize how deeply he cared for her. Olivia tried to remember her father displaying such open affection toward her or her brother, even once. Dinners had been cold, tense affairs, and she never dared speak up during the meal, much less chatter on about her day.

Shaking herself from such self-pitying thoughts, she turned toward the bureau and removed her nightgown and began undressing. The gown had barely settled around her feet before Aunt Eula tapped on the door and poked her head inside.

"I see she's fast asleep."

"Yes," Olivia whispered. "I wish you would stay in here with her. I could take your room."

"No need to do that," her aunt dismissed the suggestion. "She'll be fine."

"But I don't know anything about children."

"Merciful heavens, you were a little girl once. Don't you remember?"

"Not really," Olivia admitted. "Will she sleep all night?"

"Of course," Eula assured her, backing out of the room. Just before the door closed, she added, "Unless she wets the bed."

Chapter Six

Olivia slept fitfully, jumping at every sound, but the little girl never woke up during the night. Finally, she dozed off and slept soundly. Sunlight streamed through the gauzy curtains that framed her windows, and Olivia couldn't help yawning as she peered over the edge of the bed to check on the child.

The trundle bed was empty! Olivia bolted from beneath the covers and snatched the blanket from the tiny bed. Nothing. She dropped to her knees and peered under the bed. Nothing. She scanned every corner of the room and even searched the armoire in case Sarah had climbed inside to hide. Olivia's insides quaked. Dear Lord, the child had disappeared! What in the world would she tell Matthew?

She snatched her dressing gown from the peg and scrambled down the stairs as she dealt with the sleeves and the sash.

"Aunt Eula!" she called out when she reached the bottom of the staircase. "Maddy, where are you?"

"We're in here, dear!" Eula's bright voice reached her ears and Olivia's bare feet nearly slipped out from under her as she turned toward the dining room.

"I can't find—"

The sight of Sarah seated at the dining-room table, eating a biscuit dripping with jelly, made Olivia weak with relief. She caught hold of the back of a chair and tried to slow her breathing.

"What's wrong, dear?"

"I didn't—" she began, but her words dissolved when she realized how foolish her reaction had been. Naturally, Eula had come to claim the child for breakfast and left Olivia to sleep. She felt like a goose. "Oh, I just didn't realize Sarah was downstairs already."

"And already dressed," Eula pointed out, glancing at her niece's bare feet and haphazardly belted robe. "You'd better be getting dressed yourself. You two have a big day ahead of you."

"What do you mean?" Olivia sank into a chair and gratefully accepted the steaming cup of coffee Eula poured for her. "I'm expected at the mill this morning, and then—"

"Sarah can go along with you," Eula said by way of dismissing Olivia's objections. "I have two separate committee meetings at the church. I'll be there most of the day, and a child can't be expected to sit through all of that.''

"But Maddy can—"

Eula shook her head. "Today is her day off and she's going to visit her sister."

Olivia nodded. Maddy's days off meant as much to her as the salary she now drew. All day Sunday, half a day Saturday, and all day Tuesday, except for the time she spent preparing breakfast, although they were subject to change without notice. Olivia couldn't ask her to stay home just because she felt awkward around the little girl.

Olivia glanced at Sarah to find the child eyeing her with undisguised skepticism, but she couldn't blame her. What did she know about children?

She was trying not to resent her aunt's good intentions, and under different circumstances, Olivia probably would have done the same thing.

There were many in the community, men *and* women, who found themselves left to raise families alone, but most had relatives to help them manage. Those who didn't usually remarried as soon as possible, just as Nancy said. Something twisted inside her at the thought of Matthew marrying again out of haste and necessity, but the thought of him marrying for love was no less comforting.

The mill was a noisy place, filled with men's voices and whining machinery. Sarah's bottom lip began to quiver and she shook her head when Olivia bid her inside the entrance.

"Don't be afraid." She tried to think of something reassuring to say. "It's just a lot of saws and—"

Sarah's eyes widened in alarm and Olivia shut up before she had the child so frightened she wouldn't go near the place.

At last she held out her hand and smiled. "Come along, Sarah, nothing's going to hurt you."

The little girl took her hand without hesitation, and Olivia was startled by the feel of those tiny fingers clamped around her own. How easily the child trusted her, and she felt the need to be worthy of such faith.

She squeezed Sarah's hand and led the way inside the office. The clerk, Homer McNeely, bolted from his chair even before she closed the door.

"M-Miss Chandler!" he stammered. "We just about gave up on you coming in today."

Olivia frowned slightly. "I'm just a little later than usual. You know I would have sent word if I weren't coming in today."

Chagrined, he nodded. "Yes'm, I knew that."

"This is Sarah," Olivia said by way of introduction and explanation. "She'll be visiting with me for a few days, and I brought her to see the mill."

Homer relaxed somewhat and smiled. "Howdy-do, Miss Sarah."

Sarah tightened her hold on Olivia's hand and huddled close to her side. Olivia felt her heart swell at the gesture, though being preferred to Homer was no vote of confidence. She smiled down at the little girl. "Why don't we go upstairs and you can see where I do my work?"

Sarah nodded, but Homer bounded from his desk and blocked the way. "I don't think your office has been swept out yet. Wait here and I'll go up and do it."

"Don't be silly." Olivia brushed past him. "I don't mind a little dust."

He caught hold of her arm and pleaded, "Miss Olivia, wait!"

"Have you taken leave of your senses?" she demanded in a hushed whisper.

He shook his head miserably, dropping his hand. "No, ma'am."

"Then stand aside."

"Yes, ma'am."

Olivia led Sarah upstairs. Just as they reached the top step, she heard voices coming from her office. The first she didn't recognize, but there was no mistaking the second.

"I'm sure you'll be very pleased," Rodger said with a confidence that bordered on arrogance.

The second party was not impressed. "I expect no less."

Olivia turned the doorknob slowly and opened the door without a sound. The room was filled with cigar smoke and the stench nearly choked her. Both men stood facing the large window with their backs to her, and Rodger was using his cigar to point out the finer points of the mill.

"I'm sure you know the facility is the largest of its

kind in the area. We can produce more lumber in a week than most in a month."

Olivia closed the door none too gently, startling Rodger so that he dropped his cigar. The stranger turned around, cool as a cucumber, and smiled. "You must be Miss Chandler. We've been expecting you."

He was older than she had first thought, at least in his fifties, but his face was more weathered than it was aged. The slight graying of his hair at the temples emphasized the piercing blue eyes that quickly assessed rather than stared. It was obvious he was capable of being intimidating if the need arose.

Olivia didn't intimidate easily. "I doubt that. Otherwise, you wouldn't be filling my office with a lot of foul-smelling smoke."

Rodger had managed to retrieve his smoldering cigar from under her desk and scrambled to his feet, abashed, and hastily brushed ashes from the sleeve of his jacket. "Olivia, this is Michael Sullivan. He's interested in purchasing lumber for—"

"For your textile mill," she concluded. "Very ambitious of you, building a new factory so far from river traffic."

"I see you make it your business to investigate any newcomers to your town, Miss Chandler," he said, his polished English accent making the statement sound like a compliment. "I suppose the freight trains can accommodate textiles as well as they can your lumber and cotton."

Olivia knew the difference between a compliment

and a challenge. "You've done a little investigating as well."

He nodded. "However, I wasn't aware that you had children."

Olivia glanced down at Sarah and felt her face flush. "Oh, no. Sarah is only visiting me for a short while."

"That's Matthew's little girl, isn't it?" Rodger was incredulous. "You're keeping Matthew Bowen's child?"

"For the time being," she countered. Inwardly she groaned. Rodger would carry the news home and Ada would have it all over the county by noon tomorrow.

"Rodger and I will finish our cigars outside," Sullivan said, tactfully breaking the awkward silence. "I'm anxious to see the rest of your facility."

Normally, Olivia would have dismissed Rodger and conducted the tour herself, but she couldn't leave Sarah behind with a stranger or take her along. The child would be terrified of the screeching saws and workmen shouting to be heard above the noise.

She smiled and nodded, grateful for the diversion. "Good day to you, then."

They were gone, but the foul stench of cigar smoke lingered in the air. Olivia crossed the room and opened the window, hoping for a strong breeze. She glanced back to find Sarah watching her. The child was swallowed up by the enormous scale of the room and glanced about uneasily.

"I've just a little work to do and then we can go," Olivia explained as she settled behind the enormous mahogany desk. Once seated, she could barely glimpse the top of Sarah's head and realized the child couldn't see her, either. Knowing only too well how imposing that desk could be, Olivia peered over the edge and suggested, "You can come around here with me, if you like."

Sarah rushed to Olivia's side and clung to the arm of her chair, her eyes wide. A stack of pay vouchers waited for Olivia's signature, and she had the work orders for the next week to review. The little girl's eyes were riveted on every stroke of Olivia's fountain pen, admiring the precise lettering. Inside the drawer, Olivia found the stub of a pencil and a blank sheet of stationery and showed Sarah the proper way to hold the pencil.

Sarah carefully drew a line across the top of the paper and glanced up at Olivia for approval.

"Very good," Olivia praised, and the child beamed with pride and accomplishment. "Do you like to draw pictures?"

Olivia sketched a cat with pointy ears and whiskers and a house with a smoking chimney. Sarah eagerly took the pencil and proceeded to create her own characters while Olivia continued with her work. The little girl's brow puckered in concentration, and Olivia couldn't help smiling whenever she glanced over at her.

At last the work was done and Sarah beamed with pride at all they had accomplished. Olivia rose from the desk and moved to close the window. Voices met her ears.

"Now don't concern yourself with Olivia," Rodger was saying. "She's hard-headed and contrary, but she does have good business sense—for a woman, that is."

He was talking with Sullivan, she knew it even before she heard the man ask, "Then why doesn't she deal with the customers?"

"She doesn't know enough about the business and doesn't want to embarrass herself," Rodger explained. "She always listens to me, and I know a good opportunity when I see it."

Olivia closed the window quietly and watched Sullivan shake hands with her cousin and march out of the lumber yard. Rodger stood watching him for several seconds before turning back to the mill, a supercilious smile on his face. The fool. He wouldn't know a good opportunity from a hole in the ground.

Rodger turned toward the warehouse instead of the office building and ducked inside. Olivia could dismiss idle bragging on his part, but his furtive assurances to Sullivan raised suspicions she couldn't ignore.

If he was up to no good, flying off the handle and confronting him now would only alert him to her suspicions and make her look like a fool if he were not. The best thing she could do would be to let him play his hand and see which way the wind blew. It was unsettling to think someone so close to her was not above going behind her back, and she hoped Rodger would prove her misgivings to be unwarranted.

Forcing a smile, she turned back to Sarah. "Why don't we go back to my house? I'm sure Miss Eula is home by now."

Sarah glanced back toward the desk. "How 'bout my pic-sure?"

"Your picture?" Olivia repeated. "What about— oh! Your picture. We must take it with us to show Miss Eula."

Sarah smiled and gingerly claimed the scrawled sheet of paper and held it out to Olivia. Once outside, she and Sarah found a safe place for the picture behind the buggy seat and started for home.

Halfway through town, Olivia remembered a package waiting for her at the mercantile and drew the team to a halt. She hefted Sarah down from the buggy and led her inside the store. The tiny bell jingled above her head as they stepped inside, and she nodded in acknowledgment of the shopkeeper's greeting. The store was eerily quiet, and Olivia glanced up to find at least seven or eight women staring at her in undisguised shock.

She steeled her gaze, and they all looked away, each feigning interest in some insignificant piece of merchandise. Turning her attention, Olivia didn't miss the hushed whispers and bristled at the thought of being the subject of petty gossip. The sound of someone clearing her throat startled her.

She turned to find Eugenia Jennings at her side. "My, my, Olivia, who do you have with you today?"

She didn't bother returning the woman's simpering smile. "This is Sarah."

"Matthew's little girl? Well, hello, Sarah," Eugenia cooed. "Are you visiting with Miss Olivia today?"

The little girl backed away from her and clung to

Olivia's hand. Eugenia was not at all discouraged. "She certainly seems attached to you, Olivia. Does this mean that you're going to be her new mama?"

"Of course, not," Olivia snapped, realizing too late that her hasty denial would feed the gossip mill just as well as a confirmation.

"That's a shame." Eugenia shook her head sadly. "Poor Matthew. All alone with a child to raise. I can't believe you'd pass up the opportunity."

She felt herself stiffen at the remark. "The matter is none of your business, and I resent your prying and insinuations."

Eugenia's eyes widened with exaggerated innocence. "Why, dear, I don't know what you mean."

"You know very well what I mean." Olivia deliberately lowered her voice. "How dare you imply that I would use a child for such a purpose?"

"Well, Olivia, you own everything else in town. I don't see why you don't just buy yourself a husband."

"That's good advice. I'll remember it when yours brings his cotton to market."

Eugenia paled visibly, remembering too late with whom she was dealing, but Olivia didn't relent. It was her turn to smile sweetly. "After all, why should I buy a husband when I already own yours?"

Her spite found its mark, and the woman's eyes narrowed with impotent fury, but she dared not reciprocate. Instead, she returned to her friends with as much defiance as she could muster and led them out of the store before relating her version of the encounter.

Olivia glanced down at Sarah and smoothed the child's wispy curls away from her face. Try as she might, Olivia couldn't think of anything to say to alleviate the tense mood that had spoiled an otherwise pleasant afternoon. Instead, she made a feeble suggestion that Sarah peruse the sparse selection of toys Parson's had in stock.

The plain truth was that she just couldn't do this. No one would ever believe she was keeping the child for the sake of kindness alone. She would have to find a nurse for Sarah and take her back to her father. The child would still be cared for and Matthew wouldn't lose any time in the fields.

"Here's your package, Miss Olivia."

The storekeeper's voice startled her, and she was mortified to realize he had probably heard the entire exchange between Eugenia Jennings and herself. Why had she let that woman goad her into such a petty confrontation? She might have had the last word, but Eugenia would have the satisfaction of knowing her accusations had been deeply disturbing.

Still more troubling was the knowledge that news of her keeping Sarah would be all over town by nightfall, and the natural assumption would be that it was part of some desperate hope of winning back the man who had spurned her not so many years ago. She simply could not allow it, especially when she found herself sorry to think the remotest possibility didn't exist.

*   *   *

For two days Matthew hated himself for leaving Sarah with strangers. It was mostly guilt for not being able to care for her himself, but he would have felt somewhat better if she had been better acquainted with either Olivia or her aunt. Nothing, however, could ease his conscience over ignoring her cries to go home and leaving her behind. He couldn't forget the pitiful picture she made, clutching her doll and fighting back tears, and he didn't know if he had the heart to do it again.

But his concern forced him to visit the Chandler home, to assure himself that she was being cared for and to reassure her that she would be coming home soon. If the weather held out, he would have the crops planted in a matter of weeks. After that, he would be better able to manage caring for Sarah himself.

Dusk was just beginning to settle as he made his way up the front steps of the Chandler house, and before he could knock the sounds of laughter reached his ears. He recognized Sarah's infectious giggle, but her words were impossible to understand coming from behind the house. He forgot about knocking and searched out the voices.

He found Sarah and Olivia on the back porch. From his vantage point he could see an expression of intense concentration on his little girl's face. She was lying on her stomach, scrubbing a charcoal pencil over a large sheet of paper, her eyes flitting up to Olivia, whose face warmed with a smile—a smile he hadn't seen since he was little more than a boy. He stared in silence for many moments, as if he were gazing through a window into the past.

Her hair had come loose from its pins in the late afternoon breeze and the errant strands fanned her face and caught the radiance of the setting sun, turning the soft brown locks russet flecked with gold. She leaned forward and pointed to some mark on the paper and they laughed again. Sarah quickly resumed her work.

Olivia straightened up and reached out to smooth a lock of hair from her face, only to have the breeze unsettle it. She turned away from the breeze and froze at the sight of him. She knew at once that he'd been watching her; the horror in her eyes said so, and her face grew flushed.

Sarah looked up at him, startled and delighted both. She leapt to her feet and cried, " Daddy! Daddy, look what I got!"

He scooped the little girl into his arms and hugged her tight. "What have you got, darlin'?"

The carefree expression disappeared from Olivia's face and she struggled to her feet before he could offer to help her stand. She smoothed the wrinkles out of her skirt and her smile disappeared along with them. In a stiffly formal voice, she managed, "Good evening."

"Good evening," he returned, stung by her summary dismissal. Whatever game she had been playing with Sarah was over, and she certainly wasn't going to include him.

Sarah began to twist in his arms, wanting down to show him her new toys. He knelt beside his daughter and listened to her breathless account of finding the sketch pad at the store and bringing it back to Olivia's house. He noticed she was wearing another new dress and a matching ribbon in her hair.

"I trust you'll be joining us for dinner?"

Olivia's guarded statement could hardly be considered an invitation, but he had come to spend time with Sarah, not her. "If it's not an imposition."

"Of course not." She didn't wait for a reply. "I'll let Maddy know we need another place setting."

With that she turned and disappeared inside the house Forcing his attention back to Sarah, Matthew carefully studied the drawings she had been working on, amused at the images Sarah picked out of the jumbled mass of lines and squiggles.

"Careful, Daddy, don't tear the paper."

"I'll be careful." An old quilt had been spread out on the porch and he followed her when she plopped back down. "When did you learn to draw?"

"Livvy showed me," she explained, returning her attention to her artwork.

He gave her a gentle pat on the back, struck by the pride and affection in her voice.

Livvy.

* * *

Somehow Olivia had survived dinner seated across from Matthew, painfully aware of his eyes on her and wondering if he questioned her motives for caring for the child.

Tonight Sarah had not cried to go home with him, but she pleaded with her father not to leave.

"I can't stay here," he tried to explain. "I have to take care of the animals and work in the field."

The explanation mollified her enough to prompt a good-night kiss without further protest.

Olivia helped her into the lacy nightgown that fell to her feet and brushed her hair. Once Sarah was settled in the tiny trundle bed beside her own, Olivia readied herself for bed but doubted she would sleep a wink that night.

She lay in the darkness, listening to the rain pattering against the windowpane, and found herself thinking of all the plans she'd made, waiting for Matthew's return. She begged him not to speak to her father, knowing the man would find some way to ruin everything, until the war was over and they could marry right away. After all, they were going to whip the Yankees in six weeks, and that wasn't such a long time to wait.

Pushing the painful memories aside, Olivia drew the sheet up to her chin and thought of all she had to do the next day. Finding a nurse would be difficult, especially without having everyone in the county know what she was about.

The arrangement wouldn't be permanent, and finding an older, experienced woman willing to uproot herself without a guarantee of longtime employment would be difficult. There was no other choice but to seek an older, mature woman if she was to live in Matthew's house for any length of time. A younger woman might get ideas about making the situation permanent, one way or another.

Indeed, Matthew was still considered quite the catch by postwar standards. He still had land and a home, and any scars he carried from the war were not visible. Many men had returned home to find their wives and sweethearts unable to accept the ghastly results of cannon fire and shrapnel.

Lightning flashed in the night sky and thunder boomed loud enough to rattle the windowpanes. Olivia turned away from the window and tried to go to sleep.

"Livvy?" Sarah's tiny voice came out of the darkness.

"Yes?"

"Can I sleep with you?"

She understood the little girls qualms only too well, and she threw back the covers and helped the child climb into her bed.

Sarah snuggled close and Olivia awkwardly gathered the little girl in her arms. "When I was a little girl I was so afraid of thunderstorms."

"Real 'fraid?" Sarah asked in a hesitant whisper.

"Terrified. Sometimes I would hide under the bed." Another clap of thunder rumbled, nearer than the last, and Sarah huddled closer to Olivia. "But we don't have to be afraid tonight."

"We don't?"

"No, we don't," Olivia assured her. "You see, I learned that the thunder and lightning couldn't really hurt me as long as I was inside."

They lay silent for many moments, listening as the storm gained momentum and the rain pounded furiously at the window.

"Livvy?" Sarah whispered. "Did you have a mama?"

The question startled her, and she swallowed hard before answering, "Yes, I did."

"Did she go to heaven?"

"When I was twelve years old."

"My mama went to heaven," Sarah told her, as if it was some terrible secret. "She won't ever come back."

"People can't come back when they go to heaven." Olivia grappled for some way to change the subject. "Try not to think about—"

Sarah's fingers knotted in the sleeve of her nightgown, and a ragged breath escaped the little girl's lips. "B-but I don't *want* her to be in heaven."

"Oh, Sarah," she whispered as the child buried her face against Olivia's shoulder. Hot tears dampened the thin fabric of her nightgown. "Your mama didn't want to go to heaven—"

Sarah sniffed "I want her to come back and take care of me so my daddy won't burd-ing."

Olivia thought for a moment. "You mean burdened?"

Sarah nodded. Olivia could only guess how many times the child had heard that whispered when no one thought she was listening. She remembered the spiteful things Eugenia Jennings had said today and wondered how Sarah had taken them. "Sarah, your father isn't burdened. He's just working hard to plant his cotton, and so are a lot of other men."

She was the last person on earth to be comforting this child, but she held Sarah close and rocked her, repeating what Matthew had told her so many years ago. "It's all right to cry, to be sad, to wish for things to be different."

Sarah nodded against her shoulder, her sobs quieting to deep, cleansing breaths. Olivia forced herself to say what this child needed to hear. "Your mother still loves you, Sarah. Even in heaven, she won't forget you or stop caring about you."

Sarah rubbed her eyes, absorbing Olivia's words. Settling back down under the covers, Olivia gathered the little girl in her arms and shuddered with guilt.

"Livvy," Sarah whispered, "what's a orphan's home?"

Startled, Olivia was horrified to think someone dared to suggest Matthew place the child in an asylum. "An orphan's home is for children with no family or friends to take care of them. Your have your father, and he will see that you're taken care of."

Circling her arm around Olivia's neck, she said, "I got you too, Livvy."

Olivia closed her eyes. God help her, but she would find a nurse if she had to travel all the way to Richmond.

Chapter Seven

Dear Mrs. Murphy,

I am writing in hopes that you might be able to recommend a suitable governess for a family friend. The child, a girl, is three years old and remarkably well-behaved and bright. Experience and maturity are crucial, and I would prefer someone capable of tutoring in reading and music.

Please have all interested parties forward a résumé along with any letters of recommendation available.

Sincerely,
Olivia Chandler

*   *   *

"Your daddy will be here any minute. Let's get your clothes changed."

Olivia helped Sarah out of her Sunday dress and slipped a simple muslin blouse over her head. The blue jumper and sturdy shoes were nice enough, but Sarah had looked darling in the dress she had worn to church. Eula insisted the child change into everyday clothes and be ready to leave when Matthew arrived.

"He won't want to be kept waiting," she had insisted as she hurried them up the stairs. "Don't forget the hamper in the kitchen."

When the last button was secured, Olivia carefully brushed Sarah's hair and changed the ribbon to one that matched her jumper. Sarah peered in the mirror hanging over the dressing table and smiled with approval.

"You look very pretty," Olivia assured her, smoothing one last curl into place. "Now, let's go wait for your daddy."

It wasn't long before a knock sounded at the front door, and Olivia managed a polite smile when she invited Matthew inside. "Sarah's all ready to go."

"Good," he said as she closed the door behind him. "We won't have much time as it is."

She nodded and called for Sarah, who was tidying away her toys in the parlor.

"Daddy!" She rushed to him and he scooped her up in his arms.

"Are you ready, punkin'?"

She nodded, and Olivia almost forgot the hamper. "Oh, Aunt Eula packed a picnic for the two of you. Wait here."

When she returned with the basket, Sarah rushed to meet her.

"C'mon, Livvy!" The child caught hold of her hand and turned for the door. "Let's go! Let's go picnic!"

"I'm not going with you sweet—Sarah." Handing the basket to Matthew, she resisted the urge to smooth the little girl's bangs out of her eyes and clasped her hands behind her back instead. "You and your father are going to spend the day together."

"There's no reason you can't join us. Is there?"

She raised her eyes to find Matthew studying her uncertainly, and she wished she could say she had other plans. Instead, she bit her lip and tried to think of a plausible excuse.

Sarah held tight to her hand. "Please, Livvy, please!"

She looked into the little pleading face and felt helpless. She hesitated before asking Matthew, "I wouldn't be intruding?"

His face softened with a grin. "Of course not."

Olivia had only visited Matthew's farm once, after his father had died, but she hadn't stayed long or even gone inside the house. Even so, there was no mistaking the maintenance that had gone undone— the paint on the house was faded, two shutters were missing and one upstairs window was boarded up.

"There was a storm last fall," he explained. "A limb off that elm tree crashed right through the window."

"Oh, my," she murmured. Olivia wondered if that room was his bedroom, but she didn't ask. "How frightening."

Sarah was delighted to be home. She scrambled down from the wagon and ran toward the back of the house. The yard was neat and bare, and Sarah ran toward a giant oak tree. "Look, Livvy, my swing!"

"She calls you Livvy?"

Matthew was right beside her, but she didn't look at him. She knew he was referring to the irony of his child using the same pet name he had so many years before but merely said, "I suppose it's easier than Olivia."

He crossed the yard and helped the little girl into the swing. With a gentle push he set the swing in motion, and Sarah held tight while the breeze tugged at the ribbons in her hair.

Olivia turned toward the porch and placed the hamper on the top step, taking in the almost spartan appearance of the place. There were no flowers planted anywhere, just a grassy expanse of yard leading to the tilled fields that surrounded the house on three sides. To the south was the sloping pasture behind the barn where the livestock grazed.

"Watch me, Livvy!" Sarah called impatiently, swinging higher. "Watch me!"

"I'm watching." Olivia retraced her steps and bestowed her undivided attention on the child. "Be careful."

"I'm sorry I didn't have anything better planned for the afternoon. I thought it would be a good idea for her to spend some time at home." Matthew paused, hesitantly adding, "I hope it wasn't improper to invite you here."

She was surprised at his concern, but then, they had both been brought up under the same strict code of what was and wasn't acceptable for a lady. "Oh, don't worry about me. Aunt Eula says one of the best things about being an old maid is not having a reputation to guard."

Olivia could have bitten off her tongue, but the words were out before she thought twice. Eula could joke about things like that and get away with it, but Olivia feared she sounded self-pitying. She forced a smile in spite of the look of dismay on his face.

"I didn't mean—" She wasn't sure how to apologize for the remark or if she even should. "There's nothing inappropriate about my being here with you and Sarah. In fact, I appreciate being included."

Sarah finally tired of the swing and gave Olivia a tour of the farm, introducing her to several barnyard animals. To her amusement, they all had names and knew when they were spoken to. As a child, pets of any kind were never allowed in her home, and Olivia declined the opportunity of petting a pig or shaking hands with a rooster.

Just inside the barn, Sarah cried out for Olivia. "Hurry, Livvy! Oh, look!" Olivia peered over the child's kneeling form to find a mama cat dutifully tending four tiny kittens. "Aren't they precious?"

The mother glanced up at the humans and meowed her agreement. Sarah whispered to the cat and gently stroked each baby. Olivia had never seen anything so tiny or helpless.

"Their eyes aren't even open," she breathed, watching the kittens blindly grope for their mother. One baby turned in the wrong direction and wailed pitifully as he searched for the warmth and security of his mother.

Sarah carefully placed the frightened kitten at his mother's side and he quieted right away. The tour resumed, and Sarah led her through the vegetable garden to where the neat rows met the tilled expanse of the cotton fields.

Olivia glanced over her shoulder and asked Matthew, "How is the planting coming along?"

"Very well." He moved to stand beside her and gaze out across the land. "Thanks to your help."

She was struck by the pride and reverence in his expression as he studied the sprawling land. The place meant so much to him, more than the worth of the land or the promise of a lucrative harvest, and it shamed her to know that she had been reluctant to help him.

He glanced down at her. "I'll never be able to thank you enough."

She looked away, uncertain how to respond. Instead, she let Sarah lead her back toward the house, calling for her daddy to follow. They spread a faded quilt on the porch and ate the picnic lunch. Olivia was glad to see that Maddy had packed twice as much as they could eat. She would leave the remainder for Matthew to have the next day.

When they had finished eating, Sarah lay with her head resting on Olivia's lap and drifted off to sleep. When she was sound asleep, Olivia eased the little girl onto the quilt and began repacking the food into the basket.

"Tom Jennings told me that you and his wife had quite a row the other day."

The statement shattered the companionable silence, and Olivia gaped at him, horrified to think what tales he'd heard, let alone Eugenia's insinuations regarding her motives for keeping Sarah. Straightening her shoulders, she did her best to sound disdainful. "I didn't realize men were such gossips."

"Tom's afraid you'll hold Eugenia's insults against him. He's barely making it, Olivia. It wouldn't take much to ruin him."

She got to her feet before he could stop her. "Tom Jennings wouldn't give a damn what his wife said to me if it weren't for the fact that I own the gin."

"And the mill, the store and the bank."

"I don't own the bank," she snapped.

"You might as well. Old man Perkins doesn't want you moving your money, and he'd foreclose on his own mama if you wanted him to."

She only stared at him, wishing she could deny what he said. She had no intention of hurting Tom Jennings. He would get a fair price for his cotton, the same as everyone else. She wasn't, however, above letting him worry all summer long, dreading the moment he would pay the price for his wife's spite-fulness. The relief he would feel would do nothing to warm his heart toward the woman who caused him so much grief.

The idea had been appealing to Olivia, until now, with Matthew looking at her with such reproach.

"Let me tell Tom there's nothing for him to worry about."

She whirled around, turning her back to him. "It would be most improper for you to speak on my behalf to anyone. The gin is my business, and I'll run it as I see fit."

She made her way down the steps, wishing she'd never come here with them. She eased into the old swing, surprised at how sturdy it felt, and stared down at the worn patch of ground at her feet.

She flinched at the feel of his hands on her shoulders as he tried to apologize. "I shouldn't have asked you that, but Tom is a good friend of mine."

"I—" Olivia fought the tremble in her voice. "I understand."

His thumb traced the taut muscles at the base of her neck and she shuddered at the intimate touch. "Hold on," he told her.

"Hold on?"

"To the ropes," he explained, guiding her hand to the knotted ropes on either side of the swing. Gently, he drew the swing back against him, letting her back rest against his chest for just a moment, and nudged the swing forward.

When she made no complaint, he gave her a firm

push that sent her sailing over the worn ground. Olivia gasped at the feel of the breeze on her face and held on to the ropes for dear life. Just when she felt unsteady, he caught her and said, "This time, point your toes."

She did, and the swing carried her higher than she would have thought possible. Holding tight to the ropes, she let her head tilt back slightly but enough to see the clouds peeking through the green canopy of oak leaves. She felt giddy, light as a feather, and all that held her to the earth was the hard wooden seat and the feel of his hands on her back as she pushed higher and higher still.

At last, the swing slowed and he caught her, gently bringing the swing to a stop. She was breathless and held tight to the ropes, not trusting her legs enough to stand just yet. Taking her hands, he helped her to her feet and drew her near, brushing a kiss across her knuckles.

The touch of his lips against her skin sent shivers racing up her arm and along her spine. He studied her face for a moment before lowering his mouth to hers, barely brushing her lips with his own. Olivia tensed, knowing the kiss would be a dreadful mistake.

As if to reinforce her foreboding thoughts, a clap of thunder startled them both and she pulled away immediately. "Oh, goodness. We'd better get going before the bottom falls out."

He caught her by the hand and drew her against him, not waiting for her consent, and kissed her. Just as before, she was helpless to resist the waves of desire that rippled through her. She knew she should pull away, forbid him to touch her, and she would loathe herself later for not doing so.

He sensed her retreat and drew her closer, his arm circling her waist, and he deepened the kiss. Her lips parted beneath his and she raised a hand to his cheek, shuddering as her senses were bombarded by the taste, the scent and the feel of him. The feelings were new and enticing yet achingly familiar.

His lips left hers and found the sensitive flesh just below her ear. Olivia gasped at the gentle graze of his teeth along her throat, his breath hot against her skin when he whispered, "You're no old maid, Olivia. We both know that."

She stiffened at his words, uncertain if he was mocking her or insinuating an unspoken claim on her. With as much dignity as possible, she extracted herself from his arms and pinned him with a cool, disdainful look. "Do you really think I need to be reminded of that? Especially by you?"

Just as she turned back toward the porch, heavy raindrops began to pummel the ground. Sarah was still sleeping on the pallet, and Olivia once again began to gather up the remains of their picnic. "We'd better get going if you're going to see me home before nightfall."

A sudden boom of thunder drowned out his reply and startled Sarah from her peaceful nap. Abandoning the task, Olivia hurried to reassure the child that everything was fine. "Come on, sweetheart, let's go back to my house."

"We'll have to wait out the storm." Matt scaled the steps, his shirt splattered with dampness. "There's no sense in the three of us getting soaked for the sake of your pride."

No sooner than he spoke, the lightning flashed across the sky and thunder shook the columns of the porch. "Let's get inside."

The screen door slammed shut behind them, and Sarah flinched in his arms but remained asleep. Olivia moved about the kitchen warily and removed her hat and gloves.

"I'm sorry about this—"

"Don't apologize." She waved off his concern. "It can't be helped."

"The storm was sudden, and I doubt we would have made it before the road washed out."

"It's all right," she insisted, but her restless pacing betrayed her apprehension.

He wasn't looking forward to having her stay overnight any more than she was, but it couldn't be helped. "I need to put Sarah in her bed."

Olivia glanced up and nodded.

"I'll be right back."

Again, she only nodded, and he turned toward the stairs without further comment. As he placed Sarah on her narrow bed and drew the faded blanket over her sleeping form, he was reminded how much he missed having her home. He couldn't ask for a sweeter child, and he felt more guilty than ever for sending her away from home, even temporarily.

At least Sarah was fond of Olivia, and, despite every attempt to appear ambivalent, Olivia was quite taken with the child. The situation would be ideal if things weren't so awkward between him and Olivia. Would his timing with her always be so bad?

He didn't regret the kiss, not in the least, and her ardent response really hadn't surprised him. Once again he'd pushed too far and said the wrong thing, causing her to pull away from him and regret her actions.

He could never have guessed that an afternoon thunder shower, sudden as it might have been, could turn into a downpour, washing out the road and leaving her stranded at his house. For the night.

The kitchen was empty and eerily quiet, and he found Olivia on the porch, sitting in an old rocking chair that creaked with the slightest movement. She glanced up at him, thankfully without wariness, and managed a slight smile.

"It's always so peaceful after a storm," she said, by way of explaining her being outside. "They say the night air is bad for you, but I find it somewhat refreshing."

He let the door close behind him and crossed the porch to sit across from her on the swing. The old chain groaned beneath his weight, and he suspected she felt a good deal safer out here than inside the house with him.

"Olivia, I can't tell you how sorry I am about this."

"I told you before, it can't be helped."

"Coming here for the day was probably foolish, but I don't want Sarah to forget where her home is."

"No, it wasn't foolish at all," she insisted, her voice much softer this time. "I simply had no business tagging along."

"Sarah enjoys being with you," he told her. "And so do I."

"Oh, Matthew, don't say things like that."

Before she could look away, he saw the pain in her eyes, and he cursed himself for hurting her. Again.

"Because of what happened so long ago?" he prompted. "Or because of what happened this afternoon?"

"It wasn't that long ago," she insisted, ignoring the second half of his question.

"Ryan knew your father would never approve of our getting married and would probably disown you if we did." This was the first time he'd had a chance to explain things to her, and he didn't mince words. "When you didn't answer my letter, I thought it was because you despised me."

She shook her head. "The letter was three months getting here, and by then I wasn't sure where you were or if you were even still alive. Everything fell apart toward the end of the war." She paused for a moment. "I did answer the letter right away, but it was already too late, wasn't it?"

She raised questioning eyes to his, and he knew she was ready to hear the truth. He couldn't swear to the day, but she wasn't asking specifics. Taking a deep breath, he said, "Yes, it was too late by then. I told myself it didn't matter, since your father would never have permitted us to marry."

"But he died." Her words held more regret than accusation. "I should have let Ryan know, but I was afraid he would desert the army to come home and take care of me."

"He would have." Matthew had no doubt of that. Ryan had no sense of reason where his sister was concerned. "He loved you dearly."

"Deserters were hanged without trial unless they were shot on sight. I wouldn't risk that happening to him."

He understood, but she was still waiting to hear the rest of it. "Three months after Ryan's death, I took a bullet in the shoulder."

She gasped. "I didn't know—"

"It wasn't serious, but it took a surgeon to get it out." He leaned back in the swing, trying to remember just exactly how things had happened. "She was a nurse in the field hospital, and she offered to write a letter to someone for me since my arm was in a sling."

Olivia ducked her eyes, but he saw the heartache in her expression.

"When I told her there wasn't anyone," he went on, "she asked me who Olivia was."

"Me?"

"It seems I talk in my sleep, especially when someone is cutting into me with a knife."

Olivia rose from the chair and crossed the porch. "So she *knew* about me? That we were engaged?"

"She also knew that I broke the engagement," he added. "It wasn't her fault, Olivia. I was lonely and feeling sorry for myself. I figured once everyone knew the engagement was off, you'd have a dozen men clamoring to take my place."

A dozen men, handpicked by her father.

She stood with her back to him, and he rose to his feet when he heard her sob. "Olivia, what is it?"

"I never told anyone about the letter," she whispered. "Not a soul."

"You never—" He couldn't believe it. "Why not?"

"I knew . . . somehow . . . that you had written those words out of obligation to Ryan, and once you returned home and learned that my father was . . ." Her voice trailed off and she shrugged slightly. "I planned to surprise you . . . at the station."

"Oh, Livvy," he breathed, sickened to realize that every person waiting at that depot thought Olivia had come to meet her betrothed. "I would never have humiliated you like that deliberately. I certainly never expected you to be waiting for me."

"Papa would never have allowed it."

Indeed, her father had refused to allow Olivia to accompany Ryan to the station when he left for the army. If there was anything Father couldn't stand, it was an emotional scene, and God forbid one in public.

"Did you love her?" The moment the words were

spoken, she desperately wished she could take them back. It was the one thing she was afraid to know.

"She was a good person," he said without hesitation. "I couldn't leave her behind knowing she was going to have a baby."

"Your baby," she whispered.

"Yes, my baby," he said. "We married for the child's sake only, and Rebecca knew that as well as I did."

Olivia turned away at the mention of her name. She didn't want to see grief on his face or hear longing in his voice and know it was for another. She drew a breath and managed a strangled reply. "I'm sure you made her very happy."

"Would you be happy married to a man you didn't love?"

Her fingers dug into the wooden railing. "What makes you say a thing like that?"

"It's the truth. Neither one of us wanted the marriage, but we both had to face the consequences."

Chapter Eight

The storm had left its mark on the countryside just as the night had left its mark on Olivia. Tree limbs and debris were scattered across the yard, and her emotions were torn to shreds. Early morning fog was just beginning to vanish now that the sun was risen fully in the east, but Olivia saw nothing clearly.

Indeed, this morning she was more confused and hurt than ever before. In her mind, she envisioned a very different sequence of events. Always she'd imagined Matthew being seduced by a wanton female and forgetting all about her. Once she had her claws in him, he had to marry her and abandon Olivia.

They'd talked all night, but she hadn't had the nerve to ask him what he would have done if he'd learned she was waiting for him, with no father to stop her from marrying him. Would he have come home to her, or honored his obligation to the mother of his child?

Matthew had ridden off on horseback nearly an hour earlier to inspect the road and determine whether they would be able to travel safely today. She could only hope they would; surely Aunt Eula would be sick with worry, and Olivia berated herself again and again for not leaving so much as a note explaining her absence.

She slipped back inside the kitchen, where Sarah was finishing breakfast, and smiled at the memory of Sarah insisting that Matthew not do the cooking, confiding that he burned the bacon every time. Olivia wondered if her own efforts were any less disappointing.

"How is everything?"

"Good," was all she would say, swinging her bare feet under the table. "I like Maddy's waffles. She puts blueberries in 'em."

"I like them, too."

Olivia began gathering the dishes and placed them in the basin as she had seen Maddy do at home. Tears stung her eyes and she squeezed them tight, not wanting Sarah to see her upset.

We married for the child's sake.

The child. Sarah.

What would have become of the little girl if Matthew had abandoned her mother? Any woman bearing a child out of wedlock would be shunned, put out by her family, considered little more than a whore, but the child would suffer worse. Upon her mother's death, Sarah would have gone from being a bastard to an orphan, winding up in an asylum or worse.

No, Matthew had done the right thing and, glancing now at the little girl with mussed hair and syrup on her face, she was glad he had. The tight knot of bitterness she'd carried for so long cracked and something eased inside her, knowing Matthew had not wronged her. If anything, she had wronged him.

Sarah took her hand and led her across the yard and past the barn toward the chicken coop. Once there, Sarah efficiently went about unlatching the door and coaxing the chickens outside. "Here, chick. Here, chick, here."

The birds needed little encouragement and raced into the grassy area that already bore signs of their scratching and pecking. Sarah showed Olivia where the chicken feed was stored and how many scoops to pour into the bucket. After a few clumsy attempts, Olivia was able to scatter the cracked corn evenly and the chickens descended in a cloud of flapping wings and tail feathers.

Three fat geese came waddling up the hill, infuriated at the thought of missing out on the feast, and honked loudly in protest. One in particular began pecking at the hem of Olivia's skirt, and she cried out in dismay. Sarah giggled and shooed the bird away as her father had taught her to do.

"Now we can gather the eggs." She handed Olivia a wire basket and led her inside the coop, warning her to be careful where she stepped. The eggs, some brown, some white, were warm to the touch, and Olivia tried not to think how recently they might have come from the chicken.

She whirled around at Sarah's gasp, but the little girl motioned for her to come and see. Far in one corner, Olivia could hear a faint chirping and saw three tiny chicks amid a pile of eggshells on a bed of straw. Two more eggs sat undisturbed, but Sarah pointed at one and smiled.

The egg trembled slightly and the shell began to crack. Olivia watched in fascination as a tiny beak began to emerge from the brown shell and the chick struggled to free himself. The egg split in half and he tumbled into the straw, quite startled by his new world.

"My goodness." Olivia was amazed by what she had seen.

"Daddy will have to move them, once the mama comes back."

"Whatever for?"

"So nothing will happen to them. A fox or a possum might get to them, or even a snake."

"A snake!" Olivia cried. "You mean there are snakes out here?"

Sarah nodded. "Daddy killed a big old snake out here one day and hung it over the fence."

Shuddering at the thought, Olivia reached for Sarah's hand. "This is no place for little girls."

The chicks began peeping louder than before, and Olivia was struck by their helplessness. She would feel awful if something happened to them, but she would feel worse if a snake came after her. "Perhaps we can just wait outside for your father. We really shouldn't leave them alone."

"Leave what alone?"

"Daddy!" Sarah cried in delight. "Look! We got baby chicks!"

Matthew made his way inside the chicken coop without bothering to hide his amusement at Olivia's wariness. She folded her arms across her chest and tried to look indifferent, but his grin only widened. "Are you ready to milk the cow?"

Stung by his teasing, she drew herself up and said, "Certainly not. I was beginning to wonder where you had taken off to."

"Far enough to make sure I can get you home safely."

When he said nothing else, she prompted, "And?"

"The road is clear," he assured her. "A few bad places, but nothing that would keep us from getting to town."

Relieved beyond measure, Olivia nodded and carefully made her way out of the chicken coop, leaving Matt and Sarah to deal with the baby chicks. When they were ready to leave, at last, Matt helped Olivia onto the wagon seat after hoisting Sarah in place. His hand lingered for a moment at the small of her back, and a shiver ran up her spine, a shiver she knew he felt.

She swallowed hard and grasped for something to say that would break the tension. "Why on earth would you hang a dead snake over a fence?"

The question caught him off guard and he tilted his head to one side for a moment before he understood. "Sarah told you about that, did she?"

Olivia nodded.

"Anytime you kill a snake, old folks say to hang it belly side up over a fence, and you'll get rain." He grinned slightly. "I never dreamed I'd get you in the bargain."

Matt turned the wagon onto Olivia's street and her laughter died as she realized that most of her neighbors were enjoying the lovely weather by either taking a midmorning stroll or pampering their rosebushes. So astonished were they at the sight of her riding in a farm wagon that they failed to even pretend not to stare.

Matt was well aware of her embarrassment. "Livvy, I'm sorry. I should have come around the back way."

"Nonsense." She held her head high and deigned to meet each gaping stare only to have her own gaze quickly averted. "I will not sneak inside my own home as if I have something to hide."

The wagon rolled to a stop in front of her house and, like a queen, she waited for him to assist her down from the seat. When he had hefted Sarah to her feet, the three of them made their way up the front walk. Olivia opened the front door and Matthew followed her inside, leading Sarah.

"Olivia? Olivia, is that you?" Eula rushed into the foyer, her eyes wide with concern. "Thank God you're home. I was just about to send for the sheriff."

"I'm fine, dear," Olivia assured her, returning her embrace. "The road was washed out by the storm, and we were stranded. I'm sorry if you were worried."

"You were stranded all night?" Olivia started at the sound of Ada Kirk's voice and turned to find her cousin and his wife standing just inside the parlor. "Just the two of you?"

Rodger and Ada exchanged a harried glance, and Rodger's disapproval was obvious. "Eula sent for me at the mill this morning. We've all been worried sick."

Olivia fought to keep her temper in check, knowing an ugly scene would only upset Eula and make the situation worse. "I appreciate your concern, but I'm home now and there is no longer any reason to worry."

"I'm just thankful you weren't driving that buggy of yours all by yourself." Eula turned to Matthew. "Such a storm would have washed that little rig away, wouldn't it?"

"Yes, ma'am."

He raked a hand through his hair, and Olivia sensed his discomfort. Damn Rodger, anyway, for bringing Ada along, but his wife would never forgive him if she had missed out on the juiciest piece of gossip since the wife of a church deacon ran off with a traveling circus, supposedly enamored with the lion tamer.

"The road was completely flooded," Matthew explained, but he was looking right at Rodger. His eyes narrowed slightly and his next words left no room for argument. "Only a fool would risk lives for the sake of propriety."

"Oh, absolutely," Rodger agreed, sparing his wife a pleading look, and hurried across the foyer to shake Matt's hand. "We're just grateful to you for seeing her home safely."

For a moment, Olivia thought he might refuse Rodger's handshake, but he finally extended his hand somewhat reluctantly and said, "It was my pleasure."

Ada's eyes grew even wider, if that was possible, and Olivia bit the inside of her jaw to keep from laughing out loud. An awkward silence fell, but Eula was unperturbed. "Matthew, would you like a cup of coffee?"

"No, thank you Miss Eula," he declined with a thankful smile. "I've got to be on my way. I just need a good-bye kiss before I leave."

Olivia froze and Rodger and Ada gaped at him in disbelief and then chagrin when he scooped Sarah into his arms and told her to be a good girl. The child assured him that she would and planted a kiss on his cheek.

Eula reached out to take Sarah from Matt, suggesting they go see if Maddy needed help frosting a layer cake, and turned toward the kitchen. Matt glanced up at Olivia, and she felt the hot flush of color rise to her face, more angered than embarrassed. He had chosen his words carefully, gauging her reaction, and was now quite pleased at her immediate assumption that he'd wanted a kiss from her.

Her sharp disappointment rankled her even further, and she stiffened with wounded pride. Somehow she kept her voice cool and impassive, and said, "Thank you again for seeing me home, Mr. Bowen. Good day."

Not waiting to see his reaction, Olivia turned to make her way up the stairs.

"So you spent the night with a man you once hoped to marry." Ada's summary conclusion made Olivia flinch when she met her at the top. "Everyone already thinks you're keeping that little girl, hoping he'll finally marry you, and now something like this? He'll *have* to marry you now."

Olivia caught hold of the banister, shocked and angered, but she knew Ada wasn't exaggerating. Most people would jump to the worst conclusion over such an occurrence, but her past history with Matthew would refute any likelihood of an innocent but unfortunate situation.

"Matthew Bowen is a gentleman, Ada." Olivia felt her cheeks flame even though she should have anticipated such accusations. "What you're suggesting is an insult to both of us."

"You just mark my words."

"Oh, I will, and I'll recognize every one of them that gets back to me."

* * *

Olivia briefly scanned the last letter in the stack before tossing it aside with the others, along with any hope of finding a suitable nursemaid for Sarah. It was obvious her mistake had been disclosing the fact that Matthew was a property-holding widower. Every woman who responded to her notice was more interested in him than the child. Most had children of their own that they expected to bring with them, as if providing Sarah with a playmate was some sort of bonus!

Sarah had had enough adjustments to make in the past months and the last thing she needed was a lot of strange children invading her home. Poor Sarah, she deserved better than that, and Olivia intended to see she had it. Time, however, was not on her side.

Every day, it seemed, the child grew more attached to her and to Aunt Eula. Olivia reminded herself that Sarah missed her mother and would feel the same toward any female. What concerned her most were her own feelings for the little girl.

She was finding it impossible to remain detached. Rather than a nuisance, Sarah proved to be a delight, and Olivia feared she would dearly miss the little girl if a nurse could be found and the child returned home. Once Matt was finished with spring planting, he would be able to care for Sarah himself and wouldn't need her help at all, and already Olivia found herself dreading that day.

It galled Olivia to admit, even to herself, that she

would miss seeing Matt as much as she would Sarah. After so many years of cold silence between them, she had forgotten how much she enjoyed his company, and caring for Sarah gave her license to spend time with Matt whenever he came to see the child.

She had been foolish, however, to tag along with them on Sunday, allowing herself to pretend she could ever be part of their world. Kissing Matt had been stupid to the point of lunacy and only served to make the situation less manageable. She berated herself over and over for wanting to believe he still held feelings for her after so much time had passed. More than likely he was confusing gratitude and sentiment with desire.

A knock at her door distracted Olivia from her troubling thoughts, and she glanced up to see Rodger peering into her office with a painfully friendly smile.

"Afternoon, cousin," he drawled and strolled inside without waiting for an invitation. "I have some news you'll be happy to hear."

"How nice." She seriously doubted that, but she faced him, waiting. "What is it?"

"You remember Mr. Sullivan?"

She nodded.

"Well, he made his order this morning." He placed the bill of sale on her desk. "He plans to start construction next week, and we're supplying the lumber."

She glanced at the numbers. "You gave him quite a generous discount."

"Well, considering how much he was willing to buy, it only seemed fair."

"What do you know about Sullivan?"

The question startled Rodger and he blinked. "Well, he . . . ah, he comes from Liverpool, but he's lived in America for the last ten or twenty years. Made a fortune in cotton export."

"And now he's moved to Georgia to start a textile mill? Doesn't that seem odd to you?"

Rodger squirmed slightly. "There's a lot of opportunity nowadays. Lots of businessmen are taking advantage of such . . . opportunities."

"I thought you disapproved of doing business with carpetbaggers."

"I do," he assured her without hesitation. "They all have political agendas; Sullivan is no carpetbagger. He's simply making a good business move."

"Taking advantage of a good opportunity, you mean." At Rodger's pained expression, she let the argument drop. For now. "I just feel we should know more about who we're dealing with when we extend ourselves so heavily."

"Well, I invited him to Sunday dinner." Rodger smiled slyly. "That should give you an opportunity to get to know him better."

"At *my* house?" Olivia was shocked by his presumptuousness. "Without asking me first?"

"Olivia, dear, we always have Sunday dinner at your house. I didn't think you would mind." He paused. "Unless you have other plans . . . again."

She could feel the color warm her face and tried

to ignore the thinly veiled query. She hadn't missed the furtive looks and hushed whispers everywhere she went in the past week. She had known more than one person had seen her early morning return with Matt and Sarah, but she had no doubt Ada Kirk had spread most of the gossip as thickly as possible.

"From here on, please ask me before inviting people to my home," she conceded. "Especially strangers."

"He's no stranger," Rodger corrected her. "He could prove to be a valuable business . . . associate."

Her head snapped up, and she refused to pretend she hadn't caught the slip. "Valuable to whom? Rodger, whatever business dealings you involve yourself in are your own affair, but don't ever think you can use your connections with me for personal benefit."

His eyes narrowed. "I'm thinking of the benefit of the business. Perhaps you should do the same."

"What are you saying?"

"Everyone in town is speculating on what happened between you and Matt Bowen." His voice held a note of triumph, and she suspected he'd been dying to tell her that all week long. "What on earth were you thinking? You had no business going out there alone with him, let alone spending the night!"

"Well, I certainly didn't plan on it!" she snapped. "How many times do I have to tell you that there was a storm—"

"And you were stranded," he finished for her. Leaning forward, his tone softened. "Look, I know you well enough to realize that you wouldn't intentionally do something so . . . improper, but there are others who might not be so willing to give you the benefit of the doubt."

"Let them think what they like; I don't care."

"You'll care when they quit doing business with us."

She hesitated. "You're exaggerating."

"Am I? Most folks, even Yankees, find it scandalous to conduct business with a woman, and unthinkable with one of questionable virtue." He pressed the point. "Most of our customers are married men. Do you think their wives will want them dealing with you?"

"This is ridiculous!" Olivia shot out of her chair, furious, and crossed the room to stare out the window. "I haven't done anything wrong! How dare anyone make such presumptions about me?"

"As long as you're keeping that child, everyone will think you're out to marry him. By any means necessary." He paused. "Is that what you're doing?"

"No!" She whirled to face him, shaken by the conversation. "I resent your questions. My personal life is none of your concern."

"But this business is," he stated. "Olivia, I've worked here since I was fifteen years old, and I don't intend to stand meekly by while you throw it all away."

"I don't care what your intentions are. The business is mine and I'll run it as I see fit."

"Even it that means running it into the ground? I'm certain Ryan thought you'd be married by now and have a husband to oversee things for you."

"Well, I'm not." She deeply resented Rodger speak-

ing so casually about her brother. God knows, she'd
prefer to be penniless rather than lose her brother.
"Ryan's will mentioned nothing about my being married or needing anyone to run my affairs. *Least* of all
you."

The last phrase was deliberately mean-spirited, but
Olivia didn't care.

"You're right, of course, Olivia." Rodger turned
toward the door, pausing only long enough to add,
"I'm sure Ryan had no doubt you'd end up alone."

She swore not to pay Rodger any mind, but Olivia
did have to consider her reputation. Her standing in
the community might actually be in jeopardy, and
sometimes that meant more than wealth. People
might not like her, but they would respect her.

For her own sake, she had to end the situation.
She couldn't afford to become any more attached to
Sarah, and the risk of her feelings for Matthew posed
the greatest danger. She couldn't delude herself that
they could pick up where they left off just because
of a little honest conversation, but pride wouldn't
allow her to invite another woman into his life.

She had to think of something that would allow
him to manage the farm and care for Sarah. Even as
she was leaving for home, the issue plagued her.

Crossing the lot behind the gin, where her buggy
was waiting, she caught sight of Sam, the mill foreman, and smiled as he tipped his hat.

"Afternoon, Miz Chandler."

"Hello, Sam. How are things going?"

"Work's never done," he stated. "Can't finish one order without two more waiting."

"That's good," she reminded him. "You and I will never be without work."

They paused while more lumber was loaded into a wagon, and Sam ordered the men to tie the load. She thought again of Matthew's situation and realized that Sam might just hold the solution.

"Sam, forgive me if I'm prying, but did I hear you say that your sister's family was living with you?"

"My *wife's* sister," he corrected her, his voice thick with resentment. "Her and her husband and five young'uns."

"My goodness, what a brood." She hesitated. "What are their plans?"

"Hell, who knows? Beg your pardon, Miz Chandler, but having a passel of young'uns tries a man's nerves."

"I can understand that."

"They came down from Memphis two months ago for a visit. My wife was thrilled to see her sister, and I didn't mind them coming for a visit. When she and the missus started making Christmas plans, I knew they weren't going anywhere anytime soon." He ran his hand along his jaw. "They lost everything in the war . . . their land, the house. Everything."

"What will they do?" He shrugged, and she suggested, "Have you thought of giving him a job here?"

"No!" He was emphatic "He'd never take orders from me, and I won't have something like that coming between me and my wife."

"What about farming? You said he owned land."

"He had a small place . . . nothing big.

"I know of someone who needs help on his land."

"Sharecropping?"

"Not exactly . . . this would be help with his own crops. Your brother-in-law and his family would have a place to live and I would see they earned enough to secure a place of their own next year. Would you ask him about it?"

"You let me know where and when and I'll have them there."

Chapter Nine

I wouldn't ask, except that Sam is in such an awkward position.

I wanted to ask you first, before mentioning anything to Sam.

The buggy jostled along and Olivia struggled to think of the best way to approach Matthew with what seemed to be the perfect solution to her problem. She didn't mean to lie to him, but if he even suspected she was doing this to help him financially he would balk. Like most men, his pride got in the way of common sense.

Mindful that there might be snakes, Olivia picked her away around back of the house, steering clear of any tall grass. Thankfully, she caught sight of him just beyond the garden. She hadn't fancied the thought of waiting hours for him to return from the field. Still, she could have used the time to gather her thoughts completely.

He was repairing a section of the fence separating the garden from the fields and took no notice of her hesitant approach.

Sweat glistened across his bare shoulders and ran down his chest in rivulets, leaving the fine dusting of hair damp against his tanned skin. She couldn't help noticing how the hair narrowed at his waist and disappeared beneath the waistband of his trousers. She swallowed hard and tried to force the words that would alert him to her presence, but he must have sensed her watching him and turned toward her.

"Olivia." He was obviously surprised and his eyes narrowed. "Is something wrong? Where's Sarah?"

"Oh, no. Everything is fine. She's attending a birthday party one of Aunt Eula's friend's is having for her grandson. You remember Mae Helen Randall, don't you?"

He nodded and reached for his shirt, slipping his arms into the sleeves but not bothering to button it. When he turned back to her, his expression was all but contemptuous. "Then what are you doing here?"

His curt manner stung, but she steeled herself for what she needed to do. "I need a favor."

His expression registered surprise. "What kind of favor?"

"Well, it's not really for me." She tried to smile, but the wary look in his eyes warned her to skip any pretense. "My foreman, Sam, has relatives who've relocated here since the war. He needs to find them a place to live, and his brother-in-law needs work. I was hoping you might be interested in having some help with the cotton and all."

"Why not just put him to work in your mill?"

He turned toward the house, and she had to hurry to keep up with his long strides. "I offered, but Sam doesn't think it would work out."

"If he's not the sort of man Sam wants working at the mill, what makes you think I'd want him around here?"

"Sam doesn't want any of his relatives working for him," she explained. "It can cause hard feelings, especially if he has to let them go."

Matt nodded but didn't say anything as he dipped water from a pail and drank, draining the dipper twice more. Water trickled down his chin and mingled with the perspiration dampening his throat and chest, following the same path toward the flat plane of his stomach.

"I still don't see what kind of favor I can do for you that would help."

His words startled her, and she realized she had been staring at the span of his naked torso exposed by the gaping front of his unbuttoned shirt. Her face flamed, but she managed a hoarse reply. "The main thing is finding them a place to live, and you have that empty cabin just going to waste."

His eyes grew wide with alarm. "I don't want a bunch of—"

"It would only be temporary," she pleaded. "Just until they're on their feet, and I thought it might be nice for you to have some extra help."

"Does he expect me to pay wages?"

Olivia chose her words carefully, knowing full well that Matthew's pride would force him to refuse any help from her. "No, of course not. Aren't most arrangements such as this based on a percentage of the crop?"

He nodded. "How much of a percentage?"

She faltered, carefully considering her reply. She knew that sharecroppers usually split the price with the land owner, in addition to buying their own seed and supplying all the labor. This situation was different. She knew he would balk if the cut was too high and be suspicious if it was too low. "Fifteen percent?"

He frowned slightly and she held her breath, wishing she could tell him it wouldn't cost him a cent.

"And if they don't stay until the crop is in?"

"Then you owe them nothing."

Finally he said, "That sounds fair."

"Sam will be so pleased," she replied.

"I haven't agreed to anything," he cut off her reply. "Tell Sam to bring the man out here to have a look around the place. If I like him, we'll go from there."

She nodded, relieved that he was receptive to the idea. Now all she had to do was turn and leave with whatever dignity she could retrieve.

"You still haven't answered my question."

She glanced up at him, uncertain of his meaning. "I told you, if they leave before—"

"I asked what you were doing here."

"Asking you about Sam's in-laws."

He shook his head. "No. You could have sent Rodger to ask me about that, or Sam himself. I want to know the reason *you* came out here."

He advanced on her and Olivia swallowed hard, knowing he wasn't waiting for her answer. It took every ounce of courage she could muster not to take a step back in retreat.

"You want to prove being around me doesn't mean anything to you. That seeing me has no effect on you at all." He stared down at her, his eyes burning into hers. "Well, you're wasting your time because we both know the truth."

Her hands came up to ward him off, but the feel of his hot, solid flesh against her bare hands startled her, causing her resolve to slip. His arms closed around her and she could feel the heat of his skin burning through her clothes. For an instant, she wondered what it would feel like against her own bare skin. The image frightened her and she began twisting out of his embrace.

He released her immediately and turned away. "You can't keep coming around me, Olivia, not if you expect me to pretend like nothing ever happened between us."

She could feel her face burn with bright color. "What happened between us was . . . was—"

"I'm talking about last Sunday."

"Last Sunday? Nothing happened—" The words died on her lips, and she realized he wasn't referring to long-ago moments of passion. So much had been said between them, breaking a long bitter silence, and a fragile trust had been formed. A trust she had broken when faced with narrow-minded gossip and insinuations.

"Do you really believe that?"

"I—" Again, he didn't wait for her answer. Instead, he turned and stalked away, leaving her to stare at his retreating back and wish she had the courage to go after him.

"Mr. Sullivan, I'm so pleased you could join us this afternoon."

"Thank you, Miss Chandler. I am honored by your invitation."

"I'd like you to meet my aunt, Eula Chandler."

Sullivan bowed elegantly, and Olivia was more than a little surprised by his sophisticated manners. She glanced at her cousin, who merely nodded in response to her welcome, and then to Ada, who didn't let on that she knew of the recent unpleasantness between her husband and Olivia.

Eula led the gentlemen into the parlor, but Ada caught hold of Olivia's arm and stopped her before she could follow the others.

"Olivia, I want you to know I'm sorry if you took offense at anything I said the other day."

But not sorry you said it, Olivia thought to herself. She only nodded and said, "Let's just forget the matter."

"Forget it?" Ada was dismayed. "Olivia, dear, you have got to *do* something about resolving this . . . predicament. And soon."

"Predicament?"

"With Matthew Bowen."

Olivia wrenched her arm none too gently from Ada's grasp. "Yes, I hear the local gossip is simply rife with speculation on what *really* happened between us last Sunday."

"Well, just what do expect people to think?"

"If I really cared, I wouldn't have gone back out there the other day, now would I?"

For a moment, Olivia was positive Ada was torn between fainting dead away and running into the street and shouting the news to everyone in town. At last, she found her voice and managed a strangled, "You did what?"

"There was something I had to discuss with him, and it just couldn't wait," Olivia replied, delighting in dangling just enough information to whet the woman's thirst for gossip. Ada reveled in her esteemed position as the local authority on the goings-on of Olivia Chandler and her sordid business. "Something personal."

Ada's eyes shone in anticipation of the knowledge, and Olivia allowed the ensuing silence to build just enough before leaning forward and whispering, "He's going to let out the old cabin on his place to Sam Pate's brother-in-law. Isn't that wonderful?"

Ada blinked, unable to suppress her disappointment, and repeated, "Wonderful."

Without another word Olivia turned toward the parlor, stopping short when she heard Sarah's voice. "Livvy! Livvy, Daddy's here!"

Olivia turned just in time to see Sarah leading Matthew from the kitchen into the foyer, her face beaming with delight. Ada was no less delighted, as well.

"Well, well, Matthew Bowen," she chimed. "How wonderful to see you. But I suppose we'll be seeing a lot of you these days."

"Thank you, Mrs. Kirk." His gaze barely flickered over her before settling on Olivia. "I certainly hope I don't wear out my welcome."

Telltale warmth rose to her cheeks and Olivia lowered her gaze, unable to meet the knowing look in his eyes.

"Matthew!" Rodger stepped out of the parlor, extending his hand. "I thought I heard your voice."

The two men shook hands and Ada tittered in mock amusement. "Mr. Bowen, I'm sure you'll always be welcome in this house. You will be joining us for dinner, won't you?"

Olivia winced, knowing everyone was waiting for her to echo Ada's invitation, but Sarah beat her to it. "Please, Daddy. Let's stay with Livvy."

Glancing down at his daughter, he shook his head. "Miss Olivia has company, sweetie."

"You're more than welcome," Olivia said a little too quickly and a little too insistently. "If you'd like."

Unable to deny Sarah, Matt agreed, and introductions were made before everyone settled around the dining room table. The conversation dwelt mostly on the weather, the optimistic predictions for a bountiful harvest, and the growing demand for cotton by northern textile mills.

"I think you're on to something, Sullivan," Rodger spoke up. "Why should we let our cotton go to benefit someone else? We might as well mill it and sell it ourselves."

"Labor is cheaper in the north," Matthew pointed out. "The larger cities are teeming with factory workers desperate for work, and they can pay top dollar for cotton."

"That's true, of course," Sullivan admitted. "But by the time the cotton changes hands a few times and commissions are paid, you're really not that much better off."

Olivia could see no argument with that. "And you think southern factories can compete with them?"

"I think it's inevitable," he replied. "The core of the south's economy has been completely eradicated. Without slavery, the cost of labor alone will bankrupt the average planter unless he can compete in the new market."

"The new market?"

"Industry," Mr. Sullivan insisted. "That's where the next economic boom will be, Miss Chandler, mark my words, and you're getting in on the ground floor."

"I am?" Rodger squirmed beneath Olivia's heated stare. "Since when?"

"Well, I know all of the details haven't been worked out." Mr. Sullivan sensed the immediate tension between the cousins. "But there's plenty of time for that."

An uncomfortable silence settled over the dining room, and Eula gently nudged Olivia's foot with her own under the table. They exchanged glances, and Eula skillfully directed the conversation to neutral ground. "Matt, I hear Sam's brother-in-law is going to be working out at your place.

"Yes, they got moved in yesterday.

"Sam says he's got a houseful of youngsters," Rodger put in. "Any of them old enough to work?"

"They're all old enough." Matt shook his head and smiled. "I don't know how much hard labor he'll get out of five females."

"Five females?" Olivia gasped, positive she hadn't heard right. "You mean that every child that man has is a girl?"

Everyone eyed her warily, except for Matt, who thought nothing of her startled response. "For now, anyway."

"For now?"

Matt only shrugged. "I think his wife intends to have them all married off by Christmas."

Olivia sank back in her chair, sickened by the irony of the situation. If it had happened to anyone other than herself, she would have laughed. Her ideal plan to help Matthew served only to deliver him into the clutches of not one but five husband-hunters.

From the corner of her eye, she could see the anticipation on Ada's face, and she wondered what excuse the woman would make to leave early in order to see that all the juicy tidbits she had gathered today were spread properly throughout the county.

Mr. Sullivan had been completely charmed by Eula, and he'd seemed reluctant to leave when Rodger and Ada did, but to do otherwise would have been impolite. Olivia was relieved to see them go, and Sarah was pleased to have her father's undivided attention.

A tiny table and chairs had been placed on the back porch, and Sarah had carefully set the table with her fancy new teapot and matching cups and saucers. She was so proud, and Matthew couldn't help but smile as she propped two of her dolls in their chairs.

Glancing up, she caught him watching her and patiently explained, "We're havin' a tea party, Daddy."

"A party?"

She nodded and began pouring imaginary tea into each cup.

Matthew accepted the dainty china cup and saucer she held out to him. The tea set was extravagant, no doubt hand-painted and costly, and he didn't like the idea of his little girl developing a fondness for things he couldn't afford.

She carefully seated herself at the table, pouring more tea from the matching tea pot and warning him not to drop the cup. "It'll break, Daddy."

Olivia stepped out onto the porch, bearing a vase of flowers. "Here, sweetie, I brought these from the garden. A table isn't set properly without fresh flowers."

Sarah smiled and bent her face toward the cluster of blooms. "They're simply *charming*."

Olivia laughed at her dramatics and seated herself beside Matthew. "She's quite the little hostess, isn't she?"

"You're spoiling her, Olivia," he warned, keeping his voice low. "A child can't have everything she wants."

"It's only a few toys."

"You've already bought her too many toys." He motioned toward the dolls and stuffed animals littering the porch. "She doesn't play with half of these things."

"She does so," Olivia insisted. "What does it hurt to indulge her a little?"

"I don't want her getting used to living like this." The hurt in her eyes knifed him, but it had to be said. "Don't make her resent me for being poor."

"You're not poor," she argued. "Times are hard for everyone."

"Not you, Olivia," he reminded her. "You came out ahead."

"I did what had to be done. No one lost their home or their land. I did that much. How dare they begrudge me making an honest living? If anything, they should be grateful."

She had been so pleased with herself for bargaining shrewdly with the Yankee tax man. A lump sum settlement was much simpler for him than trying to auction off dozens of pieces of property, and no one in Wilkes County would suffer eviction. Rather than a benefactor, everyone accused her of taking sides with the enemy. Worse than a carpetbagger, they said she was a *publican*. The worst kind of sinner, one who profits from the misfortune of their own people.

"Jesus healed ten lepers, Olivia, and only one came back to thank him."

"So *you're* preaching at me now?"

He shook his head. "Try looking at things from where they stand. Some families have owned land in this county since before the Revolution, and they don't like the idea of it belonging to someone else."

"It doesn't *belong* to me," she insisted. "If I hadn't stepped in, half the county would have gone on the auction block. All I ask is that they repay a portion every year out of their crops."

"And what if they can't?" he pressed. "Would you foreclose?"

"So far, no one's had a problem."

"So your generosity really hasn't been tested. Maybe that's what everyone is waiting to see."

Chapter Ten

"Well, well, who do we have here?"

"This is Sarah." Olivia eased the little girl into the room full of children. "Say hello to Miss Margie, Sarah."

Holding tight to Olivia's hand, Sarah remained silent and glanced about the spacious room crowded with children. Sarah enjoyed attending church with Olivia and Eula, but up until now, she had not attended the Sunday school class for children her own age.

Since her mother's death, Sarah had little interaction with her peers, and Olivia doubted Matthew realized the importance being confident and independent where social situations were concerned. Olivia's own father would have woefully neglected that aspect of her adolescence if Eula had not intervened. It was her duty to do the same for Sarah, and summer Bible school was the perfect opportunity.

"Say hello, Sarah," she prompted once again, but Sarah tightened her grip on Olivia's hand and shook her head.

"Oh, Sarah, we're so glad you're here," Miss Margie said the bright voice Olivia remembered so well from her own childhood. The veteran teacher wasn't fazed by a little reluctance. "It's almost time for our Bible story about Jonah and the whale."

Olivia smiled encouragingly. "That's one of my favorites."

"After story time, the boys and girls draw a picture showing what they learned."

Sarah's face brightened slightly, and Olivia was quick to point out what a wonderful artist she was. "She's drawn several pictures for me."

"How splendid. Won't you stay and draw one about Jonah for Miss Olivia?"

Reluctantly, Sarah nodded and glanced up at Olivia, "Are you staying with me?"

"This is a class for boys and girls," she explained, brushing a wisp of Sarah's hair back into place. "I'll be waiting for you when you're finished, and we'll go buy a frame for your picture."

At last, Sarah gave in to the lure of playing games with other children and drawing pictures of great whales, and Miss Margie rewarded her with praise for being so brave and grown up.

Olivia smiled encouragingly once again and waited until Sarah glanced back with a smile of her own, and then she slipped away while Sarah joined the other children.

Nancy was waiting for her when she stepped outside, obviously surprised to see Olivia without Sarah in tow. "I can't believe she let you out of her sight."

Olivia fell into step with her friend, making their way down the front walk of the church. "She was determined not to at first, but she'll be fine."

"Don't you worry that she's becoming too attached to you?"

"Of course, not." Nancy stopped short and looked at her with obvious concern, and Olivia tried to amend her hasty denial. "She's a sweet-natured, affectionate child and she's no more attached to me than she is to anyone else."

"She clings to you like a vine," Nancy countered. "And I haven't seen you without her in weeks. Perhaps you're the one becoming too attached. What are you going to do when it's time for her to go home?"

Olivia shook her head and whispered, "I don't know, Nancy. I just don't know."

Olivia couldn't stop thinking about what Nancy had said, or Matthew's sharp criticism of the way she was caring for Sarah. She suspected much of his disapproval stemmed from his resentment of her reluctance to chance anything more than a platonic relationship with him, but how could she?

How could she risk having her heart broken again? There was no guarantee things would turn out differently this time, and she couldn't stand the thought of everyone shaking their heads and wondering at her gullibility.

Three days passed, and Matt didn't return. Olivia told herself that this would be his busiest time in the fields, but she knew he was deliberately avoiding another confrontation with her. He would work himself near to death and then be able to care for Sarah himself once the crops were planted, and afterward he could afford to hire help.

None of which gave her comfort.

Dusk settled itself around the town, and Olivia stood on her back porch listening to the night peepers calling out to one another in the trees.

"Livvy?" Sarah's voice drew her attention. "Livvy, I don't feel good."

"Come sit beside me," she suggested, making her way to the swing. The little girl climbed onto the seat and slumped against Olivia just as she was seated. Her little body was unusually warm, but she shivered and huddled into Olivia's embrace.

With the toe of her shoe, Olivia set the swing in motion and gently massaged the child's narrow shoulders. Just as Sarah shivered again, Olivia caught sight of Maddy in the kitchen and called for to come out onto the porch.

"What's the matter?" Maddy crossed the porch

and felt Sarah's face. "Lord have mercy, this child is burning up."

Olivia felt Sarah's forehead for herself. "You mean a fever?"

Maddy nodded. "We'd best get her in out of the night air."

Olivia gathered Sarah in her arms and followed Maddy inside the house, berating herself. She should have known something was wrong and gotten Sarah inside as quickly as possible. There was nothing worse for a fever than the night air.

Maddy instructed Olivia to get Sarah into bed while she put together a remedy for fever. Sarah cried for Olivia to hold her, but Maddy insisted the child be in bed, covered up. Aunt Eula appeared in the doorway and tried to dismiss Olivia's growing concern. "Children run temperatures all the time. Why, tomorrow morning you won't know anything was wrong."

"She's burning up." Olivia struggled to keep from sounding alarmed. The last thing she wanted to do was frighten Sarah, but her own fear was getting the best of her. "Something is terribly wrong."

"Nonsense." Eula swept inside the room, clasping Olivia's hands in a reassuring gesture. "Just put a few drops of elderberry wine in a glass of warm sugar water, and she'll be fine."

"Elderberry wine is for headaches." Maddy hurried to the child's bedside, bearing a steaming cup in her hand. "I made a cup of willow bark tea; that's what she needs for a fever. Let it cool a bit and have her drink it."

"You can't make a child drink something bitter like that," Eula pointed out. "She won't get enough down to do any good."

While the two women argued home remedies, Olivia watched with alarm as Sarah's face grew flushed. When she felt the child's forehead, it was even hotter than before. "I think the best thing would be to send for Dr. McComb."

Eula took in Sarah's peaked appearance and nodded in agreement. "Maddy, would you send for the doctor?"

Maddy turned right away, but Olivia's voice stopped her. "The doctor first, and then her father."

Olivia had never been so frightened in her life. Sarah's body was limp with fever, and it seemed the doctor would never arrive. At last a shadow filled the doorway and she turned grateful eyes to find Matthew standing just inside the room.

"What's wrong?" he demanded, crossing the room to kneel beside the bed and smooth a lock of hair from his daughter's face. "What's the matter, sweetheart?"

"Daddy, hold me," she begged, trying to sit up, but his large hand gently eased her back onto the pillow.

"You stay in bed now. I'll hold your hand as long as you want, but for now you have to stay under the covers." He accepted a freshly dampened cloth from Olivia and bathed the child's face with cool water.

"She was just fine this morning," Olivia assured him and reached for the cup of willow bark tea. "I've already sent for the doctor, and Maddy said for her to drink as much of this as possible."

He nodded and took the cup, his face a mask of concern, without saying a word. She could only look on as he coaxed Sarah to drink a few swallows of the mixture, knowing she was to blame for whatever was wrong with his child.

Matthew watched Olivia move about the room, reminding him of a condemned prisoner awaiting the hangman. She was more than worried, she was frightened, terrified, and no assurances he might offer would ease her mind. Somewhere along the line, Olivia's fondness for Sarah had grown into a deep love, no less than she might feel for a child of her own.

The doctor appeared in the doorway, and Matthew took one look at the haggard old man and knew something was terribly wrong. The doctor's clothes were wrinkled and he looked as if he hadn't slept in days.

Olivia didn't seem to notice and rushed to usher him inside the room. "Oh, thank heaven you're here. She was fine this morning, just fine, and then she complained of not feeling well early this evening. She's still running fever, but she drank half a cup of willow bark tea. Aunt Eula said—"

"Olivia, let me be the doctor." With a weary smile,

he bent over Sarah and felt her forehead. "Let's have a look here, little girl."

He opened his bag and withdrew several gadgets. Matt sat down on the bed and held Sarah's hand while Dr. McComb listened to her heart and bid her to take several deep breaths.

"This little girl's got herself a case of the measles." He looked up at Matt. "So do half the youngsters in town. I'll be lucky to get a wink of sleep."

Olivia's hand flew to her mouth, but not before a gasp escaped her lips. The doctor glanced over his shoulder and then back at Matthew. "Measles aren't uncommon, but it can be serious. Keeping the fever down is the main concern."

Dr. McComb drew a tiny vial of medicine from his bag, explaining that quinine was the best thing for the fever. "Mix a tiny bit in a few spoonfuls of sugar water and have her drink it. Keep giving it to her every few hours until the fever breaks."

"That's it?" Olivia couldn't believe he was leaving. "That's all you're going to do for her?"

He smiled sympathetically but shook his head. "I've got four more families waiting on me now. Just keep her fever down and she'll be fine."

"What if it doesn't stay down?" she demanded. "What then? How do we—"

Matthew crossed the room and held out his hand. "Thank you, Dr. McComb. We'll take care of her."

The old physician smiled gratefully and patted Olivia on the shoulder. "Don't worry yourself sick, Olivia. I'll stop by tomorrow to check on her."

Dr. McComb left the room, and Olivia's gaze fixed on the slight figure on the bed. Her lips began to tremble and she turned away, burying her face in her hands.

"Olivia," he whispered, gently placing his hands on her shoulders. "Everything will be all right."

She pulled away from him. "You don't understand. This is all my fault."

"Your fault?" He caught her arm and turned her back to face him. "How could it be your fault?"

"I took her to Bible school. I thought it would be good for her to be around other children, to play with someone her own age. Now she might—"

He pressed his fingertips against her lips, silencing the terrifying possibility he refused to consider. "You don't know that's what caused it."

"You heard the doctor," she countered, digging her fingers into the fabric of his shirt. "Half the children in town have the measles."

Tears slipped down her face, and he remembered the last time she had cried in his arms. With as much resolve as he could muster, he held her at arm's length and said, "Children get sick, Olivia. Measles aren't uncommon. The doctor said she'll be fine, and he wouldn't have left if he thought she was in danger."

She drew a deep breath and nodded. "Yes, you're right. We mustn't let her fever get too high."

She returned to the bed and knelt beside the child, gently pressing the back of her hand against Sarah's flushed cheek.

"I don't feel good, Livvy," she cried.

"I know, honey, I know," Olivia crooned, smoothing a lock of Sarah's hair away from her face. "The doctor says you'll feel better tomorrow."

The night wore on and Matt remained, refusing any suggestion that he go home to rest and return in the morning. Olivia knew it was because he, too, feared the worst.

Despite their attentive care, Sarah's fever climbed higher and she slept fitfully, her tiny limbs squirming beneath the bedclothes. Olivia struggled to keep the child from catching a chill, promising her everything under the sun if she would just stay covered up.

At last, Sarah slipped into a sound sleep, but Olivia wasn't comforted by the sight of her lying so still and quiet. She knelt beside the bed and brushed her fingers over Sarah's forehead, dismayed to find it just as warm as before.

"Sleep is the best thing for her."

His voice hovered just over her head and she nodded. "Still, I'll be glad when her fever is down."

His hand settled on her shoulder and she couldn't help turning her head against his arm. The hair on his forearm grazed against her cheek and she shuddered at the feel of his skin against hers.

"She'll be fine," he insisted. "You've taken wonderful care of her."

She knew he wasn't just referring to the measles, and his approval meant a great deal to her. She might have made mistakes, spoiling Sarah with gifts and toys, but she had truly wanted what was best for the child.

"I'm happy to do it. She's a very special child."

She looked up to find him staring down at her, his eyes dark with concern. His hand left her shoulder and gently stroked her hair, combing several straggling locks behind her ear, and settling against her face. Exhausted, she leaned into his touch, and her lips brushed against the palm of his hand.

The rattling of dishes broke the spell weaving itself around them, and Eula Chandler made her way into the room without hesitation. She placed a tray of food on the bureau and turned her attention to Sarah.

Olivia remained at Sarah's bedside while Matt quickly made his way to the other side. Eula took no notice of their earlier posture. "I brought some supper for both of you."

Olivia glanced toward the window, startled to realize how late it was. Suppertime had come and gone and it was getting closer to breakfast. "I haven't even thought about food."

"That's why I brought a tray up to you." Her aunt's voice held a note of reproach, tempered by her own concern for Sarah. "You need to get some rest. I'll sit up with her long enough for you to eat and sleep for a few hours."

Olivia shook her head. "I will not leave this room until I know she's going to be all right."

"You'll just make yourself ill, and then who'll see after you?" Once again, Olivia shook her head, but Eula didn't scold her further. "Maddy is keeping some broth warm on the stove, but that can wait until she's awake."

Olivia nodded. "Shouldn't her fever be gone by now?"

Eula made her way to the bedside and studied the sleeping child, unable to resist brushing a wisp of curls away from the tiny face. Olivia wasn't fooled by the nonchalant action, and she didn't miss the fear that flickered in Eula's eyes. "Most of the time, a fever will break while the person sleeps."

"And if it doesn't?" Olivia was tired of hearing how Sarah would be fine and just needed to sleep. "What if it doesn't, Eula? What then?"

Chapter Eleven

Stifling a yawn, Olivia fought to keep her eyes open. Just when she thought the night would last forever, a faint light crept through the windows. Sarah had slept soundly but had begun squirming beneath the covers. Rising from the chair, Olivia winced at the kinks in her back and leaned over the restless child.

"Don't kick the covers off, sweetie," she crooned. She felt her forehead and found it much cooler to the touch, and the wispy curls framing Sarah's face were damp with perspiration. She glanced up to find Matt hovering over her shoulder. "My God, I think the fever's broken."

He felt Sarah's face and throat, and nodded in confirmation. "She's wringing wet. We'd better get her changed before she takes a chill."

"Of course." Relief that the fever had broken renewed her energy, and Olivia searched the dresser drawer for one of Sarah's clean nightgowns and fresh linens for the bed.

They had just finished changing the bed when Eula peeked inside. "Oh, praise be, she's better."

Olivia smiled and nodded. "The fever's down for now, but we'll have to keep an eye on her."

"She'll be fine," Eula insisted, her cheerful optimism returned in full vigor. "I'm sure the worst has passed."

"I'll feel even better when the doctor tells me that." Olivia watched Matt pulling the covers up to Sarah's chin and smoothing the damp hair away from her face. She crossed the room and sank into the rocker beside the bed. "Thank you so much for staying with me. I wouldn't have survived the night alone."

"She needed both of us," he said with a solemn smile. He studied her a moment longer before saying, "You're exhausted, Olivia. You've got to get some rest."

"Absolutely," Eula chimed in and placed a gentle hand on her niece's shoulder. "You go lay down in the spare room and leave Sarah to me."

When she would have protested, Matt took her hand and pulled her to her feet. "Miss Eula's right, and don't start making excuses."

"What about you?" she countered, shivering at the feel of his hand closing around hers. "You're just as tired as I am."

He nodded. "I'm going home to check on things there and I'll sleep for a few hours before coming back."

Eula and Matt weren't going to let her win the argument, and Olivia nodded in agreement. Before leaving the room, she did make Eula swear to wake her if Sarah's condition should take a turn for the worse and reluctantly allowed Matt to lead her into the hall.

Olivia closed the door and let her forehead rest against the solid oak. Somehow, now that the worst was over, she felt no relief. The fear and panic she'd quelled for so long reared in earnest and tears filled her eyes and burned her cheeks.

"Livvy," he whispered, gently placing his hands on her shoulders. "Livvy, don't cry; she's going to be fine."

She turned into his embrace, accepting his comfort without hesitation. Shuddering with sobs, her body was assailed by the weakness Eula had warned her about and her knees buckled under her own weight. He lifted her as if she were a child and turned toward the spare room at the end of the hall.

The room was musty from being shut up for so long, but the bed felt like heaven when he placed her on the mattress. She could barely keep her eyes open but managed to clasp his hand when he would have left her.

"I'm just going to open the window," he assured her. "Nowhere else."

She nodded and tried to stay awake. The rush of fresh air was a boon and she drew a deep breath. She felt the mattress dip beneath his weight and looked up to find him sitting on the side of the bed, studying her with concern.

"I want you to rest today," he whispered, taking her outstretched hand. "You'll be sick if you don't take care of yourself."

"I wish you wouldn't leave."

"I have to tend to the livestock, but I'll be back soon."

She nodded, reaching up to cup his face with her palm. Her fingers trembled slightly. "Hurry."

"I will." He hesitated, studying her face before lowering his mouth to hers. Her lips met his as her hands caught hold of his shoulders. She wanted to beg him not to leave, to hold her and never let go.

She felt him shudder as he held her close, and his mouth left hers to find the sensitive flesh at the base of her throat. "Tell me," he demanded, his breath hot against her skin. "Tell me, Livvy."

"I love you," she whispered. "I've always loved you."

"Come on now, sweetie. Just one more spoonful." Matthew smiled at the sound of Olivia's coaxing voice. He hurried up the stairs, anxious to see how Sarah was improving.

"Don' want it," the little girl protested. "No, Livvy."

"It'll make you get better," Olivia persisted. "Don't you want to get better and go see your kittens?"

The bedroom door was ajar, and from his vantage point he could see them without being spotted. Sarah was propped up in bed and Olivia was trying to persuade her to eat the broth Maddy had made earlier. The fact that Sarah was feeling well enough to be irritable was all the reassurance he needed that she was well on her way to recovery.

Olivia had changed clothes and not a strand of her hair was out of place now. The glaring afternoon sunlight streamed through the windowpanes, accentuating the shadows under her eyes, and she looked unusually pale. He doubted she'd slept even a couple of hours.

He tapped twice on the door before stepping inside. Sarah's face brightened at the sight of him, and Olivia turned toward the doorway, obviously surprised that he had returned so soon. Despite her prim appearance, telltale color brightened her face, and she made no attempt to conceal the fact that she was happy to see him.

"Daddy!" Sarah held her arms out to him and he made his way to the opposite side of the bed. "Daddy, where've you been?"

He crossed the room and bent to hug his daughter, relieved not to find her little body hot with fever, but he noticed the angry red splotches on her face were more prominent than before. He kissed her forehead and pulled back to study her face, noting that each bump had been carefully dabbed with something white and chalky.

"Maddy made a paste of baking soda and water for the rash, and Dr. McComb was here earlier." Olivia's voice drew his attention. "He said the worst has passed. She'll be fine, but she has to have plenty of rest. No playing outdoors and no trips."

"I want to go see my kittens," Sarah sulked and turned to her father for support. "Please, Daddy."

"You have to get better first," he reminded her in a tone that was both firm yet indulgent. Her frown deepened, and he added, "It would be too bad if you got sick all over again."

She nodded reluctantly, and he thought of the old adage that patience is a hard-won virtue.

"Will you eat some soup now?"

Sarah turned toward Olivia and accepted a half spoonful of the clear broth. She made a face but took two more sips, and Olivia was satisfied. Placing the dish on a tray waiting on the bureau, she began straightening the bedclothes, deliberately avoiding his gaze.

With a stifled yawn, Sarah rubbed her eyes and slumped back against the pillows, fighting the sleep that her body so desperately needed. Olivia squeezed her tiny hand and wished her sweet dreams, and Matt couldn't resist covering their joined hands with his. Sarah took no notice, but Olivia stilled and moved to extract herself from his touch. He held tight.

For several minutes they sat quietly, holding hands, and watched Sarah drift off to sleep. Matt's gaze was drawn to Olivia, and she glanced up just as he raised her hand to his lips. *How,* he wondered, *do you thank someone for loving your child? For caring for her as much as you do, for being there when you couldn't be.* Words were inadequate, but he vowed to show her, somehow, how much she meant to him.

She looked away, but he didn't miss the shimmer of tears in her eyes or the regret. A tight band constricted around his chest, making it difficult to breathe, and he knew he'd better think of something to say. Was she sorry she'd said that she loved him?

"Livvy, please, don't—"

"Shh." She rose from the bed and motioned for him to follow her. Outside, in the hall, she said, "I don't want to wake her up. Maddy saved some dinner for you, and I can ask her to sit with Sarah while you eat. We can talk downstairs."

He followed her down the stairs and into the kitchen. Once they were alone, Olivia retrieved the plate from the stove and placed it on the table for him. When she turned to fetch the coffeepot, she nearly collided with the solid wall of his chest. She skittered back, but he caught her by the arm and pulled her against him.

"You're avoiding me," he accused in a husky whisper.

"Don't be absurd," she countered, shuddering even before his hands cupped her face. " I just—"

Whatever excuse she might have thought of was lost as his mouth closed over hers, and her gasp of surprise only gave him the advantage he needed. He deepened the kiss, cradling the back of her head with one hand while the other slid to the small of her back, but she needed little encouragement. Raised on tiptoe, Olivia let her arms wind around his neck, and he savored the strong, primal response that urged her body closer to his.

Her fingers combed through the hair at his collar, and he inhaled the sweet, womanly scent that was uniquely hers, enhanced only by a faint touch of perfume. He buried his face in the delicate curve of her shoulder, his teeth gently nipping the flesh where her pulse throbbed. Craving the taste of her, his mouth once again sought hers, and this time her own urgency matched his.

A sound in the distance drew her attention for a moment, and he realized she was pulling away from him, gently ending the kiss. She stared up at him, and the sound came again, this time registering as the sound of someone clearing her throat. Olivia started and they both turned to find Ada Kirk peering into the kitchen, a smile of pure delight on her face.

"I declare, I told Rodger it would take *something* earth-shattering to keep you away from that gin,

Olivia.'' Already picturing herself delivering such a succulent bit of gossip, Ada was practically beaming. After all, the only thing better than gossip was an eyewitness account. "Looks like I was right."

Chapter Twelve

It was a week before Olivia returned to the mill, and even then she had misgivings about leaving Sarah. Aunt Eula and Maddy would take good care of the little girl, she knew, but that didn't make it any easier.

She needed to put in an appearance, at least. Heaven only knew what Ada had been saying, and Rodger had probably moved into her office.

"Welcome back, cousin." Rodger smiled as he crossed the front lot of the gin to greet her. "I assume this means the little one is all better."

"Almost. She'll need a few more days of rest, but Aunt Eula is staying with her." They fell into step, heading toward the gin. "Besides, it isn't fair to leave you to do everything alone.

He shrugged, as if it was nothing. "You know I don't mind."

"I appreciate all your help." She was surprised at the number of wagons, piled high with cotton, waiting to be unloaded. "Cotton in July. You know that means we're in for a bumper crop."

Already, she could hear the steady clip-clop of the mules treading the endless path that powered the pulleys that worked the press, packing the cotton into bales. She was surprised that so much had already been ginned, and the first band of sharecroppers were lined up to collect their crop.

Olivia had already decided she didn't like the man Rodger had in charge of settling the accounts, regardless of how long he worked for her father. Joe Hannah was coarse, an obnoxious bully, and she didn't like the way he ordered people around.

"Mr. Hannah, how can that be right!"

"It's right because I say it's right'"

The harsh words drew Olivia's attention and she turned toward the commotion. She recognized the hapless farmer as Albert Wallis, one of many former slaves who sharecropped land once owned by former masters. The system was hardly fair: a sharecropper had to buy his own seed and all necessary supplies with his own money, pay the landowner a substantial portion of the crop, and live on the meager profit, if any, that remained.

Few could read or write, and most found themselves at the mercy of a system designed against them. Olivia knew many cotton merchants were all too eager to take advantage of the situation, but she considered herself above such common thievery.

"It's just that"—Wallis kept his eyes downcast— "that's such a little bit of money for so much—"

"Now you're calling me stupid!" Hannah's face flushed a brilliant shade of red, and Olivia was stunned at the fury in his eyes. "Are you saying I can't add figures?"

The other men huddled together, exchanging anxious glances, The scene was getting ugly, and Olivia wanted it stopped before things got out of control. She ignored the reproachful touch of Rodger's hand on her elbow and made her way behind Mr. Hannah's makeshift counter.

"What's the trouble?" she said in a soft tone, startling both Hannah and Wallis. "Perhaps I can be of assistance."

"There's no trouble, ma'am." Joe Hannah slammed the ledger book closed and glared back at Wallis. "This boy, here, seems to think he knows a little more about running a cotton gin than I do."

"I didn't . . . didn't mean that, Miss Olivia," Wallis insisted, panic causing him to stammer. "I didn't mean that a'tall."

He was terrified, clearly distressed that Olivia had taken notice of the situation. She couldn't imagine why such a simple question had caused such an uproar. She reached for the ledger only to have Hannah snatch it from the table.

"Please, Miss Olivia," Albert pleaded, "I didn't mean to cause no trouble."

"This is between him and me, Miss Chandler." Hannah's tone was almost a warning. "And I know how to run a cotton gin."

"You don't run *this* cotton gin, Mr. Hannah, I do."

She stood her ground, ignoring Rodger's whispered plea. "Olivia, please, let me handle this later, when things have calmed down."

"Let me see that ledger, Mr. Hannah. Now."

All eyes were riveted on the confrontation, waiting to see what he would say to that.

"Very well," he said, tossing it to the table. "Suit yourself."

Olivia flipped to the last entry and studied the figures on the page. She glanced at her cousin and back at Wallis. "I'm afraid there's no mistake."

From the corner of one eye, she could see Rodger's posture visibly relax.

"You're deliberately being cheated, and so am I."

"Olivia!" Rodger was stunned. "What on earth are you talking about?"

Hannah shot to his feet, causing the table to upend, and the wary sharecroppers scattered, except for Albert Wallis. Olivia wasn't sure if it was fear or hope that kept him rooted in place, but she didn't want to subject him to any further blame for the ugly scene.

"Mr. Wallis, can you come back tomorrow?" His eyes widened at the question, and Olivia hated knowing he feared her as much as Hannah. "Please reassure everyone that their cotton will be tallied and their accounts settled once I've had a chance to go over these books.

He nodded, backing away, and doffed his battered hat. "Thank you, ma'am, thank you."

"Olivia, please." Rodger didn't bother to whisper; instead he was pleading. "You're making too much of this."

She gaped at Rodger. "How can you say that?"

"You don't know what you're talking about, lady." Hannah's face was almost purple with rage, and the warning in his voice had become threatening. "You got no right interfering—"

"Interfering?" Olivia snapped. "Mr. Hannah, I own this gin, the mill, and the outhouse in back. Anything you do on my property concerns me, so don't be surprised to find me looking over your shoulder whenever I please. No matter what you're doing."

"You'd better watch your step, lady," he ground out. "I'll not be bossed around by some uppity old maid."

"No, you won't," she agreed, "because you don't work here anymore, and don't bother trying to pick up a pay voucher."

Without waiting for a reply, she turned toward the stairs leading to her office. Halfway up, she glanced back to find Rodger rooted in place at the bottom of the stairs, gaping up at her. Mr. Hannah stood glaring at Rodger, almost expectantly.

"You gonna let her do me this way?" he demanded.

"Calm yourself, Hannah," Rodger advised. "Let me talk with her. I'm sure this whole mess can be worked out. Somehow."

Upstairs, in her office, Olivia began scanning the ledger and realized it was not the one she worked with every day nor one she had ever seen before today. None of the entries were in her handwriting and many of the names were foreign to her.

There was a tap on her office door, and she looked up to find Rodger wearing his usual placid expression. He stepped inside and closed the door, moving gingerly, as if walking on egg shells.

"Olivia, aren't you being a bit hasty?" he cajoled, clasping his hands behind his back. "After all, one little error doesn't warrant dismissing a longtime employee."

"One little error? Rodger, he was paying that man half what his cotton is worth and recording the full amount against our ledger. Now, where do you think the difference is going?"

Rodger begin to fidget with his cravat, and she didn't wait for his answer. "I won't tolerate an employee who steals from me."

"Don't you think *stealing* is a rather harsh word?" he countered, crossing the room. "We really should give him the benefit of the doubt."

"You're too good for your own good, Rodger." She

shook her head, amazed at his naivety. "If anything, he should be grateful I'm not sending for the sheriff."

"Good heavens," he breathed, sinking into a chair, "think of the scandal that would cause."

"Hmm . . . you're right. We'll have to make good for those men who were here today and saw everything, but we can't have every sharecropper in Georgia showing up with his hand out."

"I am absolutely right." On second thought, he added, "Besides, this could be just a one-time thing."

"Even if it was, what do you think my father would have done if someone had spoken to him that way? In front of that many people?"

Rodger was clearly taken aback by the question and looked away before stammering, "Olivia, your father was . . . he was . . ."

"A man?" she concluded sarcastically.

With a sheepish nod, he reminded her, "I told you there would be problems. Men want to do business with other men."

"Folks in hell want ice water, too," she reminded him. "You see that Joe Hannah is gone within the hour."

"I can't stand to know everyone in the county thinks I'm a cheat."

Matthew eased back in the porch swing and studied Olivia's exasperated expression. "No one thinks that."

"Why wouldn't they? For all I know no one has

received a fair price for their cotton, and all this time they think I've condoned the practice."

"I thought you didn't care what people thought of you."

"I don't." His comment roused her usual contrariness. "However, this time things are not as they appear. I may be a lot of things, but I don't cheat or steal from people who can barely feed their families."

"Come sit down," he coaxed, hoping to steer the conversation on to more pleasant ground. "I hear there are other things going around town about you."

She sank down beside him, alarmed by his remark. "What things?"

He placed one arm around her shoulders, drawing her close, and cupped her face with his free hand. "Rumor has it you're getting married."

She gasped, but he cut off her reply with the kiss he'd been wanting ever since he arrived. It wasn't much of a proposal, but the way her lips softened beneath his assured him that she was receptive to the idea. He held her close, even as the kiss ended, and smiled down at her.

Instead of smiling back, a troubled expression came over her face and she whispered, "Is that really what people are saying?"

He hesitated, wishing he hadn't tried to be clever. A couple of old men had questioned him, wanting to know if he was really courting Olivia Chandler, but he didn't think everyone in town was discussing their relationship. At least he hoped not, if a little gossip was going to upset Olivia.

She eased out of his embrace and rose from the swing. "I've no doubt Ada has been running her mouth to anyone who would listen."

"You're the one who said you didn't give a damn what people in this town thought of you," he reminded her once again. "I doubt a little gossip would ruin your reputation."

Her eyes widened in disbelief. "Do you have any idea what people are saying about us already?"

"No, I don't."

"People are speculating on what's been going on between us, why you're here so much, why I'm keeping Sarah for you."

He'd wondered the same thing himself. "Why *are* you keeping Sarah for me?"

"What do mean, why am I keeping her?" She turned toward him, her expression surprised. "You asked me to."

"When the hell did I ask you do that?" It was his turn to be surprised. "You sent your aunt to fetch her, afraid I'd say no to you."

"I never did any such thing." She started to say something else but hesitated, glancing toward the house into the brightly lit kitchen. "I think we've both been duped."

A mix of anger and disappointment settled in his gut. "You mean you never wanted Sarah to come here?"

"No! I mean, I didn't know you needed—" She held up her hand, delaying his response, and drew a deep breath and began again. "Aunt Eula led me to believe that you needed someone to care for the child, and that you felt I was the only person you could trust to look after her properly.''

''And why wouldn't I have asked you myself?''

She shrugged. ''I suppose it never occurred to you that I might be capable of such kindness.''

That was the last answer he expected, but it had been his first reaction when Eula Chandler presented him with the offer. Given that, he had to be honest with her. ''Maybe it never occurred to me that I deserved your kindness, or that my child did either.''

Her pained expression confirmed that she had thought the same thing, but he didn't blame her. And no one could question her feelings for Sarah now. Her feelings for him, however, might not be as clear as he thought. She'd been weak with exhaustion and nearly asleep when she declared her love for him, but now that she was thinking clearly, her doubt and reluctance were obvious.

''I guess the answer is no.''

She looked down at her hands. ''It didn't occur to me that you were really asking me.''

He gently grasped her shoulders and turned her toward him, forcing her to look at him. ''Yes, I'm asking you. I feel like I've been given a second chance and I don't want to mess things up this time.''

She ducked her head, not willing to look him in the eye, and he swore he saw her lips tremble. She didn't say anything at first, but then she whispered,

"Then I don't think we should rush into anything. That's what caused so many problems the first time."

Matthew let out a breath of frustration. "What is it you think we should wait for?"

"Don't be cross," she implored. "I just think we should take our time and be sure of our decision. We've both changed a great deal over the years, and I don't want you to be disappointed."

"Olivia—" He barely managed to stop himself from saying how ridiculous that was, and he realized that she didn't trust him not to hurt her again.

She could claim all day not to care about public opinion, but she was painfully aware of what was said about her, and even the possibility of being considered corrupt had her in a panic. She cared all right, maybe a little too much.

From inside the parlor, Olivia watched him disappear down the front walk into the darkness. She had been completely unprepared for his proposal, and his innuendo about town gossip had reminded her how painful things had been after his return from the war. Every time she entered a crowded room, conversations would abruptly cease and knowing glances would flicker over her.

They all thought she had gotten exactly what she deserved.

She had wanted so badly for him to tell her that

he loved her, but he had accepted her reluctance with little objection.

Olivia's spirits were no brighter when she left for the mill the next morning. Sarah had begged to go with her, but the unpleasant events of the previous day made Olivia hesitate. If there was to be another confrontation with Joe Hannah, Sarah did not need to be present.

When she arrived at the mill the place was buzzing with commotion and her presence was hardly noticed. She made her way inside and caught sight of Homer hurrying up the stairs toward her office.

"Homer, what's going on here?"

Her voice startled him and he whirled around, wide-eyed. "M-Miss Olivia, don't worry, we've just about got everything straightened up."

"Straightened up?" she repeated. "What happened?"

"Well, it seems some windows were broken."

"Seems? Either they were or they weren't."

"Yes, ma'am. They were."

Losing patience, Olivia motioned toward the top of the stairs. "Let's go."

Inside her office, two workmen were busy nailing boards across one of the damaged windows. Every window in her office would need the same treatment; the remains of glass snarled at her like jagged teeth in gaping mouths. Homer dashed ahead of her, grabbed a broom and began sweeping the shards on the floor into a neat pile.

Rodger turned at the sound of her voice. "Olivia, dear, I'm so sorry about all of this. I had hoped we'd have everything straightened up before you arrived."

"What happened?"

"No doubt young ruffians playing a prank. I've already ordered new glass for your windows, so there's nothing to be concerned about."

"Nothing to be concerned about?" Olivia couldn't believe how dense Rodger could be at times. "I doubt this was any schoolboy prank; the damage is too severe. Were any other businesses targeted?"

He shook his head. "We seem to be the only one."

"A bunch of hooligans wouldn't be so selective." She was barely able to stop Homer as he bent to pick up the shattered glass with his bare hands. "For goodness sake, go find some gloves."

"Olivia, you're not becoming paranoid, are you?"

She waited until Homer was out of earshot. "Paranoid? What else besides my office was damaged?"

He fidgeted with his collar. "Perhaps they were frightened away before—"

"Just as I thought. No doubt this is the work of your Mr. Hannah." She held up a hand, silencing Rodger's prompt contradiction. "He was furious at being let go, and he's obviously not above taking a little revenge."

"We can't prove it."

"No, we can't prove it, but if you see him around here again, day or night, send for the sheriff."

The room grew darker as each board was nailed in place, and it was obvious she wouldn't get any work done with all the hammering and banging. Still, she wouldn't allow the vandal any sense of accomplishment by going home in disgust and frustration. Or fear. "I have a great deal of work to do today, and I'll simply have to use your office."

"My office?" he squeaked. "What is it you need done? I'll be happy to take care of things."

"You just see that my windows are repaired." Olivia gathered several heavy ledgers from a nearby shelf and turned to leave the room, nearly colliding with Homer as he rushed inside with his gloves. "Homer, do be careful. I don't want to find one of your fingers on the floor pointing up at me."

"Y-Yes, ma'am."

She rolled her eyes and wondered how the poor fellow found his way home every night.

Halfway down the stairs, Rodger was right on her heels. "Olivia, wait up now."

She glanced over her shoulder but didn't stop. "We can talk inside. I can't hear a thing with all that banging."

Inside Rodger's narrow office, she settled herself in a chair across from the desk and began leafing through the ledgers. Without looking up, she asked, "What is it?"

"Well, just what exactly do you expect to find?"

"More than likely it's what I won't find."

"Won't?"

"Something's just not right," she insisted. "I just know it."

Matt stared out across the cotton field, a vast expanse of ankle-high green leaves rustling in the wind. The white blossoms were just now turning a pale shade of pink that would soon deepen to red and fall away to leave the tiny bolls to form and ripen in the hot summer sun.

He'd been so encouraged by the promise of a bountiful harvest that he'd decided to surprise Olivia with a proposal. Instead of delight, she'd been horrified at the prospect of town gossip regarding the two of them, and he'd had to ask the second time before getting his answer. No.

He still couldn't figure it out. She'd declared she loved him, plain as day, and made no attempt to retract her statement. She kissed him as if she cared for him, wanted him. The natural conclusion would be that they should be married.

Olivia didn't see it that way.

He thought of all that had changed since the war, and the main thing was his finances. His father had never been respectable, but they'd had money. Enough that no one turned John Bowen away from their place of business, and his mother's family had been in the area for generations.

Matt had lost a great deal in the war and had started over from scratch, like most folks. Except Olivia. Her father had practically owned the town, and Olivia had managed to hang on to everything despite the war. If anything, she had prospered. Enough to buy out the Yankee tax collectors and beat the carpetbaggers at their own game. Most folks thought that made her no better.

More than anything, he'd always believed she'd been motivated by fear, but now he had to wonder if it wasn't the money that had really mattered to her. By controlling the farm land, she insured her stake in the cotton market and her profit.

The cotton was well on its way, and he should have brought Sarah home weeks ago, but she'd been so sick, he wanted her to have the best of care until she was completely recovered. Carter's girls had already offered to look after Sarah while he was in the fields, and he knew it was unwise to allow her to become so attached to Olivia.

He also knew it was unwise to let the child become accustomed to fine living that he couldn't provide. She had more dolls than she would need in a lifetime and a chest full of fancy dresses, and Olivia was paying someone to give her piano lessons.

Perhaps he was becoming a little too attached himself. He was the last person she needed to remind her how much she had changed since the war. Everyone had changed, but Olivia bore no resemblance to the timid young girl she had been. Olivia feared losing things, and marrying him was asking her to give up a lot, but he was also offering her a chance to start over.

New beginnings.

Things would never be the way they had been, but they could still be good. He refused to accept Olivia's reluctance He would make a new beginning with her and show her that things could be better.

Chapter Thirteen

"The things I let you talk me into."

"Hush up, now," Eula scolded. "Can you think of a more pleasant way to spend a lovely Saturday afternoon?"

Olivia made no comment as she helped Sarah down from the buggy and straightened the little girl's dress. Sarah was overjoyed at the prospect of her first outing since recovering from the measles.

Today most of the town had gathered to help build a barn for Bill and Mary Ann Fleming, a newly married couple, and the work was well underway by the time they arrived. While the men toiled on the barn, the ladies were busy setting up housekeeping for the young couple.

Olivia had been surprised to receive a personal invitation. The new bride had been so sincere and jubilant, Eula scolded Olivia for even considering forgoing the day's festivities.

"Miss Chandler!" Mary Ann's face lit up when she caught sight of Olivia and Eula. "Thank you both so much for coming!"

Olivia accepted the girl's exuberant embrace. "I wouldn't miss it for anything."

Ignoring Eula's smug expression, she placed a beautifully wrapped package on the plank table bearing the growing mountain of gifts for the new couple. Mary Ann had already opened several and couldn't resist opening Olivia's. She gasped in delight as she withdrew the fine linen tablecloth.

"Oh, my goodness," she breathed. "It's lovely, just lovely."

"I'm glad you like it."

"Oh, Miss Chandler." Mary Ann hugged her again. "You're the sweetest thing."

"Please, call me Olivia."

Mary Ann turned to show the tablecloth to her friends as if it were some priceless treasure. Their awed reactions made Olivia feel conspicuous, as if she'd given something extravagant.

Most folks had learned to do without wealth, and new standards of success and accomplishment were necessary. Still they had fared better than most. Olivia had heard horror stories of entire counties with not one building left intact—nothing but blackened chimneys standing like grave markers where beautiful homes once stood.

War was so useless. She had only just learned of her brother's death when word came that Yankee troops were marching toward them from Atlanta, burning everything in their path. Her father had died, her brother killed in battle, and Olivia couldn't bear to lose one more thing. Not her home, not her town, and she had vowed that somehow she would stop it.

"Come on, Livvy," Sarah clamored, tugging at her hand. "Let's find Daddy!"

That comment made the good ladies forget all about the tablecloth, and they exchanged knowing glances. Olivia only smiled down at Sarah and said, "Of course, sweetie. Let's go."

Olivia led Sarah across the grassy lot and surveyed the rising skeleton of the new barn. Her eyes found Matt right away. Perched atop the tallest ladder, he was laughing at something another man said and wielding a hammer with easy certainty. He had removed his shirt, as most of the men had, and the muscles cording his arms and shoulders gleamed with sweat in the midday heat.

"There's Daddy!" Sarah cried out and pointed toward her father. "Hello, Daddy!"

Matt glanced down and smiled as he waved at the two of them. Still holding tight to Olivia's hand, Sarah waved back, and Olivia raised her own hand in a hesitant greeting. With a conscious effort, she turned away to keep from staring, and caught sight of Eula, already helping with the dinner.

A makeshift table had been put together with long planks and bales of hay, and every inch was covered with bowls and pots of food. Mrs. Tate had stationed her daughters strategically at the end, where the desserts were placed, each girl serving wedges of pie or cake with an eager smile. One by one they were each invited to join some blushing young man for dinner.

"Sarah, darling, why don't you join the other children?" Eula suggested. "They're all having a picnic and will be playing games after they've eaten."

"Are you sure that's a good idea?" Olivia held tight to Sarah's hand when she would have hurried off to join the other children. "She's barely recovered from—"

"She'll be fine," Eula insisted. "Now, the men will be stopping for dinner any moment, and I want you to fix a plate for Matthew and one for yourself. Find a nice shady spot and enjoy each other's company."

"I can't just waltz over there and invite him to sit with me."

"If you don't, someone else will."

Eula turned and led Sarah to join the other children, leaving Olivia to contemplate the alternative. Mrs. Carter still had one daughter yet unclaimed, but that didn't matter. If she wanted to sit with Matthew Bowen at a picnic, it was no one's business but her own.

With food in hand, she approached Matthew where he stood talking with two other men. She almost turned around, but he caught sight of her and smiled. "I hope that's for me."

"I remember you being partial to blackberry cobbler, and I managed to get the last serving." She would have felt foolish if he hadn't smiled even more at the statement. "Won't you join me?"

She was painfully aware of the furtive looks thrown their way as they strolled away from the crowd. They settled in a shady spot, and Matt dug into the food on his plate. Olivia carefully balanced her own plate on her knee and inspected everything with her fork. She knew she was being a snob, but since the war many women had learned to make very economical substitutes in old recipes, and just because something tasted liked chicken didn't mean that was what it was.

"Find anything?"

She glanced up at Matt, chagrined that she was so obvious. "I've no stomach for ears or tails."

He laughed at that. "Be glad you weren't in the army. You'd have learn to eat worse than that."

She grimaced at the thought. "Ryan once wrote of boiling acorns instead of coffee."

"We did that all right. Toward the end, the army wasn't furnishing any supplies to speak of, and we had to make do with what we could find or steal."

"How awful."

He shrugged, but she didn't miss the way his smile faded. "That was the least of it."

"I've heard stories." She hesitated. "I know Ryan died from being wounded in battle, but did he suffer much?"

"Olivia, you don't—"

"Did those army surgeons get hold of him?"

"No," he answered right away, and she knew it was the truth from the relief in his eyes. There was a lot he didn't want to tell her, but at least he could ease her mind with this one thing. "He died before reaching the field hospital."

"Good," she said, nodding her head. "That's good. At least his death was merciful."

Silence hung between them and Matt reached out to squeeze her hand. "This is no kind of talk for a picnic. What do you think of your first barn raising?"

"Amazing." She gazed up at the skeleton of what would be a huge barn and marveled, "All that work was done in one day?"

"You get fifteen or twenty men working steady and you can get the job near finished."

"When will it be finished?"

"As they get to it. One day is about as much as you can ask folks to put their own work aside. I think everyone enjoys the food and visiting with others. I can't believe you've never been to something like this before."

"Mary Ann is the only one who's ever asked me."

He smiled. "Well, it's the least she could do."

"What do you mean?"

"After you let them have the lumber for the barn at such a low price, they probably think you're the salt of the earth."

"I didn't let them—" She hesitated, positive she had never spoken with anyone from the family about an arrangement for purchasing the lumber.

"Oh, I know no one's supposed to know about it,

but Bill knows you and I are . . . close." It was his turn to hesitate, waiting for her reaction to the statement. When she said nothing, he went on. "Anyway, building this barn was important to him, and he's grateful you made it possible."

Olivia racked her brain, but she knew nothing had been mentioned to her about the young couple needing to build a new barn. Most likely she would have tried to work something out for them, given the circumstances, but she hadn't known anything about it. She thought back to the conflicting ledger entries and wondered how many other transactions she knew nothing about.

"Don't worry, Olivia. I won't say anything." Before she could answer, Matt set his plate aside and said, "Look who's here."

"Daddy!"

"Hello, princess." Matt lifted her onto his lap, and she hugged him. "How's my girl?"

"Daddy, when am I'm going to come home?" she whined. "I miss my kitty, and my—"

"Sweetie, don't fuss at your father. We'll go visit you kitty now that you're feeling better."

"Well, little lady, what if I said you could come home tonight?"

"Tonight?" The word was a mere breath on Olivia's lips and she suddenly felt light-headed, as if all the blood had left her head. "But she can't—"

"Carter's oldest girl said she'd be happy to look after her for me."

Olivia bit the inside of her cheek to keep from

swearing out loud. Her throat was so tight she could barely speak. "How nice of her. Of course I'll have to get all her things—"

A picture flashed through her mind, a picture of herself packing dolls and dresses into boxes and sitting alone in an empty room. She was being silly, she knew, but she wished he had mentioned this to her earlier.

"What's wrong, Livvy?" Sarah slid down from her father's lap and put her arms around Olivia's shoulder. "You look so sad."

Blinking hard against tears, she managed a smile. "Oh, it's just that I'll miss you. Very much."

"You could come with me!" Sarah's face lit up at the notion. "You could live with me and Daddy on the farm."

"Honey, Miss Olivia doesn't want to live out in the country." Matt brushed a wisp of hair out of his daughter's eyes. "She'd hate living on the farm with us."

"No, I wouldn't" she countered, realizing she'd played right into his hands. "It's just that—"

"It's just that we'd have to get married for her to do that." His explanation was directed more at her than Sarah.

"Oh, Livvy, please. Marry Daddy and live with us."

"Can I think about it?"

Sarah nodded. "You'd better hurry."

"Why should I hurry?"

"Mrs. Porter told Aunt Eula you'd better hurry up and get married before you *have* to."

* * *

Olivia carefully leafed through the pages of the ledger, scanning the entries for any mention of Bill Fleming's lumber purchase or any payment arrangements. She had meticulously maintained the records just as her father had, never failing to record every purchase, every sale. Every transaction was recorded by herself or Rodger.

Perhaps it was an oversight. With the ginning season in full swing, Rodger had been especially busy and might not have gotten around to recording everything. Even such a large order.

That was what troubled her the most. Sam Pate would never let a stick of lumber out of the mill without orders from her or Rodger.

Or Rodger.

She didn't want to believe her own cousin was capable of dishonesty, but he was the only one besides herself who had access and authority to release such a large order without payment upfront.

As if her thoughts had somehow conjured him up, Rodger knocked on the open door of her office and stepped into the room. "You'll be pleased to know your windows have been repaired and you won't be cramped in here with me any longer."

She looked up at him, still puzzled. "Rodger, do you know anything about Bill Fleming buying lumber on credit?"

"I beg your pardon?"

"I can't find anything about it in the ledger."

"Oh, yes, I remember now." He lowered his voice and admitted, "I've gotten a little behind on this month's books, but I'll have everything completed before the month's end."

She smiled and decided to play her hunch. "Why don't we make a gift of that? What with the two of them just starting out and all, he'll barely make ends meet as it is."

Every bit of color drained from his face and his knuckles turned white on the back of the chair. "Why would you do that?"

"I know I'm being sentimental, but they're a sweet couple, and I hate seeing anyone struggle."

"Olivia, you can't just—"

She watched him struggle, wondering just what he knew about the missing lumber. "Unless, of course, this is another one of your ventures you've forgotten to mention to me."

He was still pouting over her dismissal of Michael Sullivan's interest in a partnership between the gin and his textile mill. A mill that wasn't even completed, let alone making a profit.

Rodger drew himself up slowly, her meaning clearly registering on his face, but he managed to answer without hesitation. "If you start giving lumber away, we may find ourselves needing an investor, and the offer won't be so sweet. Things are already on shaky ground."

"We're doing fine, and you know it."

"Olivia, surely you must be aware of what people are saying about you and Matt Bowen."

"I am, and I told you I don't care what they say."

"Then why go out of your way to prove them right?" He held his hand up to stay her reply. "Please, hear me out. Not everyone listens to rumor and innuendo, but your little display on Saturday only confirmed what you've so adamantly denied."

"We ate dinner together with at least one hundred other people looking on."

"You were just a little too cozy, and as you said, everyone was looking."

She rolled her eyes. "Good heavens, Rodger, you make it sound—"

"Folks will be reluctant to do business with you. Even Yankees will think twice before dealing with a woman of questionable virtue."

"Is that what you think?"

"No, I believe you," His voice lacked conviction. "But my opinion means nothing, and I would be shirking my responsibility by not addressing the matter."

"What responsibility?"

"Olivia, try to understand." The patience in his voice grated on her nerves. "There have already been several occasions on which I was called to act on your behalf as your nearest male relative."

"Only because of foolish laws that allow a woman to own property but not to sell it. You acted on my behalf out of necessity, not responsibility."

"The law doesn't see it that way." He folded his arms across his chest and drew a deep breath before saying, "I cannot allow you to run this business into the ground. If you don't stop carrying on with Bowen—''

"Rodger Kirk, it will be a cold day in hell before you *allow* me to do anything." She couldn't believe what she was hearing. "And don't ever give me an ultimatum like that again."

"You're not giving me much choice, Olivia."

"Just what do you intend to do?"

"If necessary, I can take the matter to court. I will be appointed trustee over all holdings in your name, and see that things are done properly."

"I don't believe you." Fear and anger surged inside her, and she fought to remain calm. "You can't do something like that."

"Yes, Olivia, I can, and many wonder why I haven't done so already."

Olivia knew she shouldn't let Rodger's carrying on upset her so, but she couldn't forget the look on his face. He'd been serious, she had no doubt, but what troubled her most was his confident expression. Somehow, he *knew* he could take charge of her holdings and "see that things were done properly."

If he didn't sell the business out from under her, he would probably squander the profits. Without the gin, she would be a penniless old maid, forced to teach piano lessons or take in sewing just to survive.

She had to know if what he said was possible, and if it was, she had to do whatever she could to protect herself. If there was nothing to fear, she refused to worry needlessly. One visit to the courthouse was all it would take.

"Olivia, my dear, how nice to see you."

"Thank you, Judge Stone." Olivia smiled as the older man grasped her hands and welcomed her inside his office. "I appreciate you seeing me on such short notice."

"Don't think a thing about it," he assured her. "It's always a pleasure to see you."

Barton Stone had been her father's friend and attorney as long as she could remember, and she could trust him to tell her the truth and advise her wisely.

"Well, I need some advice."

"Of course, of course. What seems to be the trouble?"

She tried to sound matter-of-fact. "I need to know if my control of my business and property could be revoked, just because I'm a woman."

"Olivia, how much did you know about your father's business before he died?"

The question caught her off guard. "Not a great deal, but I've managed well enough. That's not what—"

"Ian Chandler was one of the shrewdest businessmen I've ever known. If he spent a nickel, you could bet he'd get back a dollar in change." Judge Stone adjusted his eyeglasses, as if trying to see her more clearly. "It was never his intention for you to run the business."

"Yes, I'm certain of that." She didn't flinch at the

harsh statement, a fact she couldn't deny if she tried. The only mention of her in her father's will was a brief clause that named a modest monthly allowance to be given to her brother or husband, if she had one, for her needs. "Heaven knows, I wish my brother had returned from the war and taken over himself."

"But he didn't. Your father's death left everything to him, and his death left everything to you." He shook his head at the irony, and Olivia could only guess that her father never knew of Ryan's will. "It also left you sadly without guidance."

She struggled to remain polite. "Surely you haven't been listening to gossip about me.

The old man's face grew pink, but she didn't wait for his answer. "I can't believe you think so little of me."

"It's not that, my dear," he insisted. "But an unmarried woman should never allow herself to become entangled in such a . . . sordid predicament."

"Rodger seems to think it might affect the business."

"I'm afraid he may be right. It's unbecoming for a lady to conduct herself so . . . freely." He paused. "Always, she must stay clear of scandal and not allow the slightest stain on her character."

"I daresay there are few successful businessmen in the state of Georgia who could withstand such scrutiny." Olivia felt her patience slipping, and she paused long enough to collect her thoughts and remind herself that Judge Stone was her only possible ally. She couldn't afford to alienate him. "I just don't see why I'm to be held to a higher standard."

"Business dealings are not something in which women were ever meant to participate." He shook his head, as if unable to even imagine the possibility. "There simply is no standard for women, but surely it shouldn't be the same as that for a man."

Olivia didn't see why not, but she refrained from sharing such a radical thought. "So you're telling me that it doesn't matter what I've done, but what people think I've done."

"It isn't fair, my dear, I know that, but the damage may already have been done."

"But if you know it isn't true . . . Rodger's motivations are clearly in his own interest."

"Rodger is certainly not the man your father would have chosen. He intended to see you marry well, but, like most of us, he thought he had all the time in the world." Judge Stone heaved a sigh and shook his head. "I'm afraid that, without a husband, there is nothing to prevent Rodger from—"

"Just because I'm a woman?"

Husband.

"He can just take charge of my life?"

Husband.

Judge Stone had the decency to look chagrined, but he assured her, "Even I would be hard pressed to refuse such a petition, and another judge wouldn't think twice."

"Well, it seems I've nothing to worry about." She

rose from her chair and let the old goat clasp her hand. "You see, Judge, I'm getting married."

"You are?"

Under different circumstances, Olivia would have been insulted by the shocked expression on his face, but she managed to smile. "Yes. I just haven't had the chance to tell anyone."

"How wonderful," the judge assured her. "I presume I will have the honor of performing the ceremony."

"I think that would be just wonderful."

Chapter Fourteen

Courage had never come easy for Olivia, but she now needed every ounce she could muster. Twice, Matthew had insinuated a proposal but never spoken of his feelings for her. She couldn't wait for love any longer.

She knew she wouldn't find him in the house, even though it was late afternoon, but she hoped to find him near the house. This time she would have to wait if she didn't.

She found him inside the barn, brushing one of the horses and talking with George Carter. Evidently, Mr. Carter was interested in buying the horse, and there was some good-natured debate over the animal's worth. Neither man noticed her coming into the barn, and she debated waiting outside until they were finished bargaining.

"Hello," she said in a pained whisper. If she waited, she would leave, and she spoke again, this time managing more than a whisper. "Hello, gentlemen."

They turned at the sound of her voice, and Matt was obviously pleased to see her. "Olivia, this is a surprise."

"I need to talk with you."

"Of course." He tossed the curry comb aside and crossed the distance between them. "What is it?"

She glanced back at Mr. Carter, who was listening as expectantly as Matt. All her carefully chosen words escaped her, and she could only look away, wishing she hadn't done this.

"I need to talk to you," she repeated. Lowering her voice, she added, "Alone."

Matt glanced over at Carter, but before he could say a word, Mr. Carter grinned slightly and said, "I need to be getting back to the house, anyway. I'll see you tomorrow, Matt."

The two men shook hands and Carter doffed his hat toward Olivia before taking his leave. Matt waited. "Well, what is it, Olivia?"

She hesitated, feeling suffocated by the warmth and the scent of the animals. A cow balled just behind her, and she almost changed her mind. She might have given up on love, but she wasn't going to accept a proposal standing in a barn.

He followed Olivia outside and gazed down at her expectantly.

"Isn't there somewhere we could talk in private? The house, perhaps?"

"Mrs. Carter and her girls are cleaning house for me today."

Olivia felt her insides clench in panic. If she was going to do this, she had better do it now. Today. Before Matt fell under the influence of all that housekeeping and good cooking.

"Oh, well, I suppose here is fine—"

"I know a place," he said reaching for her hand. "Come on."

He led her down the hill just past the barn. The trees grew closer, and soon they were surrounded by massive oaks, shaded by the billowing canopy of green leaves. Sunlight crept in where it could, dappling the mossy earth with golden specks of light. She hesitated as the path narrowed and the brush tugged at her long skirts, but he held tight to her hand and she made herself follow.

She heard the water before they reached the stream, but the sight was still a surprise. The water looked cool and inviting and made the afternoon seem even warmer.

"When I was boy, I'd sneak down here every chance I could get." He neared the bank and gazed at the water rushing over the rocks, smooth and shiny from years of wear. "Mostly to fish, but sometimes I'd take a swim. Pa caught me swimming alone once and wore me out. Said if he wanted me drowned, he do it himself."

"How awful."

"Not really. I never went swimming by myself after that." He grinned at her. "Ryan loved this place."

"I always envied his visits with your family," she admitted. "He'd stay with your family for days at a time. I suppose you swim whenever you wish now."

He grazed the back of his hand along her cheek. "Don't have anyone to go with me."

"I can't swim," she countered.

"We could go wading." His fingers lingered against her throat. "Just get our feet wet."

She shook her head and wanted to laugh at the suggestion. He ignored her and went about removing his boots and socks. She settled herself on the stump of what must have been a very old tree. It was wide enough that she didn't have to scoot over for him to sit beside her.

With a wicked grin, he reached for her feet before she realized his intent. "Come on, Livvy. It'll be fun."

He caught the back of her calf in one hand and slipped her shoes from her feet. When his fingers found the band of her stocking she tried to stand up, but he held tight and stripped the garment down and off. He ran his hand over her ankle and barely tickled the bottom of her foot.

"Come on in," he coaxed, even as she tried to pull away. "I dare you."

"In this dress?" she scoffed.

"Not necessarily."

"That's not funny."

His hand disappeared under her skirt, sliding up

her calf and settling over her knee while his free hand traced the line of her face. "I'm not laughing."

His mouth covered hers, and the kiss was slow and patient. Only when her arms slid around his neck did he draw her into his embrace, and the kiss grew passionate but no less tender. His lips left hers and sought out the sensitive places along the curve of her jaw and the hollow of her throat.

She gazed up into the trees, feeling the same dizziness as she had that day on the swing in his yard. She wanted this, she really did, but she wondered if a loveless marriage wouldn't be better than a one-sided love. Could she live the rest of her life hoping every day would be the day he decided he loved her?

Hadn't she been living that way for the last three years?

"Why did you ask me to marry you?"

The question caught him off guard, and he stared at her, as if trying to discern her true reason for such a question. "What do you mean, why? I asked you because I want to marry you."

"Why? Why do you want to marry me?"

He reached out and grazed her cheek with his fingertips, the light touch making her shudder. "Because I need you."

She needed him, too, but she wanted him to love her. She reached up and caught his hand, holding it against her face. If he loved her, the truth wouldn't matter, but she didn't dare risk him refusing her.

"Then the offer is still good?"

Still cradling her cheek in one hand, his free arm

circled her waist and pulled her to him. His lips touched hers, and she sank against him, unable to disguise the aching for his touch, and her arms slid around his neck and his own embrace tightened.

"Livvy," he groaned, trailing biting kisses down her throat. "Livvy, please don't do this if you're not sure you want me."

He drew back, and searched her face with a look so intense it made her tremble. "Yes," she whispered, wanting to tell just how much she needed him, how much she loved him. Instead, she told him what he wanted to hear. "Yes, I do want you."

He smiled slightly, but the look in his eyes grew more intense. Her answer pleased him, but he wanted more. He kissed her again, holding her close, and his hands explored the contours of her back, her waist, and cupped the curve of her hip, pressing her against the hard ridge of his arousal.

Olivia's heart began to race with the realization that he wanted more than words to seal their commitment. She steeled herself, knowing he was entitled to such expectations, and she was determined not to allow faded girlish delusions to stand in the way of what was expected of a woman. She raised her lips to his and kissed him, welcoming the warmth that spread through her entire body as he deepened the kiss.

Gradually her misgivings and reluctance melted away, and she was lost in the sweet passion assailing her from within and without. The heat of his body burned through her clothes and made her skin tingle in anticipation of his touch. He cupped her breast in the palm of his hand, and she gasped at the feel of his thumb grazing the sensitive peak.

Without warning, he lifted her into his arms and made his way into the shadow of an ancient oak tree. Easing her down on the soft bed of moss, he knelt beside her and worked the few remaining buttons of his shirt loose and tossed the garment aside. The sight of his naked chest made her insides quake, and she raised a hand to trace the broad line of his shoulder.

Settling beside her, Matt caught her hand in his and pressed his lips into her palm before taking her in his arms for a kiss that left her breathless. His fingers sought and found the tiny buttons of her bodice and made quick work of them.

He lowered his head and barely touched his tongue to the hard nub of her nipple, straining against the thin material of her chemise. She bit her lip to keep from crying out and held him close, her fingers twined in his hair. He deftly loosened the ribbon and parted the thin lace, his warm breath fanning over her bare breasts. The feel of his tongue against her flesh undid her resolve, and she gasped in pleasure so intense that it bordered on pain.

His fingers found the open seam of her drawers and she arched beneath his tender touch. He coaxed her body open to his gentle exploration, finding the very core of her being, and she tried to pull away. He kissed her, gently at first, until she stilled beneath him and he resumed the exquisite torment. His lips traveled the length of her throat, grazed the ridge of her collarbone and then caught the aching peak of her breast, grazing it between his teeth.

It was too much. The feel of his tongue against her flesh, the heat growing between her thighs. Olivia clutched frantically at his bare shoulders, as if she were falling in a dream and desperately sought to awaken before hitting the earth below. She tensed and felt her mind and body shatter without ever touching the ground, drifting slowly as bits of flotsam onto a still pond.

Her head fell back against the soft bed of moss, and she fought to slow her breathing, but her heart raced madly. Her eyes drifted open to find him watching her with eyes so smoldering with desire that she shivered to think what more she had yet to experience.

"Oh, Livvy," he groaned, brushing damp strands of hair away from her forehead. He kissed her, searching out the ties securing her undergarments, and swept aside the last of her clothes. He stroked the sensitive flesh of her inner thigh and gently eased her legs apart

She had hardly forgotten the way his body felt against hers or the sharp pain of having him inside her, but the first contact of his heated flesh against her own banished any fear.

Raking her nails across his shoulders, slick with sweat, she raised her hips, seeking more of the glorious sensation. He groaned deep in his throat and caught her hips in his hands, holding them still, and drove deep inside her.

She stiffened slightly as her body adjusted to his length, and she saw the strain on his face as he fought for control. She raised trembling fingers to his cheek and assured him, "I want you, Matt. Please don't stop."

She had unknowingly given him the words he needed, because his control snapped and his hips rocked against hers. He slid one hand to her thigh and eased it up and over his hip, guiding her into his rhythm, and she gasped as her body quickly braced for another surge of intense pleasure.

The muscles in his arms bunched beneath her fingers and she could do little more than hang on as wave after wave of pleasure washed over her.

His own movements quickened to a frenzied pace and he grasped her hips and buried himself to the hilt, his body shuddering with release. He collapsed, bracing his weight on his forearms, and his forehead fell to rest on hers. "Oh, God, Livvy."

"Did I—" She swallowed. "Were you pleased with me?"

"Oh, yes." He chuckled, easing off her and rolling onto his back. "It scares me to think it can get any better."

She sat up, not certain if he was teasing her. "It can?"

He laughed again, but she liked the idea.

For an hour, at least, Matt had dozed on and off, but it was too damn hot to sleep soundly. He glanced over at Olivia and admitted part of the reason he couldn't sleep was his body's aching awareness of her presence. He longed to pull her into his arms, but just holding her wouldn't be enough

He couldn't dismiss the nagging doubts about making love to her, but the feel of her warm and willing in his arms had banished all logical thought. He'd ruined things once before by letting lust get the better of him; he could only hope she wouldn't awaken embarrassed and remorseful over what had happened.

This time, however, it wouldn't matter. A surge of angry possessiveness dispelled his concerns. Olivia could have all the regrets she wanted, but she would marry him. He hated to admit it, but he'd actually taken comfort in the knowledge that she would have had a lot of explaining to do if she'd married another man.

He eased out of bed and crossed the room to stand before the open window, hoping to catch a cool night breeze, and he frowned at the sight of light in the distance. Almost a coral glow like sunrise, but he was facing south and he knew that light could mean only one thing. Fire.

"Livvy, wake up." He returned to the bed and brushed a lock of hair from her face. "Wake up. honey."

She sat up, somewhat startled. "What is it?"

"Something's on fire, to the south." He stepped into his britches and fastened them quickly. "Someone's barn or house."

"Where are you going?"

"To help put it out," he explained, slipping his shirt on over his head. "A fire like that can spread for miles."

"You can't leave me here alone."

He smiled and bent to kiss her forehead. "I'll be back as soon as I can. You'll be fine."

She shook her head, throwing back the covers. "I'm coming with you."

She was dressed and waiting for him by the time he had the horses hitched to the wagon. "We need to hurry."

Help had already arrived before they did, but the fire raged out of control. Matthew swore and drew the team of horses to a halt. "We'll have to leave the wagon back here. The horses won't go near the fire."

She nodded and scrambled down from the wagon without waiting for his assistance. They hurried toward the crowd of folks rushing around like ants, desperate to do anything they could to help.

"Stay back," he warned her.

Matt wasted no time in joining a line of men passing bucket after bucket of water to be thrown on the fire. There was no hope of saving the barn, but everyone was determined to prevent further damage.

Olivia had never seen such a sight and she stared in morbid fascination as the flames snaked from the hayloft and gnawed at the roof of the barn. Only when a shower of sparks landed near her feet did she consider the danger and hurry to safety

Several women were gathered on the porch, trying

to comfort a sobbing girl, and Olivia gasped as she recognized Mary Ann Fleming.

"It's gone," she wailed. "Everything's gone."

"Mary Ann, what happened?"

Olivia's question startled all of them, and a half dozen pairs of eyes bore down on her. She could see the reflection of the flames glittering in each accusing stare.

"What are you doing here?" An older woman Olivia did not recognize hurried down the steps and barred her from coming any closer. "What brings you all the way from town?"

"We saw the fire and came to see if we could help."

"We?" Olivia recognized the second woman glaring down at her. Eugenia Jennings. "I'll just bet you don't mean you and that old maid aunt of yours."

Too late, Olivia realized the consequences of coming here with Matt. It hadn't occurred to her that she would be seen, be recognized. There was only one conclusion to be drawn from an unmarried woman being in the company of a man in the middle of the night, and that conclusion was the truth.

"I hardly think that matters at a time like this."

"Of course, you wouldn't." Eugenia glanced back at Mary Ann Fleming and shook her head. "Still, it's awfully convenient that you just happened to show up."

"What do you mean?"

"Tell her, Marry Ann." Eugenia's voice held an unmistakable note of triumph. "Tell her what they said."

The girl sniffled. "They said we'd have to *pay* for the next barn, or have it burned down, too."

It was late the next afternoon when she arrived at the gin, exhausted from the harrowing night, and she didn't plan on staying long. She had spent the morning with the sheriff, convincing him that she knew nothing about the Flemings' barn being burned, and he assured her he would find the culprits.

Barn burner. Was there anything the people of this town didn't think her capable of doing?

She had barely settled behind her desk when Rodger barged in without bothering to knock. He closed the door and stared at her with undisguised reproach. "You did again, didn't you? You went out there—"

"Rodger, I am in no mood for your lectures."

He crossed the room and braced his hands on her desk, glaring down at her. "You spent the night out there with Bowen. Are you going to tell me it was because of the weather?"

"I'm not going to tell you anything," she snapped. "I don't answer to you or anyone."

"Olivia, people *saw* you last night. Three o'clock in the morning and you show up with Matt as if you were going to a square dance. Half the town is talking about it."

"Only half? You must not have told Ada yet."

"This isn't funny, Olivia."

"No, it's sad . . . a young couple loses everything

they have and all the people in this town can do is talk about is my whereabouts."

"You're forcing me to take unpleasant actions."

"And just what do you intend to do? Have me declared incompetent because I slept with someone?" Anger made her forget caution. "If that's the case, every man in the state of Georgia is a raving lunatic."

"I don't want to cause you any further embarrassment, but I have a responsibility—"

"Not anymore, Rodger. I'm relieving you of your *duty* toward me."

His anger seemed to dissipate, replaced by shock. "You what?"

"I'm getting married," she informed him. "As a married woman, my husband will be the one to answer for my actions and run my affairs."

Rodger paled at the statement and sank into the nearest chair. "You're going to marry Bowen?"

"I thought you'd be glad to hear it," she couldn't resist saying. "You're all the time complaining about the burden of being my nearest male relative and having so much responsibility."

"Olivia, you're rushing into this." He withdrew a handkerchief from his pocket and dabbed at his upper lip. "I'm sure, under the circumstances, it seems the right thing to do, but two wrongs don't make a right."

"There aren't any wrongs in this matter, Rodger."

"Has it even occurred to you that he may be marrying you just for your wealth?" He was grasping at straws. "Perhaps this whole business of wanting you to care for his child was part of some scheme to trick you into marrying him."

"I thought taking care of Sarah was part of *my* scheme to marry Matthew." She couldn't disguise her amusement at his incredulity. Obviously he had underestimated her. "That's the trouble with gossip. You never can keep the stories straight."

"Laugh all you want, Olivia, but I'm not going to let him waltz in here after all this time and take over just because he got under your petticoats."

"Rodger!" She had expected him to be upset, even angry, but she was stunned by the rage in his eyes. "I suggest you take the rest of the day off, before we both say things we'll regret."

He bolted to his feet and glared down at her. "What I regret is ever helping you in the first place. You can't run this place without me, and it may be time you learned that for yourself."

"But Olivia, weddings are supposed to be special occasions."

"I know that." She hated disappointing her aunt, but Olivia was determined to keep the ceremony small and simple. "I'm only inviting the people who truly care about me and Matthew. Anyone else would just be there out of curiosity."

Eula didn't try to deny the possibility. Indeed, the entire town was buzzing with the news that Matthew Bowen was going to marry his former sweetheart after all these years, and some folks were laying odds on whether or not she'd actually get him to the altar this time.

There was also a great deal of speculation as to why Rodger was staying away from the mill. Ada had done her best to make certain everyone knew his side of the story—that Olivia was impossible to work with. She doubted he had told his wife the truth of the matter, otherwise Ada wouldn't be tempting Olivia to spread the truth.

"If I were you, I'd let them look. See what a beautiful bride you are."

"I have nothing to prove to those people," she insisted. "Only myself."

"So you're a gettin' married up again." Jess Perkins eyed Matthew with a good deal of speculation. "A man needs a woman when he's got a youngun to raise."

"And a rich one's even better," another man added.

Laughter broke out and Matt tried to smile at the good-natured teasing.

Harry Rankin slapped him on the back. "I say good for you, old son. Not too many men in this county would cozy up to a woman prickly as a porcupine—rich or not."

"I guess you feel you owe it to her. What with her being an old maid and all."

"That's enough, fellas." Matt signed the receipt

for his supplies and quelled the banter with a look. "Just remember, she's going to be my wife, and I won't stand for anything vulgar going around about her."

He turned before anyone could respond, but Tom Jennings followed him outside and helped load the wagon. "Don't let those old coots bother you."

"Olivia is pretty sensitive about gossip. I'd appreciate it if you asked your wife not to be spreading any talk about the two of us getting married."

Tom nodded, his expression solemn. "I made Genie swear not to say anything about Olivia showing up with you out at Flemings'. I can't afford to have Olivia Chandler against me. Did you ever find out if she's got hard feelings about what my wife said before?"

Matt leaned an elbow against the wagon. "I talked to her about it. I don't think you've got anything to worry about."

A grin split Tom's face. "Especially now with you running things."

"Me? What are you talking about?"

"Once you get hitched, everything will belong to you. The mill, the gin—hell, boy, you got it made. I just hope you'll remember who your friends are."

"I see those old coots aren't the only ones who like to gossip."

"Ah, come on, Matt. We been friends since we were boys."

"And you ought to know better than to think I'd marry a woman just to make my life easy."

A commotion at the end of the street drew Matt's attention and he glanced up to see men scurrying out of the mill.

"Somebody get Doc McComb!" one man shouted. "And hurry!"

Matt arrived just in time to see Olivia rush inside the mill.

"What happened?" she demanded of Sam, the foreman.

"The saw musta threw a belt," he said, motioning toward the man on the ground. "The timber slipt and caught him right across the forehead.

Another man had stripped off his own shirt and had the garment pressed against the fallen man's face, trying to stop the bleeding. Olivia's face grew pale and Matt feared she would faint.

"Come on, Livvy. This is no place for a lady."

She resisted at first, but he kept a firm hold on her arm. He led her out of the building into the fresh air.

"Don't carry on so. Accidents like that happen all the time."

She gave him an impatient look, as if he didn't know what he was talking about, and shook her head. "Not here. Not that kind of accident."

"What do you mean?"

"Of course we've had accidents. Men fall or drop heavy loads, but this was . . . We keep the machinery in perfect condition, and I can't believe—"

"You think someone tampered with he saw?"

She grew flustered. "That does sound silly, doesn't it?"

"You're just upset because someone was hurt, that's all." He pulled her into his arms and brushed a kiss against her forehead, breathing in the sweet scent of her perfume. He remembered how sweeter still her bare skin tasted, and it seemed as if it would be an eternity before she would really be his. "You won't have to bothered with this place much longer."

She pulled back slightly, a startled expression on her face. "What do you mean?"

"You're going to be a married woman," he reminded her. "You won't have time."

"I can't just turn my back on everything."

"I know, I know." He pressed a gentle finger against her lips. "You'll find someone to take over first. Rodger will take care of everything."

She only smiled tremulously

Chapter Fifteen

Olivia sat quietly in her office, listening for the least little sound, but all she heard was silence. The mill had long since shut down and all the workers had gone home. She hated being there alone, but there was too much work already left undone. Too much to leave until tomorrow.

Closing her eyes, she pinched the bridge of her nose between her thumb and forefinger and tried to ease the dull pain settling behind her eyes. She hated to admit that Rodger's absence was already making a telling difference, and she even felt a little guilty, realizing she hadn't given him enough credit for all that he did.

After only three days, she was woefully behind on

the accounts, and farmers were clamoring for their money, while the workers were blaming her for faulty machinery. Poor Homer tried to help her as much as he could, but his standard answer to just about every question was, "Mr. Kirk always takes care of that."

It was equally disturbing to realize how little she knew about her own business, and her ignorance left her vulnerable to accusations that she couldn't run the company. No doubt, just as Rodger had intended.

The sound of breaking glass startled her out of such thoughts, and she jumped up from her chair. Crossing the room, she eased the door open and listened only to silence.

A muffled noise came from the downstairs. and she made her way toward the clerk's office.

"Rodger," she called. "Rodger, is that you?"

She paused and listened again. "Rodger, what are you doing?"

Two dark figures froze at the sound of her voice before turning to reveal faces she had never seen before in her life.

"Who are you?"

"Just stay back, lady, and you won't get hurt."

"Don't you threaten me. I'm sending for the sheriff and you can explain yourselves to him."

She turned, suppressing the urge to run. The last thing she wanted was to appear frightened or threatened. She'd barely gone ten yards before a hand clamped around her arm and whirled her around to meet the glaring face of one of the intruders.

"You just forget all about that sheriff, lady," he warned, "or I'll give you something to tell him about besides burglars."

She understood him perfectly. Panic welled up inside, and she swallowed back a scream, desperately trying to remain calm. "Let go of me."

"Let her go, man," his accomplice urged. "We ain't getting paid enough to get hanged."

His grip tightened on Olivia's arm. "We ain't gonna get hanged."

Her hard-won control snapped, and she fought desperately to escape his hold, but her scream was muffled beneath his palm. A narrow catwalk ran between the office and the gin and warehouse, and another branched off from there toward the mill.

Her captor turned toward the mill and dragged her along with him.

Once inside, she saw him raise his fist but couldn't duck fast enough. The blow left her staggering and he hauled her to the back of the warehouse. The second blow sent her tumbling to the ground like a rag doll. Vaguely aware of the two men looming over her, Olivia fought to remain conscious.

"Damn it, I told you, I don't want no part of a killing."

"You want to leave her here to send the law after us?"

"Well, what can we do?"

"We finish the job we came here to do. What happens to her will be an accident . . . an accident we don't know anything about. Come on."

Olivia knew she had to get out of there, but she couldn't let them know she was conscious. Her head throbbed and she couldn't move without causing the pain to worsen. She waited until she heard them turn around and their footsteps grew fainter, but she could no more sit up than she could stand up. She slumped forward, hoping she could crawl to the stairs, but spots swirled before her eyes and blackness enveloped her.

Dusky shadows followed Matthew as he made his way up the walk toward the Chandler house. He and Olivia had decided to tell Sarah about their decision together, and he couldn't wait to see her reaction. The child absolutely adored Olivia, and he had no doubt how Olivia felt about Sarah.

Before his foot touched the top step, the front door burst open and Miss Eula stared out at him. "Where's Olivia?"

"Olivia?" he repeated. "Isn't she home?"

"No, she hasn't returned since this morning." Motioning for him to be quiet, Eula stepped out onto the porch and closed the door. "I thought she might be with you."

"No, ma'am. I saw her earlier today, but she was still at the gin when I headed back home."

"I'm worried about her, Matthew. Please, go into town and see if she's all right."

* * *

No sooner than the mill came into sight, Matt knew something was horribly wrong. He could see men scurrying to and from the building, hear them shouting and cursing, and then he smelled the smoke. He swore under his breath and urged his horse into a run.

He stopped two men, asking about Olivia, but no one had seen her.

"Miss Chandler? She wouldn't be here this time of night."

"Yes, she would."

He shouldered his way through the crowd, shouting once again, "Has anyone seen Olivia?"

Inside her office, he found her shawl and her reticule, and his heart sank. A ledger lay open on the desk, as if she expected to return to it. He swore out loud. She shouldn't be working in the cotton gin in the first place.

He made his way back outside, pushing through the men thronged in the street. Most were passing buckets of water in a feeble attempt to douse the fire. Thick black smoke billowed outside when he opened the door, but he dashed inside, covering his face with a handkerchief. He didn't waste breath shouting for her and scrambled to his knees to avoid breathing any more smoke than he could help.

He caught sight of her sleeve. Her body was limp,

her face covered with soot, and a nasty cut marred her forehead.

He shook her slightly, but she made no response, and he felt her throat to find she was barely breathing. He scooped her into his arms and hurried through the thick smoke

Once outside, several men rushed forward, offering to help, but Matt would not release her until he knew she was safe. Dr. McComb shouted for him to get her inside the physician's office, and Matt rushed inside, placing her on a narrow cot.

The old doctor felt her pulse and lifted her eyelids, all the while sternly instructing her to answer him when he spoke to her. She broke into a fit of coughing and tried to roll over on her side, but Matthew managed to hold her still. Dr. McComb listened to her heart and lungs

"Olivia, answer me, " he ordered. "Do you know where you are?"

She nodded and coughed again.

"Say it, girl. I need to know if you can speak."

"Yes, I know where I am," she gasped, her voice little more than a hoarse whisper. "How did I get here?"

"Try to remember what happened." Matthew held her hand. "What were you doing in that warehouse?"

"She can answer those questions later," the doctor interrupted. "Right now she needs to rest. All that matters is that she's alive."

"Olivia!" Eula gasped, rushing into the room and

sinking to her knees beside her niece. "Oh, sweet-heart, are you all right?"

She nodded weakly. "Where is Sarah?"

Eula gently touched her fingers to the angry gash across Olivia's forehead. "She's just fine. I left her with Maddy."

"Now, folks, I know you're worried about Olivia," Dr. McComb spoke up, trying to keep her calm, "but I want all of you to wait outside while I tend to that cut and make sure there aren't any other injuries."

Olivia felt as if she'd been run over by a team of mules. Her head throbbed, but her vision was clear. She shuddered to think how close she'd come to burning alive, but she was more troubled by the knowledge that her life was still in danger. Once her attackers learned that she had survived, they might decide to finish her off.

Someone had sent them, just as someone had sent the men to burn the Flemings' barn, and another surge of anger bolted through her at the thought. And she would be damned if she would let a pair of thugs intimidate her. The trick would be finding out who had sent them.

Eula eased inside the room and placed a tray on the bedside table. "You really need to eat something."

Olivia only nodded.

"I know you don't want to tell me, but I want to know what's happening at the mill. Are you in some sort of trouble?"

"Of course not," she answered, ignoring the doubt in her aunt's eyes. She took a cup from the tray. "I was only working late and had the misfortune of being the one to discover the fire. I should have sent for help rather than try to investigate alone."

"You should have been at home." Eula studied her. "Just what exactly is Rodger pouting about?"

Before she could answer, the door to her bedroom opened barely an inch and she heard Sarah's timid whisper, "Can I come in?"

"Of course, honey."

The door swung open wide and Sarah dashed inside the room. She came to a halt just before reaching the bed, as if unsure of her surroundings. "Nobody let me see you when you came home."

"I'm sorry about that." Olivia held out her hand. "I'm fine now and you can see me all you want to."

Sarah hesitated, and her reluctance gored Olivia. The child's lip trembled slightly. "Daddy said you got hurt."

"Not bad, honey. Just a little bit." Olivia sat up on the bedside to prove her words and held out her arms. "I'm just fine."

Sarah lunged into her embrace, clinging to her as if her life depended on it. Olivia stroked her hair and whispered, "Don't cry, sweetie, please don't cry."

"I don't want you to go to heaven," she sobbed. "Stay here and take care of me."

"Oh, Sarah," she managed, though her throat tightened around the words. "Honey, did you think I was going to die?"

"I saw Daddy put you on the bed, and your eyes were closed, and you didn't answer me when I called." The words came in a rush of sobs and hiccups. "He said you were just sleeping, but you always wake up when I need you."

Olivia glanced toward her aunt, hoping for a sign that things hadn't really been that bad, but Eula turned away and wiped her eyes.

"The doctor gave me some medicine that made me sleep," she explained calmly, horrified to think of the image she must have presented to a child who'd already seen the death of a loved one. "That's why I didn't hear you."

Sarah leaned back and studied Olivia's face, doubt still clouding her eyes. She raised trembling fingers to the puffy bruises along one side of Olivia's face. She tried not to wince when the child touched her cheek, and she could just imagine how wretched her appearance must be.

"The bruises will go away in a few days," she promised. "I'll be right as rain."

"Don't you go back there," Sarah pleaded. "Promise you'll stay home where you won't get hurt."

"Sarah . . . honey, I can't . . ."

She was grateful when the door opened and Maddy made her way inside. Grateful, that is, for a moment. Maddy studied her with undisguised censure and disapproval. "I told you. You got no business down at that place. Maybe now you'll believe me."

With a jerk of her head toward Sarah, Olivia said, "Let's discuss the matter some other time."

"The sheriff is downstairs and wants to discuss the matter right now," Maddy informed her. "What do you want me to tell him?"

Eula didn't wait for Olivia's answer. "Tell him she simply isn't able to see anyone."

"Says he needs to talk to her, and he'll come upstairs if she can't come down."

"In her bedroom?" Eula blanched. "Good heavens, what sort of heathen is the man?"

"It's all right." Olivia eased out of bed and slipped her dressing robe over her nightgown. "I can manage getting downstairs if it means preventing a scandal."

The sheriff was waiting in the foyer, and his stunned expression told Olivia just how odd a sight it must be to see one woman being led downstairs by two others and a child.

"Miss Chandler," he said by way of greeting, "I'm sorry to trouble you. I know this must be a difficult time."

"And I'm sure your questions are very important or you wouldn't be here."

Relief washed over his face that she understood and he nodded. "I only need a few minutes of your time."

"Let's go into the parlor," she suggested, feeling somewhat light-headed. "I think I'd be better off sitting down while we talk."

"Of course."

She settled herself on the divan while he remained standing. Under great protest, Sarah had accompanied Maddy to the kitchen.

"I need to know if you noticed anything unusual last night."

"You mean besides my warehouse being on fire?"

He smiled and started to speak, but the sounds of footsteps silenced him. Matthew appeared inside the doorway, and she smiled, grateful for his reassuring presence.

"Miss Chandler, we found evidence of a deliberate break-in. The fire was no accident."

Matthew's expression grew grim with concern and she could feel both men waiting for her answer.

"I'm sure I don't—"

"Isn't it rather unusual for you to be at the mill so late?"

Her gaze snapped back to the sheriff, and she found the accusation in his eyes as well as his words. "There were papers needing my attention."

"Nothing that couldn't wait until morning?"

"Tell him the truth, Olivia." Eula marched into the parlor and settled herself beside her niece. "Tell him."

Matthew stepped forward. "Tell him what?"

"I interrupted two men in the process of setting the fire."

"What?" Matthew demanded. "Why didn't you tell me?"

"Did you recognize these men?" the sheriff asked.

She shook her head in answer to the sheriff's question, and struggled to think of an answer to Matthew's. She prayed the men were long gone by now and their connection, if any, to Rodger wouldn't be discovered.

"I didn't want anyone to know," she said matter-of-factly.

"Olivia, for God's sake, they tried to kill you!"

"And everyone will think they did more than just that," she countered. "My injuries were minor and the damage was slight. I won't have everyone in the county speculating over the . . . extent of their attack on me."

The sheriff cleared his throat and nodded. "Most times a woman doesn't fair very well in a situation like that."

"Well, I managed to escape with nothing worse than a few bruises and I want the matter forgotten."

"If you had said something earlier, they most likely would have been caught."

"And then what?" she demanded. "A trial? That's out of the question."

Matthew studied the charred lumber scattered across the back lot of the gin. Men from the mill were busy dismantling the damaged part of the building and placing the blackened boards into a pile to be hauled away.

He couldn't forge the picture of Olivia lying lifeless on the floor, barely visible with all the smoke. If he had been five minutes later finding her, she would no doubt have been dead. Yet, all she could think of was her reputation.

"I had to see it with my own eyes."

Matt turned to find Rodger Kirk winding his way

through the rubble-strewn lot, gaping at the burned building. "But I still can't believe it."

"Believe it," Matt said more to himself. "And be thankful it wasn't worse."

"Yes, indeed. It's a good thing someone noticed the fire in time." Rodger rubbed his chin thoughtfully. "Half of this year's cotton is already baled and waiting in the warehouse. This county would have been ruined if it had all gone up in flames."

"I'm talking about Olivia." Matt had always considered Rodger irritating.

"Olivia?"

"She was inside the warehouse," he said.

"Good heavens!" Rodger's face paled visibly and his eyes widened in alarm. "Is she . . . all right?"

"By some miracle, yes. She's going to be fine."

"What in the world was she doing down here at that time of night?"

"She's been trying to run the place by herself for a week. Whatever the problem is, you had no call to run out on her and leave her to do everything alone at the busiest time of the year."

"Is that what she told you? That I ran out on her?" Rodger asked with an unmistakable sneer. "After all I've done for her, that's the thanks I get."

Matt dismissed Rodger's sniveling account, certain he was blowing everything out of proportion. The last thing he wanted was for Olivia to return to the mill while the two thugs were still out there somewhere.

"I'm sure whatever the squabble was about, you two can work things out," Matt said. "She won't be able to run the place for some time, and she'll need you to take the reins."

Rodger looked startled for a moment and then tittered with undisguised amusement. "Take the reins? Me?"

He laughed again. "And at your insistence. Isn't that rich?"

"What the hell are you talking about?"

"The last thing Olivia would want is for me to take the reins," he said by way of explanation. "Why else would she be marrying you?"

Rodger gasped, as if stunned by his own words. "Oh, dear, I let the cat out of the bag, didn't I?"

Before he could laugh again at his own humor, Matt seized him by the collar and lifted him off his feet. "You'd better explain that remark."

"See here, t-take your hands off me," Rodger stammered. "Why don't you ask Olivia?"

Matt shoved backward. "I'm asking you."

Rodger swallowed and straightened his collar. "Olivia resented me for knowing more about the business than she did."

"You cowardly bastard. You meant to burn the place down?"

"Good God, no." Rodger was unnerved by Matt's conclusion. "I had nothing to do with this, but I'm sure Olivia will accuse me. She's absolutely paranoid."

"What do you mean?"

"She's convinced I'm trying to take the business away from her," he explained.

"Are you?"

"Of course not. I've told her so over and over, but she won't listen. It's just because she's not married. I would never do that, even though I *am* her nearest male kin . . . for now."

"That's why she's marrying me?"

"Oh, I'm sure there are other reasons, as well, and you certainly don't stand to lose anything. You'll be her insurance, you might say." He paused. "I'm sure she intended to tell you about it . . . sooner or later."

Chapter Sixteen

"What changed your mind about marrying me?"

Olivia knew just by the tone of his voice what had happened. "The same reason you want to marry me. I need you."

"You need a husband," he corrected. "And any man would do. I just happened to be convenient."

She huddled deeper inside her dressing gown, wishing she could shield herself from the inevitable confrontation.

"That's how little you think of me? That I would marry any man that came along?"

"Rather than lose your precious mill, I think you would."

How could she have been so stupid as to breathe a word about her upcoming marriage to Rodger?

"That's what this has all been about, isn't it? You've used Sarah to get to me."

"You know that's a lie."

"Is it? You never so much as looked at her until you needed a way to get to me. That explains all the toys, the clothes. God damn you, Olivia, how could you do that?"

She glanced out the window and caught sight of Sarah playing on the lawn. "Do you find it so impossible to believe that she would love me otherwise?"

"What difference does it make?" He turned his back on her, and for a moment she thought he was leaving. "You can't just make someone love you and then toss them aside when they're of no use to you."

"Why not? You did."

He froze in midstride, his fingers shoved though sun-beaten hair, and he slowly turned to face her. She gasped slightly at the rage in his eyes and it was all she could do not to look away.

When he spoke, his voice was eerily calm. "I've always regretted the promise I made to your brother. Until now, that is. He told me you wouldn't be happy without money."

"Don't blame Ryan for your sins!" She rose from the chaise. "You didn't waste time finding someone else. Did Ryan make you promise to do that, as well?"

"I told you what happened." His eyes raked her, filled with contempt. "I only hope I don't find myself in the same trap again."

"You should have thought of that a little sooner. In both cases."

His eyes narrowed in anger, and she was barely able not to flinch. He was beyond anger, and she looked away, unable to stand the cold fury in his eyes. When the door slammed behind him, she sank down on the chair, trying not to panic.

She managed to keep her composure, even as she watched him cross the lawn, scoop Sarah into his arms and carry her away from the house. When they were finally out of sight, she realized that losing the gin was the least of her problems.

Olivia sat on the edge of her bed and listened to the rain pelt against the windowpanes. It was one of those sudden storms that came in the late afternoon, promising cooler weather. But afterwards the air would be even heavier with humidity and steam would rise from the sodden grass. Sometimes the sun would keep right on shining while the rain fell, and old folks would say that meant the devil was beating his wife.

The room was stifling, and she was tempted to open the window and let the storm inside with her. Instead, she slumped back on the pillows piled high against the headboard and listened as thunder rumbled far in the distance. She hoped the storm would pass; Sarah was so frightened of—

There was nothing to worry about, she told herself.

Matthew knew just how afraid Sarah was of storms, and he would—

She buried her face in one of the fat down pillows, and her chest constricted tightly with the effort not to cry. How would she ever survive this? Sarah hadn't been gone two hours and already she missed the child so much that her bones ached with want. Tears were useless and would only serve to make her feel worse, not better.

She tried to comfort herself by remembering the good times. Isn't that what one was always advised to do? Don't grieve for what is lost but be thankful for the good times? The past few months had been the happiest of her life, and the pleasant memories ran together. Picnics on the lawn, lessons about baby chicks and kittens, tea parties on the porch. How could she separate—

The tea set!

Olivia bolted from the bed and down the stairs, heedless of the fact that she was clad only in her thin shift. How could she have been so careless? Maddy looked up from the beans she was snapping, but Olivia ignored her startled expression and whatever she tried to say.

From the back porch she could see that the little table had toppled over and the forgotten dishes lay scattered on the lawn. Olivia gasped and hurried down the steps. She was drenched immediately and her bare feet nearly slipped out from under her on the soggy grass, but she managed to reach the tea set just before one tiny chair was tossed end over end.

The teapot itself lay smashed on the ground, but most of the cups and saucers were intact. Dropping to her knees, she began gathering the delicate pieces. She reached for the miniature cream pitcher that lay on its side, hoping it had somehow survived.

She drew back and realized she'd cut her hand on the jagged edge. Blood beaded across her palm to mingle with the rain and run pink over her arm.

"No," she cried out in anguish, but her voice was lost in the storm. The tea set was all she had left of Sarah, and now it was shattered. She sank facedown on the wet grass and sobbed.

"Olivia! Come back into the house!"

She glanced up to see Eula sprinting across the grass accompanied by Maddy, who struggled to keep an umbrella over both their heads. Olivia raised her bleeding palm to ward off her aunt's concern, but Eula grasped her shoulders and dragged her to her feet.

"You know better than such foolishness," Maddy sputtered, trying to fit the three of them under the umbrella. "You'll catch your death out here!"

Eula turned Olivia toward the house and helped her up the steps and into the kitchen. Maddy draped a towel around her shoulders, but Olivia couldn't stop shaking despite the welcome warmth.

Eula began toweling her wet hair and drying her face. "Don't do this to yourself, darling."

Olivia's teeth were chattering so that she could barely manage a reply. "She loved that tea set and now it's ruined because I left it outside."

"Oh, well, you can buy her another one."

"It won't be the same," she whispered. Sarah had loved *that* tea set, and a new one wouldn't hold memories of the special times they had shared. A new tea set would simply remain in the box, unwanted and unloved, like Olivia herself.

Olivia took the towel from her aunt and buried her face in the damp cloth, unable to hold the tears back any longer. Eula took Olivia in her arms and rocked her back and forth, but there was no comfort anyone could give her.

Knowing Matthew did not love her hurt enough, but knowing that Sarah still did was worse.

"Don't cry," Eula whispered. "Don't cry, dear."

"Oh, Aunt Eula, he took my baby."

Olivia rubbed her eyes and stared up at the ceiling of her bedroom. She felt slightly disoriented, unaccustomed to sleeping in the daytime, and wondered vaguely if she had slept through the night. The thought was quickly dismissed, as her bedroom windows faced west and the sun was in clear view. She was oddly disappointed to realize she had escaped only for a few hours and still faced another long, lonely and possibly sleepless night.

Not that she could blame that on a late-afternoon nap. Most nights she would fall into a fitful sleep only to awaken later, unable to go back to sleep at all, and the prospect of just getting out of bed the next morning was absolutely overwhelming.

At first she feigned weakness and exhaustion to fend off the stream of "concerned" callers inquiring about her well-being when all they really wanted was to learn some hidden, insidious detail not yet revealed. Eula chided her for rebuffing their visits, but she stubbornly refused to see anyone, retreating to her bedroom at the first sound of footsteps on the front walk.

"Nancy Potter is crushed that you won't see her," Eula would say. Or, "That nice Mr. Sullivan has called twice."

Today she hadn't even bothered to make the effort to go downstairs, remaining in bed despite Maddy's dire predictions that her hair would fall out from lying against the pillow too long.

"You just go on and lay abed all day and see what happens." Maddy also refused to bring a tray up to her when Aunt Eula made the suggestion. "I will not nurse her misery."

Olivia's misery didn't need nursing. It was stronger than she was.

A soft tapping at the door drew her attention, and Eula slipped inside the room. The false mask of cheerfulness had vanished and her forehead was knitted with concern.

Olivia set up in bed. "What is it?"

"Ada is here to see you."

"Ada?"

"She claims she's been worried sick about you and finally came to see for herself that you're all right."

Eula's mouth thinned. "I think she wants something from you."

Olivia only shrugged.

"You want me to send her home, tell her you're not feeling well?"

"No, no, don't do that." She sat up in bed and reached for her dressing gown. "She'll just keep coming back until I talk with her."

A few minutes later, Eula reentered the room with Ada on her heels.

"Olivia, you poor thing." Ada clasped Olivia's hands and squeezed them tightly. "Rodger and I have been worried sick about you."

As a rule, Olivia felt no compunction to engage in meaningless small talk, and she was even less inclined to do so today. "What do you want, Ada?"

Ada released her hands and managed a smile. "I suppose I had that coming."

Obviously unoffended, she eased herself into the chair at Olivia's bedside. "I'm glad there's no pretense between us. It will make what I came to say much easier."

Olivia's eyes narrowed.

"The plain truth is, you can't run your business without Rodger."

"I can get along just fine without someone trying to take over my affairs as if I were an imbecile."

"Olivia, I don't say this to many people, but Rodger doesn't have much backbone." She didn't bother pausing for anyone to deny it. "If anyone is to blame, I suppose it's me. I resented the fact that Rodger

wasn't made a partner in the mill. I wanted the security, for him to be more than just another worker on
the payroll. I nagged and nagged him to insist that
you make him a partner, but he didn't have the nerve
to ask you. So he tried to find another way."

"Maybe having me dead would be simpler?"

Ada didn't look the least bit chagrined. "Olivia,
you know Rodger would never have the nerve to go
through with something that drastic."

"What he did was no better than stealing," Eula
pointed out. "And from his own kin."

"If it meant so much to him, he should have asked
me."

"And what if you'd said no?" Ada challenged. "A
man needs his pride, Olivia."

Olivia winced at the irony of Ada's words. Yes, a
man needed his pride, preferring to steal rather than
beg, and live alone rather than marry a woman who
might use him for her own gain.

At last, she shrugged. "Tell Rodger he can start
back right away."

"Olivia!" Eula gasped.

Ada didn't wait for Eula's protests. "Thank you,
Olivia, thank you so much. You won't be sorry."

She only nodded and sank back against her pillow
as the woman dashed out of the room. Olivia could
feel her aunt staring at her even before she said, "I
can't imagine what makes you think you can trust
him after all that's happened."

"I don't care. I just don't want to be burdened with

that place, and Rodger does know how to run the operations."

"Yes, and you won't have much to be burdened with for long."

"Does it really matter?"

After a week, Eula insisted that Olivia go to the gin and clear the air with Rodger. If she was going to have him working in the gin, there had to be an understanding between them. No more scheming or talk of taking over. If he wanted to be a partner, he would have to prove himself.

She dreaded the confrontation and stalled for several minutes in the general store, pretending to look at fabric while everyone else pretended not to look at her. Finally, she left without buying a thing and turned toward the gin.

"Livvy! Livvy!"

Olivia froze at the sound of Sarah's cheerful voice, slowly turning to the girl darting down the wooden sidewalk toward her. The next instant the child was in her arms, winding her little arms around Olivia's neck.

"Sarah," she said, willing herself not to cry and upset the little girl. "Oh, sweetie, I've missed you so much."

"I miss you." Sarah drew back enough to plant a kiss on her cheek. "We got another cat, and she had kittens."

"More kittens?" Olivia couldn't help but notice

the dirt smudged on Sarah's face, and the fact that her bare feet were filthy. "What on earth will you do with all those kittens?"

The little girl giggled. "Daddy says we won't have mice, that's for sure."

Olivia smiled, brushing a tangled lock of hair back from her face. "What are you doing in town?"

"Daddy had to fetch some medicine for the horses," she explained, pointing toward the feed store at the end of the street. "And he brung me along."

"Brought you along," Olivia corrected gently.

"Brought," she amended. "But only if I promised to be good."

"You are a good girl, and he knows that."

"Mrs. Carter says I'm a handful."

Olivia frowned. "Mrs. Carter? Have you been staying with them?"

Sarah nodded. "She looks after me while Daddy works."

Not very well, it seems.

Finally she had to ask. "How did you get so dirty?"

Sarah glanced down at her dress and her grimy hands. "Doing chores."

"Chores!" Olivia was horrified. What kind of chores could a child so young be expected to do? "What sort of chores?"

"I fetch the eggs from the hen house, pull weeds in the garden—"

The list went on, and Olivia felt her anger kindle

against Matthew for allowing this sort of thing to happen, and she intended to tell him so.

"Your father is probably looking for you. Perhaps we should go back to the store and let him know you're with me."

Sarah scampered along beside her on the sidewalk, their hands clasped tight, and Olivia quelled each gaping stare with the look of haughty disdain she'd mastered so well. She caught sight of Matthew coming toward them, a harried expression on his face.

"Sarah, honey, don't ever wander off from me that way."

"I found Livvy, Daddy, look."

His gaze traveled from their knotted fingers up the silk sleeve of her dress and settled on her face. "I see."

"Daddy, I wanna go home with Livvy." Sarah's grip on Olivia's hand tightened almost to the point of being painful.

"No, sweetie, you have to come home with me."

Without warning, Sarah's lip trembled and she buried her face in the folds of Olivia's skirt. "P-Please, Livvy, please let me. I'll be good, I promise."

"Don't cry, Sarah." Olivia knelt to hug the little girl, heartsick at the thought of refusing her, but one look at Matthew's grim expression told her that he would not compromise. "You're always a good girl. Always."

Sarah clung to her, her tiny fingers twisting in the fabric of her sleeves. "Please, take me home with you . . . just for a visit."

"Sarah"—Matt's voice was gentle, almost pleading—"Miss Olivia can't do that."

The little girl blinked back her tears and asked, "Why? Why not?"

Olivia glanced up at Matt, and he turned away, but not before she saw the guilt and anger in his eyes. Forcing a smile, Olivia found a lace handkerchief in her pocket and dried Sarah's eyes. "Your daddy needs you, Sarah. He needs you to help him on the farm . . . to take care of all those kittens. And what about the baby chicks? If you hadn't told your father about them, some old fox would have gotten them for sure. Your daddy needs you to help him take care of things. You'll do that for me, won't you?"

Sarah nodded bravely, but her lip trembled slightly. "I will, but I miss you."

Olivia tucked the lacy handkerchief in Sarah's hand. "I miss you, too."

Matt held out his hand to Sarah. "Come along, honey. We need to get home and see about the horses."

Sarah hugged her tight, and Olivia kissed her cheek, tasting the salty tears. She whispered into the child's ear, "I love you. Don't ever forget that."

He hoisted Sarah onto the wagon seat and turned to bid good day to her as if she were a brush salesman.

She didn't wait for his dismissal. "May I speak with you? Privately."

He hesitated, following her toward the back of the wagon. When she turned to face him, he shook his head. "There's nothing to say."

"Perhaps you can explain why you're allowing your little girl to be mistreated."

"Mistreated?" His eyes narrowed. "What do you mean?"

"Don't you see how dirty she is? She told me she's expected to do *chores,* for God's sake."

"She was helping in the garden, and there was no reason to get fixed up for a trip to the store for sulfur and liniment." He glanced down at his own work clothes. "I suppose I don't look much better."

"You're a grown man; she's barely more than a baby."

"Olivia, I hate to tell you this, but children on a farm are expected to do chores, even the younger ones. It won't hurt her to get a little dirty in the process."

"A little dirty? She's barefoot and filthy, or haven't you bothered to notice?"

"I don't neglect her, if that's what you mean. She washes up every night before bed. and I make sure she's taken care of."

"You mean Mrs. Carter?" She put as much contempt in the words as she could.

"Yes, she looks after Sarah for me. She and her girls."

Olivia knew her distaste was evident. "I don't know how she can look after the ones she has, let along someone else's child."

"I suppose you should have thought of that before you moved them in on me, shouldn't you?"

"I—" She barely stopped herself from blurting out

that she had no idea the Carters were a traveling mail-order bride service, but she sensed his accusations went further. "You mean, of course, that I—"

"That you were paying Carter a salary behind my back."

"I was only trying to help Sam," she insisted, telling herself it was at least partly true. "He was at his wit's end with so many folks under one roof."

"Then why didn't you just tell me that?"

She only shrugged. "It's not their fault."

"Don't worry, I won't throw them out just to spite you."

"You will be sure they're looking after Sarah properly, won't you? For her sake, I mean."

Something flickered in his eyes, softening his expression for a moment. He stepped closer. "I know you're fond of Sarah, and I promise you no one is mistreating her. She's a poor man's daughter, Olivia. I can't give her the things you did."

"Then let me give them to her." She was pleading. "She won't even have to know—"

"I'd know."

She looked away. "What did you think would happen if we'd gotten married?"

"I suppose I wasn't thinking at all," he admitted. "You would have been miserable, Olivia."

She wanted to tell him that she was miserable now, but such a statement would only lead to tears and begging. Perhaps he wasn't miserable without her. As long as he had someone to look after Sarah, he was getting along just fine. All she could do was nod in response to his statement.

"Don't worry about Sarah. She'll be just fine."

She nodded again, and he climbed up onto the wagon seat beside Sarah. "Say good-bye to Miss Olivia, sweetheart."

One last tear slipped down the little face. "Bye, Livvy."

She watched the wagon lumber down the street. Just before it turned onto the main road, Sarah turned around on the seat and waved to her, the lacy handkerchief still clutched in her hand.

Chapter Seventeen

Olivia's fingers were beginning to cramp from signing her name over and over again, but Rodger patiently slid another stack of papers in front of her. She gave him a sidelong glance. "You certainly have been busy."

"It's our busiest time of the year," he reminded her, thumbing through the pay vouchers she'd just finished signing. "High cotton, as they say."

Was it? Olivia stopped to think and realized how late it was in the year. Wagons piled high with cotton would begin lining up at the gin before sunrise and continue long after twilight. Just yesterday, it seemed, Matthew had been fighting to get his crop planted, and now harvest was upon them.

And they were getting along just fine. Just fine without her. They didn't need her at all, and she was dying inside without them.

She scratched her name on a few more documents, barely glancing at the names and figures.

"Olivia, I'm sorry you had to come in today." Rodger scooped the last of the papers from the desk. "But I can't do a thing without your signature."

"I don't mind."

"I know you've been under a strain lately," he reiterated "Perhaps you should consider giving me power of attorney . . . so that I could take care of these tedious details without troubling you."

A faint warning sounded in her brain, but she managed to keep her expression blank. "I don't mind, Rodger. You're already taking care of so much."

"I'm happy to do it, Olivia. This place is important to me, even if it isn't mine."

She ignored the thinly veiled implication behind his remark and turned to look out the window. "Did you ever stop to think what life would be like without money?"

"What?"

"I mean, what would matter most to you if you lost every cent you had?"

"I hope to blazes I never find out."

She managed a slight smile, wishing she hadn't learned too late. Her greatest fear had been losing her security, and in the end it was worthless to her. She might never want for money, but she'd lost two people she loved more than anything on earth.

She should be happy they were doing so well, not suffering with regret and loneliness like her. The prospect of seeing Sarah again or bumping into Matthew at the mercantile was daunting. How many such encounters could she survive without falling apart in front of a store full of people?

She was sorely tempted to tell Rodger to bring any more papers needing her signature to the house from now on, but he would no doubt go directly to Judge Stone and have her declared an invalid.

"If this is all you need from me today, I think I'll go on back home." She rose from the chair. "I still tire easily."

Rodger offered to see her home, but she refused, thanking him for his concern. "I'll be fine."

Once outside, she caught sight of the foreman and waved to him. "Hello, Sam."

"Hello, Miss Olivia," he said as he crossed the distance between them. "It's good to see you."

"Thank you." She almost had to shout to be heard over all the commotion of machinery and men's voices. "I see you're keeping busy."

"The place is a madhouse," he declared. "Nonstop from dawn 'til dusk, and not a free minute in between."

"Making hay while the sun shines, I suppose."

"Yes, ma'am. Every man is scrambling to get his cotton in before rain sets in. Can't pick cotton when it's wet, and too many rainy days in a row won't let it dry out enough to pick. It'll just rot on the stalk."

"Well, it looks like everyone in the county is here today."

"There's plenty more struggling to get theirs picked. Not enough pickers to go around."

She knew she shouldn't ask, but she couldn't stop herself from casually inquiring, "How is your brother-in-law managing?"

"George? Says they're doing all they can, but Bowen will be lucky to get half his crop picked."

"Half?"

"It's just him and George. Like I said, there's just not enough pickers. It's a shame, too. He's got a bumper crop this year."

"Olivia!" Eugenia Jennings stood gaping out her front door. "What on earth are you doing here?"

"May I come in?"

Wariness quickly replaced the woman's shock, and she hesitated. "What's this about?"

"I need to talk to you."

Once inside, Olivia couldn't help but notice the threadbare carpets and faded draperies, and Eugenia stood braced for any critical remarks about her home. As a girl, she had always been haughty, but Olivia felt no vindication in seeing her reduced circumstances.

"I was out on the back porch. Why don't you join me?"

It was no invitation to tea. Eugenia was in the middle of canning tomatoes, and she went right about her work without even offering Olivia a place to sit down.

Olivia had never felt so awkward, but she tried to be as gracious as possible.

"I suppose it's more pleasant to do this outdoors." She had no idea how the process worked, but she could only imagine the open porch being more comfortable than a stuffy kitchen.

"It's cooler out here," she said by way of explanation. "Makes it easier to get things done."

Olivia nodded, genuinely amazed at the number of canning jars still waiting to be filled. Row after row of fruits, vegetables, pickles, jams and jellies were already lined up across the porch. She picked up a jar of peaches and complimented the woman on their beautiful color.

"Funny how we never thought where things like that came from, isn't it?"

Olivia nodded. "How did you learn to do all this?"

Eugenia laughed. "Necessity. Just like laundry, cooking and cleaning." She glanced down at her hands, reddened from her work. "I suppose I'll never have the hands of a lady again."

Olivia clenched her gloved hands into fists. She was no fragile gardenia herself, but she'd never faced the hard physical labor of poverty.

"What is it you need to talk to me about?"

"I had hoped to speak with you and your husband, both."

Eugenia straightened up, her eyes narrowed with distrust and a trace of apprehension. "What about?"

Olivia felt herself flinch at the look on the woman's face. Once, she had relished the idea of having prestige, having folks tread softly around her, but she sorely regretted the power she had so badly misused.

"Well," she began, forcing herself to meet the woman's gaze, "I need a favor."

"A favor?" Both women turned at the sound of Tom Jenning's voice. "What kind of favor could you want from me?"

Olivia drew in a breath as she watched him cross the lot and make his way up the steps. Of all her brother's friends, Tom Jennings had been her least favorite. He'd always been quick to tease and make fun of her. He didn't look so proud now, not in his faded shirt, patched trousers and muddy boots.

Don't get your back up.

Aunt Eula's words rang in her ears, as clearly as if the woman was standing just behind her, and it was all she could do to keep from looking down her nose at him from where she stood on the porch. Instead, she steeled herself and made her way down the wobbly steps to stand before him, his height towering over her.

"I was wondering how you're coming along with your cotton. How the picking is going, I mean."

Tom gave his wife a brief, anxious look and hesitated before answering. "As well as can be expected . . . with all this rain. Why do you ask?"

"It seems everyone is having the same problem," she began. All her practiced speeches rang hollow in her mind, and she knew nothing would cause greater suspicion than Olivia Chandler offering a helping hand. "Well, I stand to lose a fortune if all this cotton rots in the field instead getting to the gin."

"It won't do me any good, either, if that's any consolation to you."

"Not at all." She paused thoughtfully. "I cannot believe every farmer in this county is willing to let a year's work go to waste."

Eugenia's temper got the better of her. "Why don't you do something about it, Miss High-and-Mighty?"

"Genie, for God's sake, shut up!"

"I think she's quite right, Tom. It is up to me to do something about this." They were both taken aback by her reply. "However, I fail to see why I should point out what's right under everyone's nose."

"What?"

"If everyone in this county can pitch in and build a barn in a day, surely they could rally to save their crops from ruin."

"You can't pick that much cotton in a day!"

"Of course not. But if we pool all the hired pickers and every able-bodied soul who's willing—"

"We could pick this county from one end to the other in a week," Tom concluded with certainty. "Two at the most."

Olivia smiled slightly. "It is a splendid idea, but who would listen to me?"

"They'll listen to Tom!" Eugenia's eyes were bright with hope. "You can make them listen, Tom, you know you can. Please say you'll try?"

* * *

It might work.

Matt listened as Tom Jennings spelled out the plan for getting everyone's cotton picked before any more rain could ruin things. It just might work, and it was the only alternative any of them really had, other than letting a year's work rot in the field.

"How are we supposed to keep everybody's crop separate?"

"We're not." Tom faced everyone squarely. "Any man who agrees to this, agrees to put his crop in with the others, and we divide the profits evenly."

Groans of disappointment mingled with shouts of protest.

"I want everything I got coming!"

"I got twice as much land as some folks!"

Tom held up his hand to silence the crowd. "No one has to go along with us if they don't like it. Take your chances on your own, but you stand to lose everything. This way you all stand to gain something."

The crowd still grumbled but not as loudly. Several men put their heads together, and Matt glanced across the assembly to find Tom watching with an anxious expression.

"And if we sell it combined, we can just about name our price." He watched the possibilities register on their faces. "After all, they can either buy it all or we sell elsewhere . . . at our price."

Murmurs rose from the gathering of struggling

farmers, tinged with reluctant optimism, and many began nodding their heads.

"We'll send Matt to do our negotiating," a man called out from the back. "Any chance you can sweet-talk Olivia Chandler and get us a better deal?"

Laughter erupted, and Matt tried not to let his anger show. He didn't want anyone thinking he expected anything from Olivia. Before he could answer, Tom cut in, "I'll handle the negotiating. If anyone wants to come along, they're welcome."

Finally, a consensus was reached. Something was better than nothing, and the assembly adjourned after agreeing that the picking should begin at the farthest end of the county, working their way back toward town and the gin.

Tom shook Matt's hand. "Thanks for what you said. It really made a difference."

"It's a good idea. We just don't have time to mull it over." He hesitated. "Look, Tom, about negotiating with the gin, it's probably best if I stay out of that."

"Don't give it a second thought." Tom clapped him on the shoulder. "I understand."

"Just let me warn you, Olivia isn't an easy person to bargain with. She'll do whatever it takes to protect her interests."

Tom shrugged. "I can't blame her for that. I'm the same way myself."

"I wouldn't worry about her," a man on his way out stopped to say. "More than likely you'll be dealing with Rodger Kirk. They say he's pretty much running things over there now."

"Since when?"

"I don't know. That's just what I've heard."

She's got it in her head that I'm trying to take over the business, and that she needs a husband to protect her precious money. Hasn't she mentioned any of that to you?

Rodger Kirk's cavalier account of Olivia's reasoning behind wanting a husband had made perfect sense at the time, and she didn't deny any of it when he confronted her with the truth. What else could account for her sudden decision to accept his proposal? It never occurred to him that she might actually have something to fear, least of all from Rodger Kirk.

She should have told him the truth, right from the start, instead of trying to lure him into marriage just because she needed a husband. Still, he wondered how she would protect herself now, if Rodger was really a threat to her. Would she just find someone else to marry?

Word of the collective effort quickly spread, and there were few who didn't eagerly pledge their cooperation.

Not everyone was thrilled at the prospect, and it was no surprise when Rodger expressed his dismay over the matter. No sooner than grace was spoken that Sunday, he began to complain bitterly. "As if things weren't bad enough, now we have to worry about haggling over cotton as if it was gold. If they think they have us over a barrel, well, let me tell you, they're in for a surprise."

"You musn't fret over such things." Ada did her best to steer him away from the unpleasant subject. "Besides, there's nothing that can be done."

"Well, we'll just have to think of something," he countered, unfazed by her attempts to silence his whining. "Let them take their chances with the exchange in Memphis. They'll come crawling back, begging us to buy that cotton."

"We can't do that."

Olivia's quiet words startled him. "What do you mean?"

"I've already agreed that we would buy the cotton." Rodger gaped at her as if he hadn't understood a word she said. "We'll negotiate the price once the final wagonload is baled and we know exactly how much was gathered."

"You mean to tell me you *knew* about this?"

Olivia met his gaze. "Of course I knew. The truth is, I suggested the idea."

"What?" Rodger's fork clattered on his plate and he sat back, astonished. "Have you taken leave of your senses?"

Eula gasped. "Rodger Kirk, don't you dare talk that way about Olivia."

Ignoring the reproach, he continued. "Do you know what this means? We won't have a leg to stand on when it comes to bargaining for price. Good God, Olivia, they'll band together against us."

"The alternative is let the bulk of this year's crop rot in the field. Do you think that would be better?"

"For God's sake, yes!" Rage darkened his features

and he jerked his arm away from his wife's reproachful touch. "With a shortage, we can sell what we have
on hand for ten times what we paid for it!"

"And what about the families who stand to lose
everything? Their homes, their land—"

"We're not running a charity!" Rodger rose from
the table, raking his fingers through his hair, his face
grown deathly pale. "My God, Olivia, do you realize
how much this could cost us?"

"Cost us?" Her initial surprise at his volatile reaction began to fade and her own anger began to rise.
"We won't lose anything. We'll sell every pound of
cotton we can get our hands on."

"At a *substantially* lower price." He braced his palms
on the table and regarded her with an almost pleading expression. "Why didn't you discuss this with me
first?"

"Because I don't have to discuss anything with
you." In the past weeks she had given him a tremen-
dous amount of control in the business, and it was
obvious he wasn't going to relinquish it graciously.
"The way I see it, we'll have more cotton to sell than
any other broker and can name our own price."

"And you see it that way because you know absolutely nothing about the business!"

"Rodger!" Eula gasped. "Shame on you for carrying on so."

"Yes, dear," Ada put in, her voice coaxing. "Surely
business matters are best discussed at the office, not
at the Sunday dinner table."

"Rodger, I'm sorry this has upset you so." Olivia

forced herself to be calm. "There were so many families who stood to lose everything they had, and I felt compelled to help them. I'm confident no one will take advantage of my generosity."

The explanation made no impression on her cousin, and his expression was positively bleak as he took his seat.

"Come now, let's not have the whole day spoiled over this." Eula smiled at Olivia "The food is getting cold, and we have peach cobbler for dessert."

"No, thank you, Aunt Eula." Rodger pushed his plate away. "I suddenly have no appetite."

"You said you had everything under control."

Joe Hannah was even more furious than Rodger had feared he would be. He had already learned of the collective effort to harvest the cotton remaining in the fields, but thankfully he knew nothing of Olivia's involvement in the scheme. Rodger could only pray the man didn't find out before he could think of a solution. Still, there would be no lucrative profits to divide, or even to make up the money he'd already used to appease the man's ire over Olivia's dismissing him from the gin.

"I can't control what other people do, and I never dreamed anything like this would happen."

"Well, you just refuse to bargain with them." The man's dark eyes narrowed. "Tell them they can take your offer or take their chances elsewhere."

"What makes you think they won't?" Rodger

already knew he would have no say in the bargain anyway. Olivia had every intention of being as generous as possible. "Then we'll be left with nothing but what cotton there is in the warehouse, and that will be worthless."

"You'll just have to think of a way to stop it."

Rodger cursed himself silently for ever listening to this man, for ever letting his resentment of Olivia's inheritance blind him to the danger of any involvement with a man like Joe Hannah. Just once, he had thought to take what he had been denied, and he'd gotten nothing but trouble in return.

Aunt Eula was in her element and loving every minute of it. There were dozens of hungry laborers, anxious for the meals that were brought to the fields each day. Everyone contributed what they could, but it was Eula who saw that it was prepared, packaged and presented properly.

Olivia helped all she could but declined making the trek to the field on the wagon. She couldn't let Matthew see her and suspect that she had anything to do with the effort. If he even suspected she had concocted the whole thing just to save him from ruin, his pride would never allow him to accept her help, no matter how cleverly disguised.

He would think nothing of seeing her aunt among the other ladies serving the meals. Still, she was sorely tempted to tag along. Eula had reported seeing youngsters picking cotton along with the adults, and her heart ached at the thought of little Sarah laboring in the fields.

"Why don't you come along today?"

Olivia glanced up from the tray of neatly wrapped gingerbread squares and shook her head. "No, I'd better not."

"To hear you, one would think you're ashamed of what you've done." Eula shook her head. "Everyone is thrilled to death. I don't see why it has to be such a secret."

"They're thrilled to death because they think they're pulling one over on me." Olivia turned her attention to the half dozen loaves of bread that needed slicing. "If anyone knew I had anything to do with this, it would ruin all the fun."

"I don't believe that at all. They should know, and they would be very grateful."

"Hmph."

Eula folded her arms and studied her niece. "Unless there's one certain someone you don't want to know."

Olivia glanced up, irritated, and chose to say nothing.

"You can't live your life avoiding him at every turn."

"What alternative do I have?" This she asked more of herself. Seeing Matthew hurt deeply, and she didn't think she could survive having to deny Sarah again. Olivia couldn't forget the child's tearful pleadings or the way Sarah's tiny hands clutched at her clothing, and she wouldn't put the child through that kind of misery again.

*   *   *

The heat was unrelenting, and the dark clouds that gathered on the horizon offered no relief. Matthew watched them inching their way closer and closer, growing darker and more threatening. A storm right now would negate all the hard work they had done.

For nearly two weeks they had labored well before sunup until the last bit of twilight disappeared, using lanterns to light the way. Without complaint, they worked tirelessly, men and women, alongside hired pickers. The reward was the sight of the wagons, piled high with snow-white cotton bolls, leaving the fields for the gin.

The only thing that rivaled the sight of the loaded wagons was the arrival of the ladies from town at noontime. Everyday they delivered enough food for everyone to have a full meal and saw that no one went without. Matthew had caught sight of Eula Chandler more than once, but never Olivia.

Each time, he felt oddly disappointed and cursed himself for a fool. She would have nothing to do with him if she did venture out to the fields, and he didn't know what he would say to her if she did. He wasn't feeling the least bit vindicated by the evidence that she had only wanted a husband for business reasons.

The last thing he needed was guilt over Olivia losing her business. He was already plagued with guilt over Sarah's unhappiness. The little girl hardly ever smiled anymore, and he could interest her in nothing at home. Even the kittens scarcely drew her attention.

Almost every day she begged him to take her to see Olivia. At first, she cried when he said no, and not for the toys and clothes left behind at Olivia's house. *I want my Livvy,* she would sob.

Damned if he didn't want her, too. Just to be with her, see her smile, share her laughter.

"The wagon's back," someone shouted, drawing him out of his somber thoughts. "It's back, still loaded with cotton."

One by one, the pickers stopped their work to gaze at the sight. The wagon came to a halt and the driver jumped down from his perch. Tom Jennings met him halfway, and Matt could tell from their gestures and expressions that something was terribly wrong. Deciding to find out for himself, Matt made his way toward the wagon, many others following him.

Soon, over a dozen people were gathered around the wagon in time to hear the driver explain why he was returning the cotton to the field.

"They turned me away at the gin."

"There's got to be some kind of mistake." Tom glanced back at the wagon, piled high with cotton, and insisted, "You must have misunderstood."

"The man told me to take the cotton back where it came from and don't bring no more. Now, how could I misunderstand that?"

Matt's insides turned cold. He had expected to meet resistance, but not out-and-out refusal. They had been sending wagons to the gin for well over a week now, every day, and nothing had been said to indicate that there was a problem.

Those around him were shocked and angered at the news, and their voices rose in despair.

"I knew this would happen."

"We'll lose everything!"

"Why? Why are they doing this?"

"Now, just hold on!" Tom faced the crowd, holding up his hands to silence their cries of outrage and panic. "There's got to be some kind of mix-up at the gin. I'll go down there myself and see what the problem is."

"I'll go with you," Matt said.

Chapter Eighteen

With the draperies drawn against the heat of the afternoon sunlight the parlor was almost dark enough to warrant lighting a lamp, but Olivia decided against it. She had no desire to read or stitch on her needlepoint. Instead, she let her head rest against the back of the divan, tempted to lie down since no one was home.

Aunt Eula had been gone for over an hour, and Olivia regretted not going with her. The pickers were on the opposite side of the county from Matthew's land and it was unlikely he would be anywhere near the field. The men had been splitting their time between picking the cotton and the numerous chores that could not be neglected.

Chores. Olivia hated to think what tasks Sarah might be expected to shoulder during this time. Eula had promised to keep an eye out for the child in the fields, but Olivia wasn't sure she wanted to know. What could she do?

A sudden pounding at the front door startled her out of her drowsy state and she hurried to open the door.

"Matthew!" she gasped at the sight of him. "What are you doing here?"

"We need to talk."

The steely tone of his voice made her wary. She stood back and said, "Come in."

He stalked into the foyer and declined her invitation to the parlor. "What I came to say won't take long."

She nodded.

"When are you going to learn that your money doesn't give you the right to toy with people's lives?"

Olivia's heart sank. He knew. Somehow he had discovered her part in the effort. Would he really ruin it for everyone?

"Neither does your arrogant pride."

"What the hell does pride have to do with this?"

"You're not the only one who stands to gain from this," she pointed out.

"So you're willing to destroy every family in the county just to spite me?"

Olivia was taken aback, the conversation suddenly making no sense to her. "How am I spiting you?"

His eyes narrowed. "Don't play innocent with me.

No one would have refused that cotton unless you told them to do so."

"Refused your cotton? When?"

"This morning. Weren't you there?"

"No. I haven't been to the gin in days." Without waiting for his reply, she said, "But Sam knew you would start bringing what you had this week."

"How would he know that?"

Too late, she realized that Matt's anger had nothing to do with her arrangement with Tom Jennings. Evidently, there had been a misunderstanding at the gin. One she could remedy with one trip to her office.

"Don't become overwrought, Mr. Bowen. I'll speak with the foreman and see that your cotton is accepted."

She turned toward the parlor, mustering as much disdain as she could manage, but he caught her by the arm and whirled her back to face him. "How would Sam know I would be bringing cotton in this week?"

"It's harvest time," she said with a shrug, but he held tight to her arm. "Everyone is bringing their crops in."

"Olivia, what's going on—"

"Will you please just leave?" She was all but shouting, but she didn't care. If she could stay angry, hopefully she wouldn't cry. "Let go of me and get out! Don't you know I never want to see you again?"

"Is that so?"

She forced herself not to back down, and his breathing matched the fierce pounding of her heart. He hauled her up against him and caught her chin with his other hand, forcing her to look up at him.

"Yes," she ground out. "That's so, you arrogant—"

Whatever else she planned to say was smothered beneath his mouth, and her gasp of surprise only served to further his advantage. Matt deepened the kiss, holding her close, and Olivia wound her arms around his neck, clenching her fingers in his hair. Hurt and anger were passions no less powerful than love and desire, and they both sought vengeance on the other.

He meant to master her, anchoring her head against his shoulder, but she would have none of it. Her lips matched his move for move, and she welcomed the foray of his tongue against hers as a spider might welcome a fly into its web. She felt him shudder against her, and the anguish she knew would follow refused to wait, her heart already aching, her arms already empty.

There was no use being defiant; she wanted him too much, needed him too much. Loved him too much.

Without warning, she pulled away from him. Her legs were shaking, and she caught hold of the arm of the sofa to keep from falling. "Please, Matthew, please just leave. We're only making things worse."

"I didn't come here to hurt you. I just wanted to know—"

"I'm sure whoever turned the cotton away didn't know what they were doing. I'm sorry to disappoint you, but it wasn't me."

"You weren't even there, were you?"

She shook her head. "I haven't been to the gin in over a week."

"Why? Aren't you feeling well?"

"I'm fine, it's just—" She saw the dread in his eyes, and anger surged within her. "No, I'm not pregnant, more to my relief than yours."

"Then why?"

"I just don't care anymore," she told him. "I don't care what happens to that gin. I almost wish it had burned to the ground." Before he could respond, she hastened to end the discussion. "I'll go to the gin later on and straighten everything out."

"I think you'd better get down there right now."

"Now?"

"Yes, now. And I'm going with you."

Olivia didn't see how things could get much worse. She needed a chance to speak privately with Sam to find out what had happened, but Matt had no intention of letting her out of his sight until the matter was resolved. Surely he would forgive her scheme since so many stood to benefit.

Tom Jennings was waiting for them in front of the gin, and Olivia didn't miss the suspicion in his eyes. "What's this all about, Miss Chandler?"

"That's what we've come to find out," Matt told him, keeping a firm hold on her arm as they approached the entrance. "There's been some kind of mistake."

Several men had followed him and Tom into town and were gathered outside the gin, demanding answers.

Someone was shouting to be heard over the mob. "Now, I won't tell you again. If you want to deal with me, you'll do it on my terms." The crowd fell silent. "Man to man . . . no groups or combined crops."

Olivia froze at the sound of Joe Hannah's voice, and the accusing glances that flickered toward her spurred her to intervene.

"What's going on here?" she demanded, shouldering her way through the crowd. The crowd parted, and she saw Hannah barring the entrance to the gin. "What are *you* doing here?"

He grinned and said with a sneer, "I could ask you the same thing. A woman with your reputation ought to know better than to show her face in public."

Ignoring his crude insult, Olivia caught sight of Rodger wavering in the shadows. "Rodger Kirk, what is this man doing here?"

"Please, Olivia, just go home and let me handle things."

"Just how do you intend to do that? By letting this common thief work for us?"

"I don't work for you, lady. Rodger here is going to make me a partner."

"Over my dead body," she countered.

"That can be arranged." Hannah caught hold of her arm and shoved her toward Rodger. "You'd best keep her under lock and key—"

Whatever he was going to say was cut short by the

sharp crack of Matt's fist connecting with his jaw, knocking him to the ground. The crowd gathering around them swelled, and shouts of approval and encouragement for Matt rose in the air.

Olivia saw anger and disbelief on Hannah's face, even as Matt loomed over him, warning, "Don't you ever touch her again."

Hannah staggered to his feet, wiping the blood from his lip with the back of his hand. Panting hard, he growled, "You son of a bitch."

He lunged forward, and Olivia cried out and would have rushed forward if not for Rodger catching her around the waist. "Stay out of it," he pleaded. "You shouldn't even be here."

Matt surprised his opponent with a hard fist to the belly and another on the chin before he could catch his breath. The second blow sent the man reeling once again, and Olivia winced as he collided with the wall and crumpled to the ground. Momentarily dazed, Joe Hannah shook his head and slumped forward but refused to stay down.

None too steady on his feet, he did manage to stand, this time brandishing a crude knife. Olivia screamed and Rodger tightened his grip on her, even as she twisted against his hold.

"Let's see how quick you are now," Hannah taunted, waving the blade and advancing on Matt. "Let's just see."

Matt never took his eyes from Hannah, even as he seized a forgotten scrap of lumber propped against the building. Twice Hannah lunged toward him, but Matt sidestepped the blade aimed at his abdomen.

The length of wood caught Hannah at the base of his neck and he stumbled, dropping the knife. Matt kicked the weapon far from reach and swung the plank once more. The blow put Hannah on his knees, his nose cupped in one hand and blood seeping from between his fingers.

Tom Jennings rushed forward and caught Matt by the arm. "The last thing we need right now is a killing."

Winded, Matt nodded and tossed the splintered wood to the ground, and Rodger finally released Olivia now that the obvious danger had passed. She paid no heed to her cousin's shouts for someone to go for the doctor. She rushed to Matt's side.

"Is this why you haven't been at the mill?" He turned on her. "You're letting that bastard run things?"

"Of course not," she insisted, but he wasn't listening. "Please, Matt, I didn't know anything about him being here."

He said nothing, leaving her to plead with Tom not to disband the effort.

"I don't need any doctor!" Hannah shrugged away from the men struggling to help him to his feet and shoved Rodger aside when offered assistance. "I done warned you what would happen if there was any more interfering."

"And I told you there would have to be a compromise."

"To hell with you and compromise!" Hannah stormed away from the gin, wiping blood from his face with the back of his hand.

Olivia wanted to strangle her cousin. "What kind of compromise?"

"I'm begging you, Olivia." Rodger tried to lead her aside. "Please, just let me take care of things."

"It's true, isn't it?" she demanded. "He said you were going to make him a partner. Is that what you mean by taking care of things?"

Rodger wouldn't look at her, wouldn't meet her eyes, and her heart sank. "What have you done, Rodger? My God, what have you done?"

Olivia was startled at the sound of voices in the foyer. She rushed down the stairs to find Rodger ranting to Aunt Eula, but he was so out of breath nothing he said made sense.

Finally, he caught his breath and turned to Olivia. "Do you have any idea what you've done?"

"What do you mean?"

"Did you or did you not order the gin to accept all that cotton?"

"Of course I did." Rodger had taken off to placate Hannah and Olivia had send Tom Jennings back to the fields for the rejected cotton, and she had told Sam Pate not to refuse another wagon, even if she was dead.

His anger vanished and for a moment she thought

he might faint. "Didn't I ask you to let me take care of things? I know how to handle him."

"Rodger, tell me what's going on."

He opened his mouth, but words failed him. He sank to the bottom step and let the truth win out. "I promised Joe Hannah that we wouldn't deal with the farmers, that we wouldn't buy their cotton."

"Joe Hannah? The gin is none of his business. Why on earth would you promise him something like that?"

"I owe him money, Olivia. A lot of money." Rodger raked a hand through his hair. "The broken windows, the fire. It was all meant to scare me . . . not you. It was his way of letting me know that he wasn't going to take no for an answer."

"How do you owe him money?

"When your father died, I honestly thought I'd be the one running the gin." The statement held no accusation. "I'd worked there since I was twelve years old, and with Ryan away in the army, it was only natural for me to take over."

Olivia sank down beside him. "Until Ryan died and left everything to me."

Rodger nodded. "I felt cheated, Olivia."

"So you decided to take the business away from me?"

"No, I swear it. I just assumed that once you were married you'd make me a partner and let me run the business for you."

Olivia propped her elbows on her knees and braced

her forehead against her open palms. "Well, that didn't happen."

"No," he agreed. "It didn't."

Olivia hadn't forgotten those awful months after Matthew's return. She refused to cave into her misery, burying herself instead in the daunting task of running her father's business. Her determination had been so strong that she might have succeeded on her own, but Rodger had patiently shown her everything she needed to know, never once asking anything for himself.

"It never occurred to me that you might be unhappy with the arrangement," she confessed. "You should have said something."

"You were so angry and hurt, I was afraid you would throw me out altogether." When she didn't deny it, he added, "But that didn't give me the right to take anything from you.

"I had worked out several deals for lumber and decided to keep them for myself. A little business of my own, on the side."

"With Mr. Hannah," she guessed. When she glanced up, he nodded. "And he got greedy."

"The man's a thief," Rodger said, his voice bitter with contempt. "He started making all kind of threats, and I didn't doubt him for a moment. I gave him a job at the gin, put him in charge of buying cotton and let him keep half the profits."

"Until I messed that up."

They both smiled reluctantly, and Rodger said, "You certainly did."

"That's when the threats turned into actions?"

"Yes. I didn't know what to do, but I knew I had to get my hands on enough money or he would kill me."

"So you decided to take the business away from me."

"Olivia, I was desperate." Rodger sank down on the step beside her. "The only thing that would hold him off was the prospect of me controlling the mill. I just needed to buy a little time."

"There's never enough money to buy time."

Rodger nodded, his shoulders slumping forward, and she couldn't help feeling sorry for him. He looked so defeated.

"What are you going to do now?"

"I don't know, but I hope to God he hasn't found out we're buying that cotton after all." He paused. "Did everyone hear you?"

"I'm sure they did," she told him. "I made no secret about being there; in fact, I was looking for you."

"Let's hope I find him before he knows what happened. I'll try to stall him. Maybe he'll believe I'm planning to double-cross you."

"And then what?" Olivia placed a gentle hand on his shoulder. "Rodger, this man is no threat to you now. You've told me everything, and I'll back you up against him. Tell him to leave you alone."

A mirthless laugh escaped his lips. "If only it was that simple. If I don't pay him the money he wants, he'll kill me."

"My God, Rodger, you need to tell the sheriff."

"No!" Rodger was adamant. "There's nothing I can prove against him that I haven't done myself."

"Surely you don't believe him."

Olivia shared her aunt's misgivings about Rodger. "He may not be telling me the entire truth, but he's afraid of something."

"He's brought this on himself."

"And on me, as well." Olivia faced her aunt. "I can't take the chance that Rodger won't panic and blame everything on me or Matthew. I have to tell him what's happened. I won't risk Sarah being where there's trouble."

"Good heavens, what might happen?"

"Who knows what this man is capable of? He considers Matt an enemy now." She slapped the reins and turned the buggy away from town, toward Matthew's farm. "Damn Rodger for being so stupid!"

Chapter Nineteen

When she arrived, there was no sign of Matt. Inside the kitchen, the stove was cold, and Olivia told herself he had to return before nightfall to tend to the animals. Already she was warring with her conscience over what to tell him when he arrived. She was ashamed that he and Sarah were in danger because of her, but he had to know.

She wouldn't lie to him, but he might refuse to let her handle the situation if he thought she was in danger, as well. Rodger would panic if Matt confronted him, and Olivia knew she could handle her cousin alone. The sheriff would have to handle Joe Hannah, even if it meant jail for Rodger.

She found Sarah and one of the Carter girls outside

at the far end of the porch. Sarah was poking dandelions into a rusty tin can, and she placed the arrangement in the center of an overturned wooden crate. Olivia realized the little girl was setting the table for tea, patiently explaining the need for a proper centerpiece.

"Livvy!" she cried, dashing down the back steps. "You're just in time. Me and Peg are having a tea party."

Olivia caught the little girl in her arms and laughed when Sarah threw her arms around her tightly. "A tea party. How charming."

Taking Olivia's hand, Sarah led her up the steps and across the porch. "See. Everything's ready."

"Hello, Peg," she said to the older girl.

Peg grinned and said, "There's not really any tea."

Mismatched cups and saucers, all cracked and chipped, were carefully arranged in two place settings, and a dented watering can served as the teapot. An overturned wooden bucket served as a makeshift chair for her doll, and Sarah smiled up at Olivia. "There's only two saucers, but I got three cups."

"You have." The gentle reproach died on her lips and she felt her throat tighten. Forcing a smile, she said, "Everything is beautiful."

Sarah reached for the watering can and pretended to fill the cups. Peg didn't have much of an imagination and turned her cup upside down to prove to Olivia it was empty.

"Peg, I plan on visiting with Sarah for a while," she said by way of excusing the girl. "If you have anything you need to do, I'll be happy to wait for Mr. Bowen to return."

Peg was more than a little grateful to be relieved of her duty and dashed home, saying good-bye over her shoulder. Olivia fingered the dandelions and laughed when Sarah said, "She's no fun at all."

It was nearly dark and Matt still had not returned. Olivia was growing restless. She tried to entertain Sarah as best she could, and they made supper from what she could find in the kitchen and ate picnic style on the back porch. Sarah was delighted, but Olivia grew more concerned as darkness drew near.

She was afraid to take Sarah home with her. She knew she could leave the child with Mrs. Carter, but she still had to warn Matt.

Across the pasture, Olivia could see lights burning in the windows of the Carters' cabin, and she considered the possibility that Matt might have stopped there first. At first she considered walking over and to see for herself, but she resisted the idea. Peg would have to explain leaving Sarah with her, and he would come home right away.

The darkness and mosquitoes finally drove them inside, and Olivia lit one of the kerosene lamps. The soft light warmed the room, and she settled in the old rocking chair in the corner. Sarah climbed into her lap and denied being sleepy despite her stifled yawns.

In the quiet, Olivia's thoughts wondered. Silly thoughts about what it would be like to be a wife and mother, waiting for her husband to return home after a hard day's work.

Olivia had nearly nodded off herself when she heard hoofbeats approaching the house. Thank God, Matt was home.

She stroked Sarah's hair and listened for the sound of footsteps at the back door. Instead, she heard fierce pounding on the front door.

"Bowen! Open this damn door!"

Olivia's insides quaked at the sound of Joe Hannah's voice.

"I know you're in there! I seen the light from the end of the road."

Sarah stirred, and Olivia gently pressed her fingers against the child's mouth. "Shh, baby," she whispered, praying he would leave.

"I'm here to make a deal with you, Bowen!" The man's voice was almost taunting. "You tell all those farmers to take what we offer them for the cotton or your lady pays the price."

It took a moment for the words to sink in, but Olivia realized Hannah had no idea she was there. All she had to do was keep quiet until he left. He began pounding on the front door again, and Sarah, startled by the racket, was fully awake.

"What's the matter?"

Olivia barely closed her palm over Sarah's mouth before she could say anything else. The little girl's eyes grew wide with fright and Olivia begged her to be quiet in a ragged whisper.

Her reassurances were shattered by the sound of

breaking glass, and Sarah's frightened cry was barely muffled against Olivia's hand. They had to get out of there before Hannah barged in on them.

"This is your last chance, Bowen!" Hannah shouted, his voice much clearer through the shattered front window. "Face me now or I'll burn the place down."

Olivia had no doubt he meant to do what he said. She had to get Sarah out of there, but she couldn't allow Hannah to destroy Matthew's home. Holding the child tight, she slipped out onto the back porch and lowered Sarah to her feet.

"Sweetie, you're going to have to get away from here." She brushed wispy bangs away from her face and tried to sound reassuring. "You can see the Carters' house from here, can't you? See the light in the window?"

Sarah looked in the direction Olivia was pointing and nodded.

"Good. Now you run as fast as you can and tell Mrs. Carter I said for you to wait there for your daddy."

"No! It's dark. I can't—"

"Nothing's going to hurt you. Just go the same way you go in the daytime and never take your eyes away from the lights."

"You come with me."

"No, Sarah." Olivia spoke as firmly as she dared, not wanting to frighten her more than she already was. "I have to go back to my house and . . . see about Aunt Eula. Now, you go to the Carters as fast as you can and I'll watch until you get there safe."

The child nodded reluctantly and dashed down the back steps. She only stopped once, turning to see if Olivia was still there. She watched until Sarah disappeared in the darkness and breathed a prayer for her safety.

Back inside the house, she could hear Hannah's railing and steeled herself to deal with the bastard. He might be bigger and stronger, but it would be no trick to outsmart him, as long as she kept calm.

"You hear me? Tell that lady of yours she'll pay the price."

She opened the front door and stepped outside. "Tell me yourself, Mr. Hannah. I'm listening."

For a moment he was too startled to speak, gaping up at her in disbelief. Then a slow, satisfied smile played on his lips. "Well, well. Fancy finding you here."

His nose was swollen and shapeless, and she couldn't resist saying, "Shouldn't you see a doctor? I think your nose is broken."

"I didn't come out here to discuss my health."

"Then what do you want?"

"I want what's coming to me!"

"Then why not take the cash and be on your way?"

His eyes narrowed, and Olivia knew her hunch was right when he asked, "What cash?"

"The cash in the safe at the gin," she explained. "Rodger said you refused to take it and leave town."

"He never offered me any money from the safe, only what he could scrape together." He hesitated. "How much are you talking about?"

"I'm not sure. Last time I counted it, there was at least ten thousand."

The man nearly choked. "Rodger said you was busted!"

"Well, the money was there this morning," she countered. "Unless Rodger gave it to you."

"Or kept it for himself."

"I wouldn't know."

"Well, why don't we just go see for ourselves?"

"So, you're willing to take the money?" she asked. "And leave town?"

He hesitated. "That depends. I don't think you've got a dime to hand over."

Olivia only shrugged. "There's only one way to find out."

The night was a warm but welcome change from the sun's burning heat. Matt shook his head, declining the bottle of whiskey that was being passed around, and knew they would be lucky if half the men remained sober through the night. He well understood the cause for celebration. The cotton harvest was nearly complete and already they had salvaged more than anyone had thought possible.

The revelry was tempered with the knowledge that there were those determined to thwart their effort. Word had spread quickly of the confrontation with Joe Hannah, and suspicions were sprouting up everywhere.

Matt and Tom had assured everyone that no more

cotton would be refused, but they agreed not to take any chances. Armed guards were posted around the cotton waiting to go to the gin.

"Rider approaching!" the man stationed nearest the road called out.

Those armed with rifles rallied to stand shoulder to shoulder,

The horse was weaving as the rider struggled to stay in the saddle. The animal came to a sudden halt, and the rider tumbled to the ground. Matt groaned inwardly. Just what they needed, another drunk. Several men bent to help him to his feet, but he remained where he fell.

"Hey, Bowen!" someone shouted. "This man says he's looking for you."

Matt glanced at Tom before making his way to the small crowd gathered around the fallen man. To his surprise, Rodger Kirk lay on the ground looking up at him. "Matt, please, you've got to do something."

Someone had beaten the hell out of him. A nasty cut nearly the length of his face was bleeding and one eye was swollen completely shut.

Tom swore under his breath. "What happened, man? Who did this to you?"

Matt knew who had done it, and Rodger was damned lucky to be alive.

Rodger waved away the canteen someone held to his lips and struggled to speak. "Help me . . . help me find Olivia. She should have been home hours ago."

Matt felt his insides grow cold, and he grabbed Rodger by the collar and yanked him to his feet. "Where did she go?"

Rodger groaned and sagged against him, unable to stand on his own. "Eula said she went to your house . . . to warn you, but she hasn't returned."

"Warn me about what?" Matt shook the man. "Answer me!"

"I tried to stop him . . . I swear it."

"You mean Hannah?"

Rodger nodded weakly.

"And now you think he's after Olivia?"

Again he nodded, but Matt didn't wait to hear the rest of Rodger's explanation. With a hard shove, he sent the man tumbling to the dirt. He hadn't been home since early that morning. Anything could have happened to Olivia on her way to his place or while she waited for him, and now Sarah was probably with her.

He gathered the reins of Rodger's horse and swung up into the saddle.

"Matt, wait!" Tom Jenkins rushed forward. "Let me go with you."

He turned the horse toward the road. "Follow me, if you want, but I can't wait."

They arrived to find the house dark, but signs of Sarah and Olivia's presence were everywhere—the dishes on the back porch, an abandoned picnic basket and Sarah's favorite doll slumped in the rocking chair. Matt felt the kerosene lamp on the table and found it still warm to the touch. They hadn't missed them by long.

Tom stood in the front room and motioned to the shards of glass littering the floor. Matt ripped the faded curtain from the window and stared at the jagged windowpanes. He was torn between rage and fear, unwilling to contemplate the possibility of Sarah being at the mercy of that bastard. If anything happened to her, Matt would never forgive himself for not killing Hannah when he had the chance.

"The Carters are bound to have heard something." Tom took the curtains from his hand and tossed them aside. "Let's go find out."

George Carter was standing outside the tiny cabin, waiting for them. "Bowen! What the hell is going on?"

Matt didn't stop to answer, leaving Tom behind to explain. He marched through the open doorway and felt weak with relief at the sight of Sarah sitting at the table.

"Daddy!" She ran toward him and threw herself into his arms, and he could feel her slight form trembling with sobs. "Oh, Daddy, we waited and waited for you."

"I know, I know." He stroked the child's tangled hair and breathed a sigh of relief. Thank God, Sarah was all right. He could deal with anything now, as long as his baby was all right. "Where is Olivia?"

"She had to get home," Mrs. Carter explained.

"Sent the youngun down here by herself . . . in the dark. Now if you ask me, that just ain't right."

Matt would have shared the woman's disapproval if not for the fact that Olivia was so fiercely protective of Sarah and would never have taken such a chance unless a greater danger presented itself. He raised Sarah's face to his and asked, "What happened, baby?"

"She said to wait here for you and . . ." Sarah glanced around her, a guilty expression on her face. "And not to say anything to the Carters."

"Anything about what?"

"Some man came looking for you, Daddy," she explained. "Livvy said he would go away, but he broke the window."

Her lip began trembling, and Matt gathered her close. "It's all right, sweetie. I promise you, everything will be all right."

Matt glanced up at Tom and the Carters and found his own concerns mirrored in the grim set of their features. At last, Tom spoke quietly. "Rodger said Olivia wasn't home."

"We'll find her," he vowed.

The gin was abandoned, as Olivia knew it would be, so far past dark, and she felt her bravado slipping as Hannah gripped her arm, propelling her up the stairs to the office. Once inside, he refused to allow her to light even so much as a candle.

"Unhand me." She snatched her arm from his

grasp. "I'm the only one besides Rodger who knows the combination to that safe. If you want the money, I have to see how to work the dial."

"What do think I am? Stupid?" he growled. "Everyone in town will notice a light burning in this place this time of night."

"Did you think they wouldn't notice a fire?"

"It would have served you right if you'd burnt right along with the place," he said. "You got no business meddlin' in men's affairs. Now, get that safe open."

"In the dark?"

He hesitated before reaching in his pocket for a match. He struck the match and held the tiny flame over the dial. Olivia's hands were trembling so that she doubted she would be able to work the combination.

The glow from the match suddenly died and she heard Hannah swear under his breath. He struck another match. "Hurry up!"

The tumblers clicked loudly and the heavy iron door opened just as the match died. She reached inside and breathed a prayer of thanks that her father's pistol was exactly where she had left it.

She knew better than to brandish the weapon in such close proximity and risk having the pistol snatched from her hands as well as losing the element of surprise. Instead, she fumbled through the documents stored in the safe with one hand and carefully slipped the pistol into the pocket of her skirt with the other.

"Oh, my God," she whispered after searching the safe. "It's gone."

"What do you mean?"

"The money is gone," she said, and the fear in her voice was no pretense. "All of it."

Shoving her aside, Hannah reached inside the safe and raked the contents onto the floor. "Look again!"

"In the dark?" she countered. "After you scattered papers everywhere?"

"All right!" he growled. "I'm lighting a lantern, but you best not make one false move."

Another match flared and he fumbled with the lamp's glass chimney. The wick glowed orange and sputtered before glowing brightly.

She knelt to the floor amid the scattered papers and feigned searching in earnest. Olivia knew to the letter exactly what was in that safe, but she made a great show of shuffling through everything. At last she said, "The cash is gone."

"You said it was in there this morning!"

"I've been gone all day," she insisted, the weight of the pistol in her pocket keeping her from panicking. "Rodger is the only other person with the combination to this safe."

"So I'm supposed to believe he's got the money?" Hannah sneered. "I already seen Rodger today, and if he had any money, he took a hell of a beating to hang on to it."

Olivia swallowed back a gasp of alarm. "Why should I be concerned? Either way, my money is gone."

Hannah's eyes narrowed, but she didn't miss the spark of surprise. "What are you going to do now?"

"Well, I can't give you money I don't have."

"You can make Rodger give it to me."

"If you couldn't beat it out of him, what makes you think I can?"

"I'm through wasting time with you." He turned toward the door. "Let's go."

"No."

He shook his head, as if he hadn't heard her right. "What did you say?"

"I'm not going anywhere with you," she informed him, wishing she felt half as brave as she sounded. "I agreed to come here with you and give you the money. I can't help it if the money's gone, but I'm not going anywhere else with you."

He advanced on her, reaching for her arm. "By God, yes, you are."

Taking two steps backward, Olivia made sure she was well out of his reach before aiming the pistol right at his heart. "Get out of here, Mr. Hannah. You can take your chances with the sheriff or I'll kill you where you stand."

Olivia gripped the pistol with both hands, her finger trembling against the trigger, and he laughed. "Go ahead, lady. Fire that thing and see if you don't blow your own head off."

Her eyes narrowed, blinking back angry tears. Just once in her life, she shouldn't have to prove herself. Even her own brother thought her so incompetent that she couldn't survive without her father telling her what to do.

He laughed again, and she realized his disregard of her capability was her best defense. "All right. I'll prove it."

Chapter Twenty

It took all her strength, but she squeezed that trigger and saw his eyes widen in surprise just before the shot was fired. The force of the shot knocked her backward, dazed for a moment, and she landed hard on her back. Hannah cursed and blood stained his shirtfront, but he was still on his feet.

Olivia's ears were ringing from the blast of the pistol and from the fall, but she managed to sit up. Frantically, she began searching for the pistol. She could only pray that someone had heard the gunshot.

"You lose something?"

She glance up to find him looming over her, blood coursing from the wound, staining his sleeve as well, and he gasped for air, reminding her of a winded horse. "Well, you shot me . . . but you didn't kill me.

"She won't have to."

Hannah turned at the sound of Matt's voice, and Olivia let her head fall forward in relief. How had he known? How had he found her? It really didn't matter, and she tried to get to her feet as he crossed the room. If Matt knew to come looking for her, that meant Sarah had told him about Hannah being at the farm. Sarah was safe.

With his uninjured arm, Hannah caught Olivia by the hair and yanked her to her feet. She struggled against his hold, but his fingers tightened in her hair and she feared her neck would snap from the strain. She went still at the feel of cold steel at her throat.

"Get back, Bowen," he growled.

"Just let her go." Matt spoke softly, but the blade was biting into her flesh and her control was slipping. "Your fight is with me. Not her."

"The fight is with me."

Rodger made his way into the room, stunning all three of them. Olivia gasped at the sight of her cousin. His face was bruised, one eye swollen almost shut, and he limped as he crossed the floor of the gin. He paused only long enough to retrieve Olivia's lost pistol and cock the hammer.

"Now let her go." Matt reached for Olivia. "You're outnumbered at best."

"Stay back, Bowen." Rodger leveled the gun with Matt's chest. "Stay back."

Hannah began to chuckle, twisting his fingers

tighter in Olivia's hair. "It don't pay to put much faith in the boy, does it?"

"Over there." Rodger motioned for Matt to stand beside Olivia and pointed the pistol right at her. Hannah chuckled again and released her none too gently. Matt caught her when she would have stumbled, and his arms locked around her. She felt the blood rush from her head and tried to speak. "Rodger, please. What are you doing?"

"Something I should have done a long time ago." He spared a glance at Matt. "You were right, you know. I am a cowardly bastard. Always have been."

Matt eased his hold on Olivia, moving to stand between her and the other men. "Rodger, don't do something you'll regret."

Olivia's heart was pounding so hard it nearly drowned out the sound of Rodger's morose laughter. He flexed his fingers, as if getting a better grip on the pistol. "Regret? I'm through with regrets."

In one fluid movement he turned toward Joe Hannah and fired the pistol. The man staggered backward, and Olivia knew he was dead before he hit the ground with a sickening thud. The wound in his forehead was barely visible, but a pool of blood was already forming beneath his skull.

Matt pulled her into his embrace, turning her away from the gruesome sight, and held her tight, whispering, "It's over. You're safe now."

She savored the feel of his arms around her, burying her face against his shoulder. "Oh, God, how did you ever find me?"

"Sarah told me what happened."

"Is she all right?" Olivia breathed, searching his eyes. "Tell me the truth."

"She's fine. I swear." He brushed a lock of hair away from her face. "Just scared to death something had happened to you. We both were."

She didn't know what to say to that, but he didn't wait for a reply. His lips claimed hers, and she kissed him back with all the strength she had. From somewhere way in the distance, she heard pounding footsteps and men shouting, and she reluctantly allowed him to end the kiss.

Tom Jennings and at least a dozen other men stormed inside the office, taking in the scene with wide-eyed amazement. "God A'mighty, Matt, what happened here?"

Olivia twisted her head to see her cousin standing over Hannah's prone figure, muttering to himself. Rodger looked so forlorn, Olivia feared he would turn the gun on himself. She crossed the floor and calmly took the weapon from his hand and turned to the men. "Joe Hannah abducted me and would have killed me, but Rodger arrived just in time to save my life."

Rodger gaped at her. "Olivia, that's not—"

"Don't be modest, Rodger." Matt clapped him on the shoulder. "You saved this town a lot of trouble by killing that sorry bastard."

"That's right, Rodger." Tom stepped forward and shook his hand. "I'll just go get the sheriff and let him know you've done his work tonight."

The other men chorused their agreement, each stepping forward to commend Rodger, and Olivia slipped away from his side and eased into Matt's embrace. "You don't mind letting him be the hero, do you?"

Matt only shrugged. "He shot him, not me."

"I think it will mean a great deal to him. Now and later."

Matt brushed his lips against her cheek. "All that matters to me is you."

Rodger sank down beside her on the top step and raked a hand through his hair. "I certainly made a mess of things, didn't I?"

She barely spared him a glance, wondering if he had any idea what his foolishness had cost her. "It's over and done with, Rodger. We'll make the best of things."

They sat watching as the sheriff concluded the investigation he felt compelled to conduct, despite concurring statements from the three witnesses. There wasn't much to say, but a lot to be grateful for.

Rodger brushed the dust from his trousers. "We can't buy that cotton. Olivia, we just can't."

She turned her head once again, this time taking in the sight of his battered face, and compassion for him tugged at her heart. Poor Rodger; she had every right to be angry with him, but he'd been bullied all his life. As a child, other boys teased him mercilessly because his mother forced him to take violin lessons, and she knew working for her father all those years couldn't have been easy.

She reached out and brushed her fingers across a particularly nasty bruise over his right eye. "Rodger, don't worry. We can stand not to make a profit once in a while."

"That's not what I'm saying. We can't buy because we don't have the money."

"What?"

"I borrowed against this year's cotton to build the warehouse," he explained. "The fire in the mill put a stop to production long enough to lose contracts. The money had to be returned."

"So you borrowed more," she concluded. "Robbing Peter to pay Paul."

"The factors will foreclose. We'll lose everything."

"How can they foreclose if we have no assets?"

"We have the deeds to half the land in the county."

"We can't let them do that."

"What choice do we have?"

She didn't say anything for a moment or two. "Do you suppose Mr. Sullivan might still be interested in buying into the cotton ginning business?"

Rodger blinked. Then he laughed, and they both laughed, drawing more than a few curious stares.

The rain came at last. It came in great torrents that battered the snapdragons and zinnias in the flower-beds and left roses hanging by their mangled stems.

There would be no more cotton picked, and what wasn't washed away would rot on the stalk. In a way, Olivia was glad. She was weary of worrying about what happened to other people.

She stared out the kitchen door for the longest time, listening to the rain, and tried to make sense of all that had happened but couldn't.

She and Rodger had met with Judge Stone for nearly two hours that morning, trying to determine just how dire their situation truly was. Hopeless, it seemed, was the legal term. No creditor would consider extending their terms when foreclosure would mean getting a foothold in one of the most potentially lucrative counties in the state.

Every possible option was blocked either by lack of funds or opportunity. The only remaining assets were the deeds to valuable farmland, and to forfeit them would barely put them in the black and leave them with no working capital. They could escape bankruptcy, but dozens of families would lose their homes.

Riddled with guilt, Rodger was of little help, and more than once he broke down and sobbed with anguish over his actions. Blame didn't matter at this point, and she reminded him of that to no avail. She could forgive him, but he couldn't forgive himself.

Olivia sank down into a chair, folding her arms across the polished surface of the kitchen table, and stared at the stack of deeds. A neatly folded pile of papers that represented all she had left in the world.

"Oh, Maddy," she sighed. "What am I going to do?"

"Do you remember the time, when you were a little girl, that you got lost in town?" Maddy never looked up from the pie crust she was rolling out. Her arms were covered in a fine dusting of flour. "I suppose you were no more than ten years old."

Olivia shrugged.

"You were tagging after Ryan and got turned around and ended up down at the livery stable."

Closing her eyes, she nodded. "Yes, I do remember."

She hadn't thought of that day in years, though she'd had nightmares for weeks afterwards. Ryan and some other boys were off to find some mischief, and she had hoped to follow without being noticed. The streets were crowded and it didn't take long for her to lose sight of her brother and become disoriented.

She turned a corner and stumbled onto a slave auction in progress. Something never attended by women or children, and a rare occurrence in their town. Something Olivia wouldn't have believed if she hadn't seen it with her own eyes. Everyone's attention was focused on the platform and no one took notice of her as she neared the event.

A woman, barely more than a girl, stood on a makeshift platform, clutching a crying baby in her arms. Men were shouting to be heard over one another and the auctioneer upped the bidding, at last declaring, "Sold! To the gent in the fancy breeches."

The man he pointed to stepped forward, not liking the description of himself. "I ain't got no use for that bellowing brat. I need her for work, not worrying over a snot-nosed kid."

Without a word of protest, the auctioneer motioned for someone to take the child away, and the woman screamed, her grip so tight on the child that Olivia feared he would be torn in two before she would let go. The mother clawed at the men hauling her off the platform, desperate to reach her child, and the baby's cries rang out, frightened and hopeless.

Olivia had looked on in horror, rooted in place, and a wave of nausea swept over her along with the realization that the mother and child would never see each other again.

"Hey! Somebody get this little girl out of here!"

Firm hands caught her by the shoulders and turned her away from the awful scene.

"Good God, that's Ian Chandler's daughter. He'll have our hides."

At least three men rushed to escort her away from the spot, reassuring her over and over again that they would see her safely back to her daddy, but no one moved to help the mother or the child.

"It was horrible," Olivia whispered. "Like something out of a nightmare."

Maddy smiled softly. "That night you asked your mama why I lived here, why I took care of you."

"I asked her if you were only here because someone bought you on a platform and took you away from your family."

"Your mama never did like the word *slave,* always calling black folks servants." Maddy shook her head at the memory. "The next day you told me I didn't have to pretend anymore. That you knew I didn't really love you, and the only reason I took care of you was because I had to."

"You told me you *were* here because you were a slave, but you—"

Maddy covered Olivia's hand with her own. "But I did love you, and I loved you on my own."

A tear slid down Olivia's cheek.

"You didn't learn a thing." Maddy squeezed her hand hard and gave it a playful slap. "What did you go and do when the war was over?"

Olivia frowned. "I don't know what you mean."

"You was so scared I would take off and leave you that you offered me money, clothes, a house of my own . . . anything I wanted, just to get me to stay."

"But you were free to do as you pleased," Olivia tried to explain, distressed to think Maddy had been offended. "I couldn't expect you to stay, just because—"

"It was my choice, no matter what you were willing to give me. Would you really have wanted me to stay just for the money?"

Olivia fingered the deeds lying between them.

"I knew you loved me." Olivia smiled. "But you did take the money."

Maddy smiled herself. "You bet I did."

The rain lasted through late afternoon, tapering off to a slow drizzle, and Olivia watched in idle fascination as robins feasted on the worms washed to the surface of the neatly trimmed lawn. She had forced herself not to retreat to her bedroom. Eula and Maddy were worried enough, and they seemed to take great comfort in the thought of her enjoying a book of poetry while resting in the parlor.

It made no difference; neither room offered escape. She could hide from the world, but her troubles followed right along behind closed doors.

A hesitant knock sounded at the door and she smiled. Most likely Eula had thought of some reason to join her, and Olivia was determined not to worry her aunt. Drawing a breath, she called, "Come in."

The weather was always a safe enough subject. "I suppose it will rain all day."

"It probably will."

She froze at the sound of Matt's voice, deep and solemn, willing herself to remain staring out at the sodden front lawn. She wanted to run and hide in his arms, beg him to help her, let him shield her from the uncertain future she faced. Instead, she only nodded. "Yes, it probably will."

"Rodger should be in jail."

That galled her. He picked a fine time to criticize her cousin. "That's not your decision to make."

"No, it's yours, but you're going to let him get away with it."

"Whether Rodger goes to jail or not won't change what's happened." She relinquished her vigil at the fogged window and turned to face him. "Rodger is the only family I have left, besides Aunt Eula and Maddy, and I'm not putting him in jail."

"At least he'd have a roof over his head. That may be more than you'll have."

She flinched at the thought, despite Judge Stone's assurances that her home would be protected.

"You should have told me the truth," he said. "If I'd had any idea what was going on—"

"Yes, I should have," she cut in. She'd gone over it in her mind a thousand times. She should have trusted him. She should have told him the truth. "Although I didn't know the whole truth at the time, so I would still have been lying to you."

"You could have trusted me."

She shook her head. "I couldn't risk it. I didn't know how you might react, so I didn't dare."

"Why?"

"You were marrying me to solve problems, not take on new ones." She held up her hand. "Let me finish. I'm glad now that things didn't work out. You'd be in a mess if you were stuck with me now."

"I think it's worth a chance."

His meaning was unmistakable, but she refused to consider the idea, no matter how appealing it was. "No, if you marry me, my creditors would go after every acre of land you have."

The door to the parlor eased open barely an inch and Olivia caught sight of Sarah peering into the room. When she smiled, the door flew open wide and the little girl ran toward her, into her open arms.

"Livvy!" she cried, throwing her arms around Olivia's neck. "Livvy, are you all right?"

"Of course I am, sweetie." She drank in the sight of the child, noting the ribbon tied somewhat clumsily in her hair. She would have given anything to see Matt's big hands struggling to tie a bow in Sarah's wispy curls. "I'm so glad to see you."

"Daddy was going to come without me," she tattled, casting her father a mutinous look. "He said you wouldn't feel like seeing me."

"And you threw a tantrum," he reminded her.

"Did you?" Olivia cupped Sarah's sullen chin and ran her thumb over the tiny frown. "A lady doesn't lose her temper."

"I told you she was spoiled," he reminded Olivia. "Spoiled rotten."

"That's not true," Olivia insisted, secretly delighted. "Is it?"

Sarah's face remained solemn. "I wanted to see you."

Gathering Sarah into her arms once again, Olivia whispered, "You can see me anytime, Sarah, anytime you want."

"Can I stay with you? Just for a little while?"

Olivia glanced at Matt. "If it's all right with your father."

Sarah whirled on her father, her tiny hands clutching Olivia's, but any defiance she might have mustered deserted her when she whispered, "Please, Daddy."

Chapter Twenty-one

"That's the last for this load, Mr. Kirk."

"That's fine, Ben." Rodger scribbled something on a tablet and tucked the ledger under his arm. "Take it on down to the depot and stay there until they get everything loaded."

"Yes, sir." Ben climbed onto the tall seat of the wagon and snapped the reins, urging the mules onward.

"And get a receipt," Rodger called after him.

He opened the ledger and reread the entries as he turned back toward the gin. Matt stood in the doorway, blocking his entrance, and Rodger nearly collided with him.

"Watch where you're going, Rodger."

"I-I didn't see you." He barely managed to keep from dropping the ledger, and he hugged it tight against his chest. "What are you doing here?"

"We need to talk." Rodger's panicked expression was answer enough. "I want to know what's going on."

"There's nothing to tell."

"You had plenty to say to me before. Don't tell me you've developed a sense of loyalty this late in the game."

"I don't owe you any loyalty." Rodger hurried inside the gin, but Matt followed him.

"I don't need your loyalty, but you will tell me the truth."

Rodger backed up. "I told you, I've got nothing to say to you."

"Is this why you didn't want me to marry Olivia? Afraid I'd ruin everything for you?"

"Everything *is* ruined." He drew a handkerchief and mopped his brow. "And I really did you a favor. If you'd married her, you'd be liable for the losses."

"I'd also have final say over what happens to you. And I wouldn't be as forgiving as Olivia."

Rodger threw his handkerchief on the counter. "Don't get pious with me, Bowen. You want to know what's going on here? The only way she could keep her bargain with the cotton farmers was to sell the cotton directly to the textile mills, foregoing any commissions. She's not making a dime on any of this."

"Why?"

"So she won't have any assets," Rodger explained.

"If we had handled the sale of the cotton, the creditors could have claimed every bit of it as an asset.
The farmers would have been ruined, with or without
the deeds."

"The deeds?"

"Every last one, signed over to the borrower. She
was afraid they could be claimed as assets."

"Claimed by whom?"

"The courts." He made a grand gesture, his arms
outstretched. "All of it. "Everything. Chandler, Inc.
will be bankrupt . . . forced into receivership."

Matt was stunned. Why hadn't she mentioned any
of this to him? "Why didn't she—"

He knew the answer before he could say the words.
For the same reason she didn't tell Ryan about their
father's death. She could deal with her own misfortune, but not that of those she loved.

The courthouse was stifling, but Olivia wore her
finest suit. She would not look like a pauper, even if
the court said she was. She did remove her gloves,
tucking them into the black velvet reticule that
matched the trim on her blue brocade jacket and
bonnet. She would not look like a mourner, either.

Rodger couldn't stop fidgeting with his collar. Ada
had not come with him, humiliated to have her husband publically declared insolvent and a failure, but
Olivia suspected her presence would only add to Rodger's agitation. Discreetly, she caught his hand in hers

and managed an encouraging smile. "They're not going to hang us."

Indeed, today's proceedings were a mere formality. The business would be legally declared insolvent and any assets would be turned over to the creditors. The only assets were the equipment at the mill and the gin. The deeds were gone, and there wasn't enough cotton left in the gin to fill so much as a pillow.

Despite the lack of drama, the room was packed. Not a seat was empty and many people stood along the back wall. The Chandler name had ruled the county for three generations, and today it would be stripped of power, dignity, and esteem. Her father was undoubtedly spinning in his grave.

Judge Stone favored her with a sympathetic smile before addressing everyone with a pleasant, "Good morning."

Without another word, he adjusted his reading glasses and scanned several documents. When he looked up, he spoke directly to Olivia. "You know as well as I what this is all about."

She nodded.

"I suggest we dispense with the formalities and get this matter resolved." When she made no protest, he went on. "The court has received a petition, a bid you might say, from an outside party to pay the outstanding debt and take control of the interests."

She couldn't suppress a gasp of dismay. So soon! She had envisioned taking a few weeks to remove personal articles from her office and see that the employees were provided for, and *then* selling.

Rodger extracted his hand from her grip and rose to his feet. "Excuse me, your honor, this is the first we've heard of any such *petition.*"

" 'Tis a fair and generous offer, much better than you would manage on the auction block, and it will prevent bankruptcy." He glanced at Olivia. "I suggest you take it."

Rodger sank down beside her, his face sallow, and Olivia nodded, both to him and the judge.

"Well, there's no point in delaying. We can sign transfer papers right here."

"Now?" The question was nothing more than a squeak and Olivia cleared her throat and managed, "So soon?"

"The gentlemen are here," he explained, as if it was a minor detail. He motioned to the bailiff. "Bring them in."

The double doors leading inside the courtroom opened and every head swiveled to see just who would be assuming control of the gin and lumber mill and, essentially, control of the county. Only Olivia remained facing straight ahead, her entire body frozen, unable to move.

Suddenly, Rodger was on his feet, and Eula gripped Olivia's hand and smiled almost knowingly. Three men made their way forward, and Olivia's mouth dropped open at the sight of Matthew, followed by Tom Jennings and Michael Sullivan.

"What is the meaning of this?" Rodger demanded. His hand fell protectively on Olivia's shoulder. "Haven't you caused this woman enough heartache?"

Matt glared at Rodger. "Too much, but I intend to make things right. What are you going to do for her?"

Rodger sat down without another word, and Judge Stone cleared his throat, displeased to have any commotion in his courtroom. "Gentlemen, if you have business with this court, speak up."

Mr. Sullivan stepped forward. "Your honor, in reviewing the accounts, it is obvious that Miss Chandler could easily have spared herself this embarrassment by reneging on a confidential agreement with Mr. Jennings. No one would have been the wiser and it would have been her word against his."

"Is this true?"

"Yes, sir." Tom glanced at Olivia. "If it wasn't for her, every man in this county would have gone bust and she would have made good on the deal."

"She did better than that," Mr. Sullivan added. "She sold the cotton, taking no commission for herself, to bolster the profits."

A ripple of whispers filled the courtroom, and Olivia felt every person's stare boring into her skull.

"The least we could do is repay her."

"Am I to understand that, as a collective, the cotton farmers are buying out the gin and the mill?"

"Not a buy out, your honor," Mr. Sullivan explained. "Miss Chandler has done too much for the people of this county. No one wants to see the mill change hands."

"I have no doubt Miss Chandler is a generous and

honorable person. Unfortunately, these qualities are
what bring us here today.''

"The reason we're here today is Olivia Chandler
put her trust in/people who betrayed her over and
over again.''

Rodger slumped forward, burying his face in his
open palms, and Olivia forced herself to stand on
shaky legs, "No, Matthew, I can't let you do this.''

Judge Stone clapped his gavel on the desk. "Olivia,
you'll have a chance to speak for yourself, but I want
to hear what he has to say. Go ahead.''

"Olivia did what she had to do to hang on to her
business. It was the one thing she could count on.''
He turned to face her. "I let her down, when she
needed me to trust her motives rather judge her
actions. That's why we're here today. That's why she's
in this mess.''

"That's not true.'' She made her way into the aisle.
"I'm to blame, not you. I let the business become
more important to me than people. My father certainly did. I wanted to prove that I could run things
as well as he did, that I didn't need anyone.'' She
drew a deep breath. "I wanted to love it as much as
he did.''

"That kind of love will never make you happy.''

She laughed. "I realize that now, but it's a little
late.''

"It's never too late, Olivia.'' He grasped her shoulders. "Please, don't say it's too late for us. We've
wasted enough time as it is.''

Before she could answer, a commotion stirred at

the back of the courtroom, and they turned to see Maddy and Ada standing just inside the open doors and Sarah rushing down the center aisle toward the judge's bench.

"Is she ours, Daddy?" she asked breathlessly. "Can we take her home?"

The courtroom erupted in laughter and even Judge Stone chuckled, forgetting his gavel for once. Matt lifted Sarah into his arms and waited for the laughter to die down before answering her. "It's up to Olivia, honey. It's her decision."

"Well, if you're going to leave such an important decision up to me, you'll just have to bear the consequences." Sarah reached for her and Olivia took the child in her arms. "I can't lose either one of you. Not ever again."

"I see no reason we can't take care of that here and now." Judge Stone set aside the matter of the gin. "My clerk can have the license drawn up by the time you say the vows."

Olivia was stunned. She certainly hadn't expected this to be her wedding day.

"Judge Stone, this is hardly an appropriate setting for a wedding," Eula protested. "And a proper wedding will take at least a week to plan."

"Miss Chandler, as hard a time as they've had getting married, I strongly suggest we not let them leave here today without a ceremony."

The assembly broke into applause, and Nancy rushed forward, taking Olivia's arm. "I'll never forgive you if I'm not the maid of honor."

Judge Stone banged his gavel and silenced the commotion. "Let's begin." He cleared his throat. "In the presence of these witness, we're gathered to join this man and this woman in holy matrimony. Who gives this woman to be wed?"

"I do!" Sarah cried out. "I do. Forever and ever!"

BOOK YOUR PLACE ON OUR WEBSITE AND MAKE THE READING CONNECTION!

We've created a customized website just for our very special readers, where you can get the inside scoop on everything that's going on with Zebra, Pinnacle and Kensington books.

When you come online, you'll have the exciting opportunity to:

- View covers of upcoming books
- Read sample chapters
- Learn about our future publishing schedule (listed by publication month *and author*)
- Find out when your favorite authors will be visiting a city near you
- Search for and order backlist books from our online catalog
- Check out author bios and background information
- Send e-mail to your favorite authors
- Meet the Kensington staff online
- Join us in weekly chats with authors, readers and other guests
- Get writing guidelines
- AND MUCH MORE!

**Visit our website at
http://www.zebrabooks.com**